"Hey, Jonathan," the driver called out of the van, "come here a minute."

Jonathan stiffened. The man had called him by name. "I have to talk to you, Jonathan," the man was saying. "It's real important."

Jonathan inched a step closer and peered inside the dingy van. The man pulled off his sunglasses and tucked them into the sun visor. "There's been a terrible accident, Jonathan. I'm sorry to be the one to tell you," he said over the sound of the idling engine. "You better get in so we can talk."

"I'm not allowed to go with strangers," Jonathan said bravely.

"Come on, son. We have to talk privately," the man urged gently. "It's about your mom and dad."

Carefully, Jonathan shrugged off his backpack and climbed up on the tattered vinyl seat next to the man. "What do you have to tell me? Why didn't my mom and dad tell me themselves?" he asked.

"Son, you'd better close the door so we can talk."

Jonathan slammed the tinny-sounding door. His fingers gripped the handle, lingering, just in case he had to get away.

The man shifted the van out of neutral and it began to move down the street. . . .

DON'T SPEAK TO STRANGERS

MARION ROSEN

ST. MARTIN'S PAPERBACKS

For Morrie Rosen—my husband, my believer, my
best friend.

An Important Message to the Readers of This Book beginning on
p. 310 copyright © 1993 by the National Center for Missing and
Exploited Children (NCMEC), Arlington, Virginia, USA. This copyright material is reprinted with permission of NCMEC. All rights
reserved. NCMEC does not and has not authorized, endorsed, or
assisted in the creation of any of the fictional events conveyed in
this novel.

DON'T SPEAK TO STRANGERS

Acknowledgments

My most sincere appreciation and thanks to the following writers who guided, supported, and advised me in the writing of this book: Joann Burch, Karen Vik Eustis, Ann Garrett, Marylou Mahar, Sandra Steen, Susan Steen, Stephanie Waxman, April Halprin Wayland, and Abby Yolles.

Thanks also to Dr. Richard Eisenberg and Debi Eisenberg for their information on Atlanta and to my agent Lew Grimes for his early support and faith.

Chapter 1

JONATHAN spotted the battered vehicle when it was still almost a block away. Puffs of black smoke coughed from the exhaust of the rickety old van as it slowly rattled toward him. Instinctively he knew it didn't belong to anyone who lived on this clean, tree-lined suburban street.

He hesitated out of curiosity, trying to get a better look at the driver, but at the same time a sense of fear washed over him. He wished Brian were with him. They always walked home from school together and checked out any strange or new things along the way, but today Brian had stayed home with a cold. Jonathan's teacher, Mrs. Montgomery, said half the fifth grade had colds; it must be a spring epidemic.

The driver signaled for a left-hand turn as the van approached the spot where Jonathan walked on the sidewalk. Jonathan stopped and watched. The van turned, cutting right in front of him, into the Waldmans' driveway. At least it used to be the Waldmans' driveway. The family had moved a few months ago, and Jonathan hadn't learned the name of the new people. There was no need. They had only one child, a girl, and she was just a baby.

Slowly, the van backed out of the driveway and

then crawled forward, close to the curb. "Hey, Jonathan," the driver called through the open window, "come here a minute."

Jonathan stiffened. The man had called him by name, but still, his first impulse was to run. By the time you were in the fifth grade, you had heard the same message a million times. Every kid knew a stranger could be bad news.

"I have to talk to you, Jonathan," the man said. "It's real important."

Jonathan inched a step closer and peered inside the dingy van. The man wore dark glasses, but Jonathan was certain his face was not familiar. It was a tough, stony kind of face he would have remembered. Yet the man knew his name.

The man pulled off his sunglasses and tucked them into the sun visor. "There's been a terrible accident, Jonathan. I'm sorry to be the one to tell you," he said over the sound of the idling engine. "You better get in so we can talk."

"I'm not allowed to go with strangers," Jonathan said bravely, but he was definitely curious about the accident the stranger had mentioned. He took another step, a tiny one.

The man smiled. "You're right as rain. Name's Leon Hoffman. I'm sorry, I've been so upset about all this, I forgot you might not remember me. It's been a long time since I've been by here to visit with your dad."

"You know my dad?"

"Know him? We're close as brothers ever since the war. Yep, old Ed Grady and me go back a long ways."

He knew his father's name and the fact that Edward Grady had been in the war. "Which war?" Jonathan tested.

"Why, Vietnam. The only war the two of us fought in." Leon stretched, leaning over the passenger's seat, and pushed the door open toward Jonathan. "Get in. What I have to say isn't something we want to yell about in front of the whole neighborhood."

Carefully, as if he expected an electrical shock, Jonathan touched the door handle and then glanced over his shoulder. No one was around. He was immediately sorry he had picked this day of all days to stay after school. Even Marylou, the pest, was not lingering ten paces behind him, as she always did when he walked home with Brian. He hesitated, wondering if it might be smarter to just run away as fast as he could.

"Come on, son. We have to talk privately," Leon urged gently. "It's about your mom and dad."

Jonathan shrugged off his backpack and climbed up on the tattered vinyl seat next to Leon. The seat felt sticky, and the van smelled like the garage where his dad took the car for repairs. "What do you have to tell me? Why didn't my mom and dad tell me themselves?"

Leon folded his arms across the steering wheel and leaned his head against his wrists. His wide, hulking shoulders heaved, trembling as if he were about to cry. Jonathan noticed Leon didn't seem to have a neck; his almost hairless head was mounted directly on his shoulders.

"Son, you'd better close the door so we can talk."

Jonathan slammed the tinny-sounding door and then squeezed his legs as close to it as he could. His fingers gripped the door handle, lingering, just in case he had to get away from this giant no-neck in a hurry. It wouldn't hurt to play it safe even if Leon did know his dad.

Leon sat up and wiped his murky gray eyes with

the back of his hand. "I got to town early this morning and went directly to your dad's real estate office over on Jimmy Carter Boulevard. Boy, was he ever glad to see me. We laughed and talked and then ol' Ed—I mean your dad—said let's get out of here. He said Susan would be dying to see me, so we both drove on over to your place."

"What about the accident?" Jonathan interrupted, wondering what this story had to do with him.

"I'm getting to that," Leon said. "Susan—I mean your mom—started making a fuss, fixing a special lunch for us to celebrate getting together again after all these years. She even put candles on the table, so I said I'd go on over to the market and pick us up some wine."

He pointed to a paper bag on the floor next to Jonathan's feet. "There it is. A whole gallon of fancy white wine, the kind they would've liked. I wasn't gone long, but I did have some trouble cashing a check 'cause I'm from out of state, and when I turned the corner up there by your street and Maple, the street was blocked. There was police cars and fire engines parked every which way, so I had to pull over and stop. Then I saw it. It was just awful."

"What?" Jonathan asked, his voice beginning to falter. "What did you see?"

Leon leaned forward again, his head touching the steering wheel. The knuckles on his big, hairy hands had turned white and shiny from the way he was squeezing the wheel. "I'm sorry, boy. I'm real sorry."

"What do you mean? Was it my house?"

Leon nodded without looking up. "She burned to the ground," he said to the steering column. "Nothing left but the one brick wall and the chimney to the fireplace. The whole place is ashes."

Jonathan slid to the edge of the seat, close to the windshield, and stared over the rooftops in the general direction of his house. The sky was a cloudless blue. "I don't believe you. There's no smoke."

"Cleared up by now. There was lots of smoke a couple of hours ago."

Jonathan stared at Leon's hands, now big, nasty spiders skimming the rim of the steering wheel. He tried to think clearly. "I didn't hear any sirens. Didn't the fire trucks have sirens?"

"Sure they did. I didn't pay any attention when I first heard them. You was probably having lunch with your friends and ignored the sirens, just like I did."

The lunchroom at school did get pretty noisy some days. Jonathan felt tears stinging behind his eyes. He heard a faint, gasping sound, not realizing it had issued from his own throat. His house burned to the ground, gone. "Where's my mom and dad?" he finally asked.

Leon reached over and clumsily patted the back of Jonathan's hand. He slid his big, tarantula fingers up toward Jonathan's elbow and clutched his arm brusquely at first, then almost tenderly. "They didn't get out. I talked to the fire chief, and he said the oven or something in the kitchen must've exploded. They never had a chance. I'm sorry I hadda be the one to tell you, kid. I'm real sorry."

Jonathan was dazed. His knees trembled beneath his hands. He tried to will the shaking to stop, but he had no control. Had Leon just explained that his parents were dead? He wasn't sure.

"Maybe they ran out the kitchen door," Jonathan said. "It's close to the stove."

Leon shook his huge head. "Jonathan, I know you're in shock and this is hard to believe, but they didn't make it. The firemen found them, in the kitchen."

"Both my parents? What about Ginger?"

"Who?" Leon asked quickly.

"Ginger, my dog. What happened to her?" Tears began to slide down his cheeks. Not Ginger, too. Had he lost everything he had ever loved?

"Oh, the mutt. Yeah, your mom put her outside before she started to cook. That's right. Ginger was outside."

Again Leon reached over, this time patting Jonathan's knee. His touch was much gentler than Jonathan expected.

"Can we go get her?" Jonathan asked.

Leon shifted out of neutral and the van began to move down the street. "No, there's still fire trucks and hoses blocking the street. Besides, she ran away."

Outside the van everything seemed to be happening in slow motion. The houses Jonathan had passed hundreds of times were strange, unknown to him. He sniffed back his tears and shivered, wondering why he suddenly felt so cold. "Ginger wouldn't run away," he whispered.

"Sure she would if the explosion scared her. Dogs don't like loud noises."

That was certainly true. Ginger had spent hours hiding under his bed on the last Fourth of July. Jonathan suddenly realized Leon had turned left at Maple Street. He was driving in the wrong direction, and he was driving very fast. His tires squealing slightly on the curve, Leon veered right onto Peachtree Road.

"Where are you going? Shouldn't we try to find Ginger?"

"That dog may not show her face again for a month. The neighbors will look after her when she comes back."

"You mean Brian, my friend next door?" Jonathan asked.

"Yeah, Brian will keep Ginger for you. I'll come back and get her when she shows up."

"Come back?" Jonathan said. "Where are we going?" He read the signs zooming by on his right. Leon had followed Peachtree Road to the 285, but then left Dunwoody, cutting over to the interstate. Now they were traveling north, away from Atlanta, on Interstate 75. Jonathan stared at the man next to him. Leon seemed to have a determined grip on the wheel, and now he was driving even faster.

"To my place. You can't live in a house that's all burned up, now can you?" Leon said.

A sign along the road announced they were seventy-eight miles from Chattanooga. Jonathan's hand pressed against the door handle. If he jumped out at this speed, he would be killed, but he didn't think he wanted to go anywhere with Leon, certainly not to his place, wherever it was.

"I want to go to my grandma's," Jonathan said weakly.

"Sure kid, I know, but she can't take care of you right now. Maybe later."

Leon stretched, reaching back over the front seats, and yanked a wrinkled windbreaker from a big pile of clothing heaped on the floor. Jonathan saw the van had no seats in the rear, just loads and loads of junk.

"You're shivering, kid," Leon said. "Put this on. You don't want to get sick."

"How long do I have to stay at your place?" Jonathan asked, obediently slipping his arms into the

7

oversized jacket. "Why can't I go to my grandma's? What about the funeral? Won't we have a funeral?"

"Slow down, boy, one question at a time. Your grandma will handle the funeral. She didn't want you to have to go through something like that at your age."

"I'm ten. I went to my other grandpa's funeral when I was eight."

"Is that a fact?" Leon looked at him out of the corner of one eye and then slipped his sunglasses back on his face. "I guess kids are more grown-up nowadays than they used to be."

"Can't I stay with my grandma?" Jonathan tried again.

"Where's she living now?"

"Columbus, Ohio. Where she always lived."

"Right, I forgot. I was so upset about the fire and everything when I called her, I didn't even think where I was calling."

For the first time Jonathan turned sideways in his seat to face Leon. "You talked to my grandma? When?"

"The fire chief said I should take care of things, me being almost like a brother to your dad. I called her from your friend's house, next door."

"What'd she say?"

"She said she'd take care of the funeral, and I was to take care of you until she felt better. This kind of news ain't easy for an older person, you know?"

"That's what she said? For how long?"

"Lord, how am I supposed to know how long it'll take till she gets over something this awful? I'll call her in a couple of days and see how she feels. Meantime, you'll stay with me and Maria."

"Is that your wife?" Jonathan asked.

"Nah, I don't have a wife. Maria's my little girl."

"What happened to your wife?"

Leon coughed and wiped the back of his hand across his mouth. "Why don't you close your eyes, rest a bit. We'll talk more later."

Jonathan leaned his head back against the seat. He didn't feel very well. He understood how his poor grandmother must feel. Susan Grady was her only child, just as Jonathan was an only child. He would take care of his grandmother when he was able to move to Columbus. He would help around the house and be no trouble at all.

The van grew warm in the late afternoon sun. Jonathan was vaguely aware of a deep, hollow feeling in the pit of his stomach, but he was also very sleepy. His head ached. They had passed Chattanooga and the signs now said they were nearing Knoxville. Leon kept driving.

"I have to go to the bathroom," Jonathan said, looking over toward Leon.

"Sure, kid. We'll stop in a minute. I need gas anyway."

They pulled into a gas station, and Leon set about filling the tank. Jonathan raced around back where the man pointed out the rest rooms. Inside, he noticed a pay phone on the wall. He was certain he had a quarter left over from his lunch money. Carefully, he punched out the numbers for Brian's phone.

"Hello," a woman's voice answered. It didn't sound like Brian's mother.

"May I please speak to Brian?"

"Sorry, you must have a wrong number."

"Isn't this 342-3913?"

"Yes, but there's no Brian here."

The area code. He had forgotten the area code. By now they had gone what seemed like hundreds of miles and had probably traveled into a different area code.

"Thank you," Jonathan said sheepishly before he hung up. Tears welled in his eyes. He had wanted to talk to a friend, someone who hadn't been blown out of his life in that explosion.

Just as he finished using the rest room, Leon walked in. "Wait for me in the car, boy, you hear?"

"Okay." Jonathan walked back to the van. He wished Leon wouldn't call him boy.

Soon it was dark. Constantly checking the sideview mirrors on both sides of the van, Leon drove in silence. His eyes shifted toward Jonathan every now and then, but he didn't say anything. He just leaned into the steering wheel and followed the long, straight lines of the highway.

Jonathan closed his eyes, and the tears squeezed through. Not the usual kind of tears like when he got hurt or real angry, but a gentle stream he couldn't hold back. His sleeve was wet from wiping his eyes and his nose, but the tears kept flowing. His shoulders trembled from sobs that tore out of his heart.

"Settle down, boy," Leon said. "Crying won't help nothing. You have to be strong."

But Jonathan wasn't strong. He felt little and helpless and so very tired. Finally his tears stopped, but his chest continued to heave, painfully wrenching his stomach. He leaned his thudding forehead against the cool window and concentrated on the buzzing vibrations from the road that echoed through his head. Maybe today was just a bad dream. He wanted to feel his mother's arms around him, his dad's fingers running through his hair.

Suddenly his neck began to ache. Jonathan sat up straight, hugging Leon's jacket closer to his chest. He may have slept for a little while; he couldn't remember. Jonathan glanced at Leon, his jutting eyebrows outlined against the frosty moon-light. There was no kindness or sympathy in Leon's face. Jonathan sat very still, listening to the steady clapping of the van's tires against the black road.

Chapter 2

Leon felt a firm, steady sting as his muscles tightened across his shoulders. A dagger of pain stabbed into his forehead. He hoped this headache wouldn't be as bad as his last, but then they always were.

He uncurled his fingers slowly, permitting the blood to circulate more freely into his fingertips. The steering wheel felt hot, sticky with his own sweat. This time hadn't been as bad as when he grabbed Maria, but still he needed to get out of the van and stretch, release some of the tension that had been choking him ever since he first spotted Jonathan walking home from school today.

Just when Leon had been about to give up hope of ever finding a perfect opportunity to connect with Grady's kid, there it was. Jonathan, walking alone, on a quiet street where nobody would ever suspect anything like this could happen. Now, after all these runs down to Georgia the last few months, he had the kid. It was over.

Leon let out a deep breath. The long days of waiting and watching had finally paid off, and not a moment too soon. Judy Mae was getting on his nerves with all her fool questions about why was it taking so long, and why couldn't the judge just sign the papers and get it over with? He had run out of excuses for all the trips he had taken, but at least Judy Mae hadn't refused to take care of Maria for him during his absences. Judy Mae was always eager to help out with his little girl, but now she was starting to ask too damn many questions. Women always asked too many questions.

The van clattered on through the darkness. The boy had slept on and off, when he wasn't crying, and now Leon also felt the need for sleep. He looked sideways, glancing at the kid. Lights from the oncoming traffic flashed into the front seat, and Leon saw Jonathan's puffy little eyes were wide open.

"I know a place just ahead, soon's we cross into Virginia, where we can get something to eat. We can spend the night there, too," Leon said.

"How far is it to your house?" Jonathan asked.

"Not far. Just up into Pennsylvania."

"Where are we now?"

"A couple of miles from Glade Spring. That's where we're staying tonight."

"Where's that? What state?"

"I just told you. Virginia."

This kid asks a lot of questions, too, he thought. No problem, though. Leon was sure he had answers for anything the kid might think of. Well, almost anything. That one about the mutt had thrown him for a second. He had thought for a moment that perhaps the Gradys had had another baby. Jesus, he had been jumpy about nothing more than a mutt.

"Is that it?" Jonathan was pointing to a flashing yellow sign that announced a motel was just ahead.

"Yep, that's the best place around here. Doesn't cost an arm and a leg."

Leon pulled into the parking area in front of the motel office. It didn't look quite so seedy at night.

"Wait here," Leon said. "I'll get the keys."

The night man recognized him at once. "Mr. Kirby, I see you're back on your southern run."

Leon grinned, pleased that the clerk remembered the fictitious name he used whenever he stopped here. "Yeah, thought I'd try to scare up some business down this way. Not much happening up north right now."

The man nodded knowingly. "It's rough everywhere, thanks to those goddamn politicians in Washington. They'll have us all on our knees one of these days."

"Mind if I make a quick call, to let the little woman know I'm all right? I have my boy along with me this trip, and she worries like a mother hen. I'll pay for it."

"That's all right, you go right ahead," the man said.

Leon made a point of spending a night at this motel whenever he made a trip to Georgia. He also pretended to call home in front of one of the three desk clerks each time he stopped. He figured no one would pay any attention to the comings and goings of a regular family man. No one would ever guess the real purpose behind all these visits.

He dialed the number and waited for the recording from the Galworthy Medical Center in Altoona, Pennsylvania, to explain that all the offices were closed for the day before he began to speak into the dead line.

"Hi, hon. It's me. I'm in Glade Spring, Virginia, for the night."

He waited, giving his imaginary little woman on the other end a chance to speak.

"He's fine. He helped me on the job I did in Knoxville today. He loved helping out his old man, but I told him it's back to school on Monday. I said we wouldn't cover for more than two days of hooky,

14

even if he is learning more on the road with me than he learns in that school."

Another pause.

"Okay, sweetheart. See you tomorrow."

The clerk smiled as if he approved of Leon's being a family man. Nobody was ever suspicious of a family man.

"Sign the register, please. Room five okay?" the clerk asked.

"Sure," Leon answered. He carefully signed the name Lee Kirby and then printed the address for the Galworthy Medical Center, the one he had just phoned in Altoona. He inserted the medical center's correct phone number where it asked for home phone, just in case they checked against their phone bill, and then scribbled a phony license number after the words "Ford van." His was a Dodge van. They never checked license numbers, especially in a dump like this.

"Thank you, Mr. Kirby. You want to pay me in the morning?"

"Might as well pay you right now. Just in case we decide to leave early." Leon searched his pocket for two twenty-dollar bills.

While he counted out two dollars in change, the clerk said, "Was it airplane engines you work on?"

"Right," Leon lied. "A lot of small airports don't have enough good mechanics, so I sort of free-lance. The traveling's a pain, but they pay me extra for my time on the road. Besides, I don't have to leave Altoona more than once or twice a month."

"Haven't we seen you down here in Virginia about a dozen times during the past two months?"

"Yeah, but this was unusual. Guy at the Knoxville airport broke his arm. This should be my last trip down here for a while."

"Well, I'm glad you'll have more time at home, but

we'll miss you. We don't have too many regular customers."

Leon grinned. "Yeah, I like to stop here when I'm in this neck of the woods. Too much confusion in those big-city motels. Your place is a lot more reasonable, too."

"We try to keep our rates comfortable for hard-working men like yourself, and families."

"Well, good night." Leon picked up the keys and pushed the door open.

"We'll have hot coffee in here in the morning if you want it," the clerk called after him.

"Thanks."

Leon got back into the van and drove to the familiar bank of little rooms directly behind the office. He parked in front of number 5.

"Is this where we're going to sleep?" Jonathan asked.

"Get inside; we'll talk inside." Leon unlocked the door to the room for Jonathan and then walked to the rear of the van. He pulled out a large army duffel bag and a smaller gym bag and carried both inside.

"See, this place ain't too bad. Twin beds, bathroom, and a TV. Everything we need." Leon tossed the duffel bag next to the bed where Jonathan stood waiting. "That's your stuff."

The boy fell to his knees and tugged at the zipper. He examined the neatly folded stacks of shirts, pants, socks, and underwear before he spoke. "Where did you get all this?"

"Mostly K mart. It's all new. Your stuff at home got burned, remember?" Leon said.

Tears glistened in the boy's eyes. "How did you know my size?"

With a sense of pride, Leon thought about the number of times he had watched Jonathan and his friend, probably the kid named Brian, from a distance. He had done a good job of assessing his quarry. You watch somebody long enough, you learn a lot about them, even their underwear size. Leon guessed he probably knew more about Jonathan than the kid knew about himself.

"I just figured your size from all the pictures your folks sent me every Christmas. I knew you'd be needing stuff, so I bought it."

Jonathan discovered a toothbrush in a cellophane-covered box and a tube of toothpaste in his bag. "Thanks," he said, looking up at Leon.

"Don't mention it, kid. Your folks would've done the same thing for Maria if something had happened to me. Why don't you take a bath or something while I go get us some food? I'll be back before you know it."

Leon slipped the motel key into his pocket and tramped down the road to the local hamburger stand. He hoped they were still open. When he got closer, he saw the dirty little luncheonette was still lit up, but he walked faster just in case they were getting ready to close. He ordered two double burgers, fries, two slabs of apple pie, coffee, and a Coke. That should hold the kid for the night.

He let himself into the motel room and spread the food out on a wobbly night table between the twin beds. Leon removed the grease-stained paper from the burgers and placed them on napkins at opposite corners of the table. Then he combined the two orders of fries into one giant heap atop one of the burger wrappers. He ate a couple. Nice and salty, he thought. Just the way he liked them.

"Hey, kid," Leon called. "Come and get it."

Jonathan emerged from the bathroom in a clean T-shirt and the bottoms to the pair of pajamas Leon had bought for him. The creases from the folded package ran crosswise along the pajama legs. Jonathan's short brown hair was wet and slicked down, plastered against his head like a thin cap.

Leon studied the puny little kid who stood there looking like a puppy someone had meant to drown. He was pale, almost bleached, and at this moment Jonathan was an eerie reminder of the way Ed Grady, the kid's old man, had looked when he was first assigned to Leon's squad over in 'Nam.

Leon and Grady had come off their first patrol together. It had rained like a son of a bitch, and Grady was soaked to the teeth, enjoying the cooling rain after his first sweltering night out in the field. Leon had told him to put on his helmet, but Grady was still too green to understand the absolute terror of a Viet Cong beehive explosion that could shatter your head with thousands of metal fragments. Leon remembered how Grady had ducked like a scared rabbit the first time he heard a rocket-propelled grenade whizzing through the air. Where did those new guys—"cherries," they called them—think they were, some fucking summer camp? Leon suspected that Grady still had a lot to learn even today. Of course, now that he had Grady's kid, maybe he could speed up the learning process for his former good buddy.

Jonathan's big brown eyes were rimmed with red, but a weak smile crossed his babylike face when he saw the food. Without waiting for a further invitation, Jonathan shoved one of the fries into his mouth and took a long draw on the straw sticking out of the paper cup of Coke, but then he turned away from the food and sat down on the bed.

"What's the matter, kid? You don't like hamburgers?" Leon bit into his own burger and chewed. A rivulet of grease trickled down his wrist.

"I'm not very hungry."

"Well, what do you want? Here's apple pie." Leon held the soggy paper carton toward him.

"I just wanna go home," Jonathan said. The tears began to slip down his cheeks again.

"Listen, kid, I know this is hard for you, but you gotta hang tough. You don't have a home anymore. You're gonna live with me now."

Jonathan leaned back against the pillow on his bed. "Just until I can go to my grandma's."

"Sure, kid. Just until you go to your grandma's."

Jonathan rolled over, his back to Leon, and pulled his knees up toward his chest. Leon watched how the thin T-shirt pulsed across Jonathan's shoulders. The kid was still crying, but he hardly made a sound. Leon picked up Jonathan's untouched burger and took a bite, crunching into a thick slice of raw onion.

It wasn't good that the kid didn't eat. He was such a skinny little runt to start with. But he'll grow soon enough, Leon thought. Boys have a way of shooting up, growing all gangly and long-legged. Leon remembered the feeling of being all legs and feet when he was a teenager. Jonathan would be the same way in a couple of years; that is, if he decided to let the kid stick around that long.

Chapter 3

JONATHAN awoke early the next morning. He had been dreaming about the time his mom and dad had taken him camping at a park near the ocean. The sky seemed so much bigger at the beach, so wide and blue it went on forever until it touched down, gently skimming the edge of the ocean where a few tiny sailboats lolled in the sun. Ginger had gone wild, first jumping in the waves and then shaking herself until Jonathan was drenched. He came out of his dream and his sleep with a start, sadly realizing his parents could never take him anywhere ever again. Even Ginger was lost. He had to call Brian, or write him a letter. Brian's dad could help him search for Ginger. They would probably find the poor lost dog trembling under a neighbor's back porch.

Jonathan sat up and rubbed his eyes. Leon was still sound asleep. He crawled out of bed, gathered his clothes from where he had left them on the floor, and slipped into the bathroom, closing the door behind him. Jonathan dressed and brushed his teeth, then went back into the bedroom.

The room was dark and shadowy despite the rays of the morning sun that squinted through the slats of the dusty venetian blinds. Jonathan looked around. The carpet, the wallpaper, and the one vinyl-covered chair all seemed to be the same dreary shade of tan. There was nothing for him to do, so he sat down on the edge of his unmade bed and watched Leon sleep.

A snoring sound boiled from somewhere deep inside Leon's huge chest. His eyelids began to twitch and his eyebrows quivered slightly, but Leon still looked powerful, not at all soft and gentle the way his own dad had looked when he slept. He remembered the men who had worked for his dad at his real estate agency and some of his dad's friends who used to come to the house to visit. None of them had ever seemed as tough as Leon. Jonathan watched with fascination as Leon grunted and rolled over on his back.

Suddenly Leon began to kick against the thin sheet, churning the blanket on top almost to the floor. He grumbled something that sounded like "gook" into his pillow and slapped one arm down against the mattress. He's dreaming, Jonathan thought. Thick, blue veins bulged on Leon's arms and the backs of his hands, and his face contorted slightly. He was sweating now, his chest heaving as his breaths came deeper and closer together.

Jonathan wondered if he should wake Leon, but for some reason, he didn't want to touch him. He leaned closer just as Leon bolted upright to a sitting position, eyes wide with anger or fear, probably the memory of his dream. Jonathan jumped back, but Leon just closed his eyes and flopped back down on the bed. Leon reached under the sheet and scratched himself before he opened his eyes again.

"What? You dressed already?" Leon mumbled.

"Yes," Jonathan answered.

"Well, I guess I'd better get movin', too." Leon

stretched as he stood up, scratched himself again and went into the bathroom.

Jonathan flicked on the lamp and looked from the bedside table to the dresser. He thought all motels had telephones, but he didn't see one here. Maybe he could use the phone in the office. He had seen Leon making a call while he waited in the van last night. He pulled open the little drawer in the table between the beds. A ballpoint pen rolled back and forth over some wrinkled, gray stationery. A Bible was pushed to the back of the drawer. Jonathan picked it up and opened it. Inside he found two identical dog-eared postcards. He studied the picture of the Glade Spring Motel sparkling with row after row of gorgeous flowers planted right in front of the rooms. Even though it had been dark last night when they arrived, he didn't remember seeing any flowers. Maybe they planted the flowers in the summertime.

He turned the cards over. One was addressed to a Mr. Joseph McKaye, and it had a message about the weather and how long it was taking to drive from Maine to Florida. The other card had only the words: Mr. Joseph MacKaye where the address belonged. It looked as if the writer had misspelled the man's name and had started over on the other card. Having to start over on a school assignment, especially when he wrote in ink, was something Jonathan had done dozens of times, so he could understand such a mistake. But before he made his mistake, the writer had placed stamps on both cards!

Jonathan crossed out the name on the second card and carefully printed Brian's name and address underneath. He wrote a message, trying to fit as much information as possible into that tiny little space, and then put the Bible and the pen back in the drawer. Whoever had left the cards behind had given Jonathan a chance to contact Brian. He decided to repay the favor by mailing both cards.

He tucked the cards into a little pocket on one end of the duffel bag just as Leon came out of the bathroom. Within minutes Leon announced he was ready to leave.

Leon opened the rear doors of the van and began to rearrange the heaps of clothing and tools, scattered everywhere in a hopeless mess. "Bring your bag, boy," he called to Jonathan.

"Leon, can I mail a postcard to my friend, Brian? To ask him to look for Ginger?"

"I wouldn't be bothering your friend just yet. Give the dog a chance to come home first. I told you I'll call Brian soon's I have a chance."

"Could you call him today? Could I talk to him, too?"

Leon's lips tightened. "I don't want to call from a pay phone on the road. Costs too much. Can't you wait until we get home?"

"Okay, sure," Jonathan said, immediately sorry he was being a pest. He slipped his hand into the pocket on the duffel bag and fingered the postcards. The problem was, Leon just didn't understand how important this was. Maybe Brian didn't even know he was supposed to be on the lookout for Ginger. He pulled the cards out and hid them under the front of his shirt. "I'll be right back. I forgot my jacket."

Jonathan ran back into the open motel room. His jacket was on the bed where he had left it. He propped the postcards against the lamp on the dresser and prayed the motel people would know how important it was to mail them. Leon didn't understand, but maybe the man in the motel had kids of his own and a dog. He put on his jacket and went outside.

"You want me to lock the door now?" Jonathan called to Leon.

"Sure, kid. Just pull it shut; it'll lock. You sure you have everything now?"

"Yeah."

"Okay. Get in. We'll have breakfast on the road somewhere."

When Jonathan slid over on the seat, he bumped into his backpack. Inside, his school notebook and his math workbook were still there. He had forgotten he had been carrying his school supplies when he met Leon yesterday. Yesterday seemed years ago. It was as if he had fallen from the earth and landed in a distant, alien empire.

He tried not to think about his parents. He couldn't imagine anything more horrible than being burned to death, and he couldn't imagine what they must look like now. Whenever visions of blackened flesh gnawed at him, somehow the smiling faces of his mom and dad mercifully popped into his mind instead. He decided he would concentrate only on his happy memories and block any thoughts of the fire and their deaths forever from his mind. It was not until tears splattered down upon his hands folded on his lap that he realized he had been crying again.

Jonathan wiped his eyes and nose on his sleeve and pulled his three-ring binder out of his backpack. Neatly tucked inside the notebook, a plastic zipper pouch was filled with pens and pencils. He removed a pencil and began to write his name on a clean sheet of paper.

Leon glanced over at him. "What're you doing, kid? Writing a letter?"

"No, just my name." Jonathan didn't know why he had written his name. It just seemed necessary that he do something, anything to get his mind off his parents.

They passed through hilly farmland and then through a little town. Jonathan saw a bar named Nate's Watering Hole and a small restaurant that was open for breakfast, but Leon didn't stop. Jonathan wrote "Nate's Watering Hole" on the paper right under his name. He saw a route sign, 81 North, so he wrote that next. Sometimes he kept lists of interesting things he saw when his parents took him places, sort of like a game. Maybe keeping a list today would help him not to cry. At least it would help to pass the time.

Shortly after their stop at Hank's Diner for breakfast, a siren screamed loudly in the distance, approaching from behind. Leon flicked on his right-turn signal and slowed, exiting Interstate 81 near a place called Middletown. As they drove down the off ramp, Jonathan looked over his shoulder and saw two police cars speed by, continuing on the highway.

"Why did they have their sirens on?" Jonathan asked.

"Probably chasing someone. Speeders."

"Why'd you get off the highway? Were they chasing us?"

Leon looked annoyed. "Of course not. I wasn't speeding. I just don't like to drive with them riding my butt."

"How will we get to Pennsylvania?"

"There's plenty of roads besides Eighty-one. I like to drive the back roads anyway. Not so much traffic."

Jonathan continued to list the names of towns and rivers and businesses in his notebook. Then an official-looking sign caught his eye. "Hey, we're in West Virginia."

"Not for long," Leon said. "We'll cut over to Maryland in just a few miles."

Just as Leon had said, the narrow road wound through West Virginia for a very short distance. Soon Jonathan spotted a sign for Harper's Ferry. That name was familiar; he was pretty sure it had something to do with the Civil War. He wished now he had paid closer attention when his teacher used her long, wooden pointer to locate things on the classroom wall map. Mrs. Montgomery said a good citizen studies the geography of his country. He craned his neck but he saw no other familiar names until he saw a sign identifying the Potomac River. That he remembered. The Potomac went all the way to Washington, D.C. After they crossed the bridge over the Potomac, Jonathan saw a sign: MARYLAND WELCOMES YOU.

He grew tired of writing. Besides, there wasn't much to see along these tiny country roads, just wooden houses desperately in need of paint and colorless, gray-washed fields. The landscape seemed to fit the repetitious whining of the country music Leon had blaring from the radio.

"Don't you get lost without a map?" Jonathan asked. "My dad always uses a map."

"That why I was the sergeant and your dad was a private. There's a place up ahead where we can stop. They have a toilet in the back."

The place Leon described was the most run-down gas station Jonathan had ever seen. He wondered how Leon knew about so many gas stations and diners in the middle of nowhere.

The long drive continued. Jonathan ate some peanuts Leon had bought at the gas station, but they tasted funny. The little bag of peanuts had probably been stapled to that display card for at least a hundred years. He was ready to close his eyes against

26

the sun when he spotted another sign. WELCOME TO
PENNSYLVANIA. *Buckle Up—It's the Law.*

He began to write again. Gettysburg, 15 North,
New Oxford, Abbottstown, Thomasville. Signs
flashed by faster than he could copy all the names.

Jonathan saw an old farmhouse that had been
gutted by fire. Gaping black holes stared through
the walls where the windows used to be. That's what
his house looked like, maybe worse, but he remembered his decision and refused to think about the
fire that had changed his life.

They passed an abandoned, weed-choked, drive-
in theater and a building shaped like a gigantic
shoe. The old woman who had so many children
must live there, he thought, staring at a crooked little door in the crumbling old shoe. Things here
seemed so different from Georgia. Even the familiar
golden arches of McDonald's seemed completely out
of place.

One after another they passed tiny old-fashioned
towns separated from each other by fields and pas-
tureland. Cows and sheep ignored the ribbon of
traffic on the highway; the utilitarian houses, set
apart from the red barns with their silver silos, were
still boxed up tightly against the winter winds, even
though it was the beginning of April.

"Do you live on a farm?" Jonathan finally asked.

"Nope. Just a little spread this side of Reinholds."

"What's a spread?"

Leon grinned. "Just my place. Includes a lot of
woodland. I even got my own private road."

Jonathan's list now covered two columns.
Wright's Ferry Bridge, Prospect Road, Bible College,
Oregon Pike. He might as well be on the moon. None
of the names sounded familiar; all the houses and
barns were old and worn-looking against the gray of
the late afternoon sky.

After a while they rumbled over a little bridge that quivered from the weight of the van. Jonathan looked down into a shallow ravine dotted with tremendous rocks. Swirling black water foamed against the rocks as it rushed under the bridge.

"What's the name of that river?" Jonathan asked.

"That ain't no river. Just a creek."

"It looks like a river."

"Well, it ain't. We've had a lot of rain lately, that's all."

They left the creek behind and turned off Route 222 onto a narrow blacktop road cutting into a dark, wooded area. The sun was still shining, but the trees towered over the road like an arch, enclosing it in shadows. The van strained into a lower gear and roared up a long, hilly stretch. The tires crunched over the shoulder when Leon next turned onto a one-lane road paved with a fine layer of gravel. Like a volley from a machine gun, the tiny pieces of rock pinged against the underside of the van, echoing cruelly in Jonathan's head.

He sat up straighter and looked in amazement at the wild undergrowth tangled between the tall trees. The thick gloom of the surrounding woods extended as far as he could see. The wind stirred the treetops as Leon pushed farther into the woods.

Jonathan's eyes widened. "Where are you going?"

"This is it, boy. We're home."

At the end of the tortuous driveway sat a small, weather-beaten wood shack. A faint light glowed through the lowered window shade on one of the four visible windows. Beyond the shack was another smaller building, perhaps a garage, with an open door swinging back and forth monotonously in the wind. The ground between the two structures was strewn with the rusted hulls of dozens of ancient cars and trucks. Parts of engines and battered fenders were piled everywhere, just like a junkyard. Leon pulled up to the front of the house and parked next to an old Volkswagen. He turned off the motor.

Jonathan stared at the incredible heaps of automotive trash surrounding the little house. Who would place a house, even a shack, in the middle of all this junk? How had all this junk materialized in the middle of the woods? Was Leon kidding? That must be it; he had been brought here as a joke. But Leon had already opened his door and was getting out of the van.

Jonathan looked at the dense woodland surrounding the setting. The only color of warmth was the tiny square of the one lighted window. Shadows oozed out from behind every tree. The wind howled, creating sometimes a whisper, sometimes a groan. The woods seemed alive with enormous black creatures just waiting for a small boy.

"Don't just sit there, kid," Leon said. "Go on, get out of the van."

Jonathan saw a faint grin curl at the corners of Leon's mouth.

"Come on inside, boy," Leon said, "this here is your new home."

Chapter 4

Edward Grady dropped the phone back in its cradle. He looked across the room at his wife Susan. The crumpled tissue she pressed tightly against her mouth was the only thing holding back her tears, possibly even a scream. Jonathan had been missing less than eighteen hours, but already the dark purple patches under her eyes indicated the terror growing in her heart.

"That was the police. The copies of the photograph are ready," he said. "I'm going to go with them door-to-door."

Susan blinked back her tears. Her dark brown eyes were rimmed with red. Her whole face seemed swollen. "I'll go with you."

Ed ran his hand through his thick, sandy hair that curled around his ears no matter how hard he tried to tame it. "Do you think you should? Maybe you should wait by the phone in case somebody calls."

"Claudia will be here any minute. She'll wait by the phone. I have to do something, or I'll lose my mind."

Ed wrapped his arms around the petite, head-strong woman he loved so dearly and held her close.

"I can't believe this is happening," she said. "I

should have picked up Jonathan. Why didn't I pick him up?"

Ed stroked her hair, the scent of her shampoo pleasant and familiar, unlike the horror that had seized their minds. "Stop it, Sue. It's not your fault."

She pushed away slightly, then relaxed back into his arms. "If only I had driven over to the school. I could have waited while he took his makeup test. Mrs. Montgomery said he breezed through it in twenty minutes and had a ninety-eight. A ninety-eight . . . that's almost perfect." She began to cry again.

"You're tired," Ed said. "We're both tired."

Last night, after telephoning Jonathan's teacher as well as every single child in Jonathan's class and personally canvassing the neighborhood door-to-door, Ed had been too worried to sleep. Neither one of them had slept, and now the morning was glaring at them with the reality that their son had not gone to a friend's house after school. Something dreadful had happened.

"Did we call everyone in the other fifth grade class?" she asked suddenly. "Maybe there's a new kid at the school, one we don't know. We've got to keep trying."

"We'll find him, Sue," Ed said gently. "He'll turn up this morning. Maybe the police are bringing him home this very minute."

Susan squeezed her eyes shut. "They think he ran away. Jonathan has never run away. Why do the police keep insisting he ran away?"

"Lots of kids run away. I guess they're going by past experience."

Her eyes opened. "Not Jonathan. He wouldn't run away. I know my son."

A knock came at the door.

"That might be Claudia," Ed said. "I'll let her in."

Susan drew her sweater tighter around her slender body and headed for the kitchen. "I'll make a fresh pot of coffee."

Claudia Nowlin, their next-door neighbor, who looked like a carbon copy of Lucille Ball during her *I Love Lucy* days, opened the door and poked her head into the entryway before Ed got there. "Any news? How's Susan?" Claudia's son Brian was right behind her. "I brought Brian along. He might think of something we haven't."

"C'mon in. Hi, Brian." Ed lowered his voice. "See if you can talk Sue into staying here with you. She's exhausted."

"What about you?" Claudia said. "You look pretty beat yourself. Both of you should try to get some sleep. I'll be here."

"Thanks, but I've got to do something more physical than waiting around here." He turned to Brian, a fair-skinned redhead like his mother, with a generous sprinkling of freckles across his nose. "Did you think of any other friends we can call, a kid in another class or grade, maybe?"

"No, there's no one else. I told you, Jonathan wasn't going to anyone else's house yesterday. He was going to stay after school and make up his math test, and then we were going to play Nintendo as soon as he got home. He promised."

Ed knew Brian was right. Every parent they had called last night had contacted another half-dozen families. The networking of concerned parents was extremely effective, and by ten in the evening the word had spread to every family that had a child in Dunwoody Elementary. After what must have been a hundred phone calls, there was still no clue as to where Jonathan may have gone. Everything pointed to the possibility they feared most, but deep down inside, Ed still begged for another explanation. A brand-new friend who invited Jonathan to spend the night—maybe he told us about it, and we forgot —but that didn't ring true either. Jonathan would have called to let them know he had arrived safely at his friend's house. Jonathan wasn't with a friend.

Susan walked back into the room. "Hi, Claude. Want coffee?"

"Sure, I'll get some for all of us." Claudia hurried toward the kitchen.

Susan walked over to Brian. "Brian, have you—"

"I already asked him," Ed said. "Jonathan was supposed to play with Brian after school, just like he told us last night."

"I'm sorry, Brian. I believe you, I really do, but I can't believe Jonathan ran away, so there must be someplace we've all forgotten about."

As Susan spoke, her voice trembled. Ed fought back tears of his own. Neither of them had said the word out loud, but by now Ed was convinced they were facing a kidnapping.

The doorbell chimed; Susan almost jumped out of her skin. Ed hurried to open the door. Last night they had talked to two uniformed policemen who had organized the neighborhood search. The police combed the area, working through the night, but they came up empty. Now, two plainclothes officers stood on the porch with leather card holders flipped open to reveal their identification.

"Mr. Grady?" one of them said.

"Yes, please come in."

"I'm Detective Fernandez. This is Sergeant Denzler. Have you heard anything from your son?"

"No, nothing."

Fernandez was short, one of those thin, wiry kind of guys who seem to run on nervous energy. Susan stared at the detective, her eyes eager for news of their son, anything at all. They walked into the living room. Susan sat across from Fernandez, but Ed continued pacing. Brian kept his distance, lingering next to the table in the adjacent dining room.

The sound of the doorbell broke the tension. Ed hurried to open it. A tall, dark-haired man in a suit pressed into the doorway followed by another man who balanced a video camera on his shoulder.

"Mr. Grady? I'm Blain Richwine, WXIA. I was wondering if I could have a few words with you regarding your son."

Instinctively trying to prevent the intrusion of the TV camera into his living room, Ed closed the door to within just a few inches. "We told a reporter from the *Journal* everything we know. Right now we're busy with the police. Maybe if you could come back—"

"It's better if we get you some exposure right at the beginning, Mr. Grady. After all, time is of the essence in cases like this. We need to get a picture of your son on the early news. Do you know how many people watch the news every evening?"

Ed relaxed his grip on the door, allowing Mr. Richwine to push it open another few inches. "We gave the police his most recent school photograph. They said they'd pass it on to all the TV stations."

"Oh, yes, we have the still shot, but I'd like something more personal, to stir up the public interest, in your son's behalf, of course. What about a ransom note? Have you had anything like that?"

"No, nothing," Ed said.

Blain Richwine smiled, showing rows of perfectly shaped white teeth. "If I could just get a couple of close shots, you and your wife together, maybe you could tell us how you feel about what has happened. Tell us what it's like knowing your son is missing."

"How the hell do you think we feel?" Ed shouted,

wanting to punch this guy square in the nose, and cry at the same time.

Detective Fernandez grabbed Ed by the arm and gently pulled him out of the doorway. "Maybe you could check with me later on this, Richwine. You're timing stinks, as usual."

Richwine lowered his voice, but Ed could still hear him as he spoke. "If we show their grief to the public, you have a better chance of finding the boy before—"

Fernandez slammed the door in the reporter's face and led Ed back to the sofa where Susan sat. "Maybe we should get down to business. I'm sorry to say you'll probably have reporters bothering you all day."

"I won't let them turn this into a three-ring circus," Ed said as he placed a protective arm around Susan. Her shoulders and arm felt ice-cold to his touch through her blouse and sweater; tears quietly spilled from the corners of her eyes.

Claudia entered the room carrying a tray with five steaming mugs of coffee.

Fernandez took a cup and smiled. "Thanks, sure smells good."

Ed took the next cup and sipped. He burned the tip of his tongue without really feeling.

Fernandez hunched forward, holding a small notebook in one hand, balancing the coffee with the other. "We covered the immediate neighborhood last night. Today we're expanding the search."

"I know," Ed said, breathing easier now that the reporters had gone. "I'm going along."

"Good. The search team returned to the neighborhood at daybreak, checking through backyards, garages, and out-of-the-way places. They'll cover everything we covered last night, but in the daylight that part will be easier. As soon as we're convinced he isn't around here, we'll spread out into the surrounding communities and then into downtown Atlanta."

"Okay."

Fernandez cleared his throat. "Mr. Grady, does your son know not to get in a car with strangers?"

"Of course he knows," Ed said. "We've told him that a million times, haven't we, Susan?"

"Yes, yes, of course," she answered.

Fernandez cleared his throat again, this time louder. "There was one possible lead that turned up last night."

"What?" Susan leaped to her feet.

"You sure your son always walked home along the route you gave the officers yesterday?"

"Yes," Susan said. "He always went that way in case I had to pick him up for any reason. I usually pick up the boys if it's raining, too."

"It wasn't raining yesterday."

"No," she whispered.

"Did somebody see something?" Ed asked. Why was Fernandez torturing them like this?

"We're not certain. A lady over on Keyes Avenue, about two blocks this side of the school, observed something from her upstairs window at about three-thirty. She was busy changing her baby, so she didn't get a good look, but she saw a van turn around right in front of her house, even used her driveway. Then a boy, maybe the same age as your son, talked to the driver for a few minutes."

"Did they show her Jonathan's picture?" Susan asked.

"Yes, but she wasn't certain. Like I said, she was upstairs, looking down on all of this, but she said it was possible it was Jonathan."

Ed felt the blood drain from his head. "Was that it? The boy just talked to the driver of the van?"

Fernandez shook his head. "No. After they spoke, the boy got into the van and they drove away."

Chapter 5

JONATHAN followed Leon through the creaking screen door into a stifling-hot kitchen. A woman in a short, skintight white uniform stood at an old-fashioned stove stirring something in a pot. Her hair exploded from her head in a kinky mass of bedspring curls. Jonathan wasn't sure if she was pretty or not because her makeup was so heavily layered, she didn't look real. Her exaggerated splotches of rouge and eye makeup reminded him of the players in the school's Christmas play. She smiled broadly the moment she spotted Jonathan, and a laugh burst from her mouth.

"Well, look at this. I would've cooked something fancier if I had known you'd be bringing the boy along home," she said. "I thought this was just another week in court."

"Jonathan, this here is Judy Mae," Leon said.

Jonathan was confused. Leon had said he didn't have a wife.

Judy Mae took Jonathan's hand. "You poor thing; you must be tired from that long ride, and I'll bet you're hungry. I just fixed a nice pot of chicken noodle soup for us. You can sit down and eat some right now."

She led Jonathan to a small round kitchen table and pulled out a chair for him.

Judy Mae tapped her fingernails against the slick, heavy cloth that covered the table and frowned in Leon's direction. "I gave the oilcloth a good scrubbing. Looked like you hadn't wiped it for a week."

"You fuss too much," Leon said. "Where's Maria?"

"In there, by herself. I don't know why she don't talk more. She's too quiet."

"She'll have the boy to talk to now," Leon said. "She'll be all right."

Jonathan's eyes traveled from the yellow glare in the tiny kitchen into the near darkness of the room just beyond. In the corner a girl sat on a couch, hugging her knees to her chest. She stared at Jonathan with dark eyes so huge her face wore an expression of fright. Her long black hair was pulled away from her delicate white face, further emphasizing those enormous, haunted eyes.

"Maria, honey, come have some soup," Judy Mae called to her. "Look at who's here."

Maria didn't get up. She turned her head, looking away from the kitchen, drew her knees up even tighter and rocked her body back and forth.

"Get over here, girl," Leon said. "Come meet your new brother."

Jonathan felt a tingly sensation creep up his throat to his face. New brother? He wanted no part of this strange family, but on the other hand, he didn't know how he would ever get to his grandmother's house without Leon's help.

Finally the girl stood up and walked into the kitchen. Jonathan guessed she was several years older than he. She wore a red and yellow dress that was five or more inches too short and much too tight across the chest, and a shapeless cotton sweater of faded blue. Her long, thin legs were covered with bruises and scabs. Smudges of dirt outlined her knobby knees. She hid her hands behind her back.

"Honestly, Leon, you'd better let me take her into town for some new clothes. She's gonna bust right out of that dress one of these days," Judy Mae said.

"She has other clothes. She just won't wear them."

"Maybe I can find her something nice in the Spiegel catalog, some dresses, maybe?" Judy Mae said. "You'd like that, wouldn't you, honey?"

Maria didn't answer, but sidled up to the table and slipped into a chair. All the while, she stared down at the bare plank floor.

Judy Mae brought steaming bowls of soup to the table one at a time. She smiled with each delivery and patted Jonathan on the top of his head after she placed a bowl of soup in front of him.

"You go ahead and eat, honey."

The soup smelled wonderful, but Jonathan hesitated when he saw little greasy circles of fat floating on the surface. He stabbed one of the larger ones with his spoon until it burst into two smaller circles. He licked the spoon, expecting it to taste greasy, and was surprised to find the soup delicious, almost as good as his mom's. He dipped the spoon deeper and sampled a noodle shaped like a little bow tie. The hot broth warmed him, and he carefully spooned it to his lips, trying not to spill any on his shirt.

"Anybody want crackers?" Judy Mae asked.

She pulled a box of soda crackers from the cupboard and carried it along with her own soup bowl. Leon shook a few crackers from the box, spilling them directly on the table. Jonathan looked around for a napkin or a plate before he, too, placed his own crackers on the tablecloth.

Leon pulled a large green bottle of wine from a bag he had placed in the center of the table when they first entered the room. Jonathan felt his eyes begin to water, but he squeezed his eyes shut, holding back the tears. It was the same wine Leon had bought to share with his parents. The cork popped easily when Leon pushed at it with his huge thumb.

"Well, look at this," Judy Mae said, smiling, "white wine. I guess we do have reason to celebrate."

Celebrate? Jonathan wondered what she meant.

Judy Mae got up and went back to the cupboard for two small glasses. Jonathan recognized the faded figures of the Flintstones dancing on the outside of the two former jelly glasses. He used to have a glass just like that at home, but that was when he was little.

"Let me get milk for the kids," she said to Leon. "You were out again, but I picked up a quart this morning."

"Judy Mae, why don't you sit down and stop fussing?" Leon said.

She returned to the table with two glasses of milk for Jonathan and Maria while Leon poured the wine. Leon immediately took a long pull from his glass and then refilled it. Grinning, he raised his second glass to Judy Mae.

"Here's lookin' at you," he said, and drank again.

"And to us, sweetie pie." Judy Mae reached over and gave Leon's knee a big squeeze, and then she trailed her hand up the inside of his leg, almost to his crotch. She giggled and drank half of her wine in one long gulp.

Leon refilled the wineglasses and began to slurp soup from the side of his spoon.

Judy Mae smiled and tasted her own soup. "Good and hot," she said. She crushed a cracker into her bowl and stirred it with her spoon, trying to sink the larger pieces of cracker that bobbed to the top. "I'm glad this custody thing is finally over."

Leon glared at her. "Not now, Judy Mae. Don't let's talk about it in front of the kids."

Judy Mae frowned as she continued to sip the hot liquid. "Well, I'm glad you're home. Jonathan's sure a nice-looking boy, a bit on the skinny side, but we can fatten him up."

They ate in silence. Maria nibbled on the corner of a cracker and sipped a bit of soup from time to time. Jonathan watched Leon as he slurped and snorted, but Leon's eyes never strayed from the bowl and wineglass in front of him.

"Oh, I just remembered," Judy Mae said. "The john's busted again. You're gonna have to fix it."

"Okay, in the morning."

"You're gonna make the boy use the privy on his first night?"

The top of Leon's bald head tinged red. "For crissakes, that won't hurt him. Plenty of folks never use anything else, and they survive."

Judy Mae wrinkled her nose. "Maria, honey, you'll have to show Jonathan where the privy is." She turned back to Leon. "I'll wash up the dishes, and then I have to get back to the diner. I promised Jake I'd help him close the place if you got home early. He'll be glad you did. He's getting steamed about all the time I've been taking off."

"Tell that big bag of wind to relax," Leon said. "You can work all you want now. I won't be needing you to watch Maria while I go out of town anymore. At least not for a while."

Judy Mae stood up and kissed Leon on top of his shiny head. "But you'll be needing me for other things, won't you, honeybunch?" She trailed her fingers across his broad shoulders and giggled.

Leon's face went an even deeper shade of red. "You heard what Judy Mae said, didn't you?" he barked at Maria. "Show the boy where the privy is. It'll be dark soon."

Leon grabbed Judy Mae's behind and pulled her

toward him. She giggled again and landed sideways on his knee.

"Well, go on," Leon said to Maria.

Maria walked to the door. She stopped and turned, staring at Jonathan. He jumped up and followed her outside.

The screen door slammed behind them. Jonathan whispered, "Your dad told me he wasn't married. Who's Judy Mae, his girlfriend?"

"Leon's not my dad," she answered without looking at him.

"Oh." Now Jonathan was really confused. He was certain Leon had called Maria his little girl. "Who's Judy Mae?" he asked.

"She comes to visit, and she stays with me when Leon goes out of town. She says she's going to marry him."

"Oh," Jonathan answered, still not understanding.

He studied the piles of auto parts on both sides of the path. A rusted hood, small and rounded like a Volkswagen's, leaned against a tree. A tailgate from a Ford pickup lay balanced over a bumper. The bumper looked heavy in spite of layers of rust; maybe it came from a truck.

"What's a privy?" he said after they had walked a few paces in silence.

"A stinking hole," Maria answered.

"What?"

"It's where you have to go to the bathroom when the toilet doesn't work. It happens about once a month."

They passed the garage and walked into the woods. A thicket of tall, shadowy trees loomed all around them. Just ahead, almost hidden by the trees, Jonathan could see the outline of a small shed, not much bigger than a phone booth.

43

"How do you find your way out here at night? It's dark," he said.

"I'm used to it. There's a flashlight in the kitchen, hanging right by the door for when it's dark outside. There's one in here, too."

She opened the door of the privy and groped inside until her hand located the flashlight. She turned it on and hung it back on the nail where she had found it. "This flashlight's just so you can see inside. I'll wait out here for you."

Maria held the door and closed it behind Jonathan after he stepped into the tiny cubicle. The flashlight mostly lit up the floor, but he could see a wooden bench against the opposite wall. A regular white toilet seat was centered on the rough-hewn boards. He lifted the lid and immediately jumped back. The stench penetrated his nostrils and made his eyes water. His first impulse was to shine the flashlight down into the dark pit beneath the seat to see exactly what sort of disgusting filth filled the hole, but he decided maybe he really didn't want to know. He used the privy quickly and ran outside.

"Turn off the flashlight," Maria said. "Leon says batteries don't grow on trees."

Jonathan reached inside to turn off the light without reentering the outbuilding. "What do you do if it's raining?" he asked.

Maria shrugged her wire-thin shoulders and began to walk. "Let's go back."

When they entered the kitchen, they found Leon and Judy Mae locked together, kissing. Leon had one hand on her buttocks, the other tightly intertwined within a fistful of Judy Mae's hair. Judy Mae dropped her arms from around Leon's neck, straightened her skimpy uniform and smiled.

"Back so soon? Well, I've got to run. I'm glad

you're here with us, Jonathan." She grabbed Leon's hand. "Walk me to my car, sweetie."

Leon and Judy Mae slammed the door. Jonathan was sleepy; his arms and legs felt heavy. He turned to Maria and asked, "Where do I sleep?"

Without answering, she turned and walked away from him, into the room beyond the kitchen. He followed and, once his eyes adjusted to the dim light, saw the room was furnished with three shabby chairs besides the sagging couch. A TV tray held a small lamp, and a television set took up most of another small wooden table. Several crooked boards supported by big cinder blocks looked like a makeshift bookshelf, but there were no books. Instead, it was loaded down with cardboard boxes and stacks of rumpled junk mail. A door was positioned off center in the far wall.

"In here," Maria said. She opened the door and flicked on a ceiling light.

A twin bed was pushed into the corner next to the only window. A scratched chest of drawers held a small lamp that had no shade and a framed picture of an old woman. Like the kitchen and the living room, the bare floorboards, worn smooth and colorless as an overcast sky, looked cold and hard. A door stood open near the bed.

"What's in there?" Jonathan asked.

Maria marched into the next room and tugged on a string hanging from the ceiling. A single, exposed light bulb lit up a small yellowed sink, a toilet, and a bathtub. Still another door opened into the next room.

"That's Leon's room," Maria said, pointing toward the black space. She pulled the overhead string again, leaving the bathroom also in darkness. "Always turn off the lights, so he won't yell."

"Where do you sleep?" he asked.

45

Maria hesitated. "I like to sleep in the parlor, on the couch."

"I could sleep on the couch; I don't mind."

"Leon said you're supposed to sleep in this room," she answered.

"I've never seen a house like this one, where the rooms are all connected together." Jonathan sat on the edge of the bed and studied the floor.

Maria stood on one foot, awkwardly steadying herself by touching down the toe of her other foot. "Leon said his room was added on. They just attached it next to the bathroom." She hesitated, then added, "My old house had a hallway."

"What old house?"

"Where I lived with my parents and my sister a long time ago."

Jonathan nodded knowingly, although he still didn't understand why Maria lived here with Leon. Was it possible that her house had burned down also? "My house in Georgia was big and new. Not like this house at all."

"Yeah," Maria said, "it's different here."

"I'm glad I won't have to stay too long. I'll be moving to Columbus soon. That's in Ohio. My grandma's house is old, but it's real big, so's the yard."

"Leon says plenty of people live in little houses just like this one for their whole lives, and they don't seem to mind."

Jonathan looked at her. He thought he noticed a quiver in her lower lip. "Do you mind?" he asked. "Do you like living here in the woods?"

Maria's eyes grew larger, a seemingly impossible feat. She shrugged her shoulders and looked at the floor. "This is the only place I got," she said softly.

Chapter 6

LEON opened the door of the VW beetle for Judy Mae. Her skirt slid way up her leg as she wiggled behind the wheel. Leon eyed the flesh on her leg as it rippled then settled into place. As much as she got on his nerves, she had been useful, in more ways than one.

"I'm glad you're done with all these trips," she said through the open window. "I don't understand why a custody case had to take so long if both his parents are dead. Those judges oughta be happy you're willing to take the kid off their hands. Doesn't make sense for things to drag out like they did."

"I told you I didn't want us talking about it."

Judy Mae furrowed her penciled brows. "You said in front of the kids. The kids are in the house."

"Well, let's just drop it. The boy is now legally mine and there's nothing more to say. I don't want to upset him with a lot of talk."

"What about us, Leon? You said we'd talk as soon as you had this court case out of the way."

"Yeah, but I'm tired. It's been a long day," he said.

"I didn't mean right this second, but I would like to know where I stand. I haven't been seeing anyone else for a long time now."

Leon kicked the toe of his shoe into a clod of dirt.

"I know, and I haven't had any other women. You know I'm not going to run out on you, don't you?"

"Sure, honey, I believe you, but I want things to be right between us. We should get married. Make a nice home for those two kids you adopted."

"I don't like the word adopted," he said. "They're my kids, and that's that."

Judy Mae inserted her key in the ignition. "Well then, if we get married, they'll have you and me. Two parents, just like they had before their real parents got killed. They really need a mama, especially Maria."

"She's okay," Leon said. "You worry too much."

"Listen, you lunkhead, you still think of her as a baby. Do you know what she told me while you were gone?"

Leon's mouth suddenly felt dry. He licked his lips, then said, "What?"

"She got her first period, that's what. She's now a young woman, not a little kid."

"What do I have to do?"

Judy Mae laughed. "I bought her a big box of sanitary pads and told her what was happening. I think she understands. She didn't know about pregnancy or anything. Poor kid was scared to death when it started."

"Why?"

"Because you didn't tell her anything, that's why. She thought she had done something wrong and hurt herself. She thought she was bleeding to death."

"What did she think she had done?" Leon gripped the car door and leaned closer. "Did she say?"

"No, silly, she just thought something awful had happened to her, I guess. Shoot, if I didn't know about female ways and I just started bleeding like that, I'd think I had cancer or something."

"Oh."

Judy Mae fluffed the curls circling her left ear. "Like I said, those kids need me. They need a mama."

"Yeah, you're right. Listen, we'll talk about it the next time I come over to your place, maybe Monday, okay?"

"Okay, but I gotta work late Monday. Let's do it Tuesday."

"Sure thing, baby. I'll be there Tuesday."

"Leon, there was something I wanted to ask."

"What?"

"About the kids. You don't have any more friends who have you lined up as legal guardian, do you?"

"Well, no."

"Don't get me wrong. What you're doing is great, more than most guys would do. Shoot, I don't know any other guy who would actually adopt kids who weren't even family, but I was just wondering . . ."

"I'm not going to turn the place into an orphanage, if that's what you're thinking. It'll just be you and me and a couple of kids to help you around the house."

"And maybe a baby of our own?" she asked, prying his fingers loose from the door frame. She curled her fingers inside his. "Wouldn't you like to have a little baby of our own?"

"Sure. Why not?" Leon answered. It didn't hurt to humor her when she was in one of her maternal moods, but on the other hand, he sure didn't want to father a baby.

"You mean it, sweetie?" Judy Mae said. She bounced on the car seat, poking her head out of the window.

Leon leaned into her full red lips and kissed her, hard. Judy Mae aroused him real bad most of the time, but her constant banter was growing increasingly annoying. If only she didn't talk so much.

"We'll do it soon, won't we, sweetie?" she asked. "Let's get married real soon, 'cause I'm not getting any younger, you know. We gotta make that baby of ours before too many more years go by." Judy Mae giggled.

Leon hesitated, drumming his fingers on the roof of the car. "Well . . ."

"I always wanted to be a June bride. We'll get married in June, and then, if we're lucky, sometime next year we'll have a little bundle of joy. I hope we have a boy."

Leon didn't know how to ward off this crazy talk about marriage and babies, so he just grinned. If she didn't shut up soon, he was sure his head would start pounding again.

"Give me another kiss, you big lug." Judy Mae leaned toward him. She was all smiles as she started her car and backed away from the house.

He walked over to the van and opened the back door. He yanked out the two canvas bags. Maybe it wouldn't be so bad if he did marry her, he thought. He could talk her out of this idea of having a baby, and if he couldn't talk her out of it, maybe he could knock some sense into her with the back of his hand. She could cook for them and clean the place, give him more time to earn a living doing his auto repairs. And he didn't exactly object to the idea of going to bed with Judy Mae every night. She was old enough to know what to do. Sometimes the real young ones were more trouble than they were worth. Judy Mae was a willing lover, ready to do anything he wanted, even those things she said she had never done before. But if Judy Mae lived with him as his wife, what would that do to his plan to take the last kid? He'd have to think about it.

He had planned this whole thing so carefully, working out millions of details in his head. The planning alone had taken him years. Now that he had Jonathan where he wanted him, he had one of Mendoza's kids and Grady's only son. All he had left was Cozelli's kid, and he would be the easiest. Cozelli lived right here in Pennsylvania, a little over forty miles away.

Vince Mendoza, Maria's old man, had settled in California after he shipped home from 'Nam. Leon sure couldn't afford to run back and forth to the West Coast, so he had decided Maria had to be his first. Why Mendoza wanted to live in such an artificial world as Los Angeles, Leon couldn't imagine, but that's where Mendoza was, and Leon had had no choice. For three months he'd been forced to live there, right in the middle of the snarled traffic in the hopelessly overcrowded downtown area, waiting around for an opportunity to grab Maria. It came when he found her walking home alone on a side street not two blocks from her own house.

The long drive back home to Pennsylvania had been grueling, with the kid sniveling or crying every moment she wasn't sleeping. It had taken all of his patience not to whip the daylights out of her every time she cried. But he had remembered to control his temper, and he had spoken to her kindly for all of those three thousand miles.

That had been a long time ago. At first he had grown so used to having Maria take care of him, he wasn't in a big hurry to bring Grady's kid to his place. But he had always known he would have to do the job completely. One kid from each of them. That was the way it had to be.

Finally, about a year ago, he decided he had waited long enough. Since then, he had driven down to Georgia dozens of times, and what to do with Maria was always a problem. At first he could see no choice but to take Maria with him. Having a little girl by the hand wasn't such a bad idea when he was hanging around Jonathan's school, watching the boy from a distance, but most of the time he just couldn't think straight when she was with him. When she was hungry, she would whine, and then she started asking a lot of dumb questions. Meeting Judy Mae at the diner had solved his problem perfectly.

Judy Mae liked kids, and she was hungry for a husband to take care of her. She was looking for a way out of spending her life slinging blue-plate specials at Jake's Diner. After he had explained how he was raising a little girl he had adopted all by himself, her opinion of him had skyrocketed. To her, he was a hero. And Leon soon learned it's a lot easier for a hero to lure a woman into bed than it is for an ordinary grease monkey with a permanent layer of black scum under his fingernails.

Once she had set her sights on marrying him, Judy Mae became overly willing to please. She was always happy to take care of Maria while he went to Georgia to stalk Jonathan. Without her help, he might not have been able to pull it off, and for that, he guessed he owed her something.

But he had to be careful. Being too nice to Judy Mae could ruin his plans to get his hands on the last kid. He had to consider what was more important, and finishing the job he had set out to do was definitely more important. The stratagem he had mapped out and planned so carefully for all these years could not be considered finished until all three kids were his to take care of in every sense of the word.

Chapter 7

Jonathan opened his eyes and looked up at the cracks in the ceiling. A net of dirty cobwebs floated from one corner of the room and reconnected itself at the top of the tiny window. A shrunken, yellowish window shade hung almost to the sill, and below the shade the panes of glass had filmed over with years of accumulated grime. Dust motes danced in a narrow shaft of sunlight that squeezed through a tear in the shade. When he remembered where he was, an incredible heaviness filled his stomach.

Today was Sunday. His dad always cooked breakfast on Sundays, and he always helped. Together they whipped up blueberry pancakes or strawberry waffles while his mom pretended to be sound asleep. Jonathan set the table with their fanciest place mats, poured the orange juice, then ran upstairs to wake his mom. She always laughed and acted surprised, even though they did this every single week. Jonathan blinked back tears and rolled over to one side. He drew his knees all the way up to his stomach, trying to ease the rock-solid lump wrenching inside him.

The door to the bathroom opened and Maria poked her head into Jonathan's room. "You awake?" she whispered.

Jonathan nodded and sat up.

"He's still asleep," Maria said. She tiptoed across Jonathan's room and went into the living room. As soon as she closed the door behind her, Jonathan crawled out of the little bed and rummaged through his duffel bag for clean clothes. He went into the bathroom and brushed his teeth before he remembered the toilet was broken. He hoped the privy wouldn't be so scary during the daytime.

Jonathan found Maria in the kitchen, lighting one of the burners on the stove with a match. "What's that smell?" he asked.

"Kerosene. I spilled a little."

"What's kerosene?"

"Stuff we put in the stove. It smells awful."

He hugged his arms close to his body and rubbed them. The kitchen felt cold and looked dingy. Stacks of pots and dishes lined open shelves next to the window and above the table. The paint on the cupboards above and below a black sink was worn to the bare wood except for a few flecks of white near the hinges. Black smudges ringed the handles on the four doors and the drawers. The kerosene stove sat next to the sink, and across the room stood the oldest refrigerator Jonathan had ever seen. He remembered the jungle of plants his mom used to have hanging by the windows and over the sink at home. In Leon's kitchen there was no color, no warmth, not even a lonely geranium.

Jonathan watched Maria put a pot of coffee on the burner. She carefully regulated the flame, then wiped her hands on the front of the same dress she had worn the night before.

She looked up at him. "Leon said your parents died."

Jonathan nodded. The pain was just beginning to register. He didn't want to talk about it.

"Sorry," Maria said.

"How old are you?" Jonathan asked.

"I'll be thirteen in June."

He understood why she said thirteen in June rather than twelve. When you're that close to being a teenager, you skip the part about being twelve. Twelve is even worse than being ten.

"What grade are you in?" he asked.

Maria gave him a blank look. "I went to fourth grade back home. There's no schools around here."

"Sure there are," Jonathan said. "I saw schools along the road all the way from Georgia to Pennsylvania."

"Not anywhere near these woods. Besides, Leon says they're a waste of time. He brings me books to read sometimes."

"I'll be right back," Jonathan said. He hurried outside to the privy, wondering how Leon could get away with something like that. Mrs. Montgomery said there were laws requiring kids to go to school. Maybe Pennsylvania was different.

In the morning sun the house looked even gloomier. Whatever paint had once covered the outside had weathered away years ago. But by daylight the rusted heaps of junk lining the path didn't seem quite so threatening. If his dad were with him, it might even be fun to dig through the mountain of auto parts or to sit inside one of the deteriorating shells that had once been a car. He had to stop thinking like that. His dad was dead. He sniffed and wiped his sleeve across his nose.

By the time Jonathan got back, Leon was in the kitchen. Leon hadn't shaved or washed, and he wore old, greasy work clothes that smelled musty and disagreeable.

"I'm gonna try to unplug the john today," he said.

"You won't have to use the outhouse after this morning."

"When can I call my grandma?" Jonathan asked.

"Write the number on a piece of paper so I don't forget it," Leon answered. Jonathan noticed a vein thumping in Leon's short, chunky throat.

"I can dial myself," Jonathan said. "I call her all the time."

"You can't dial nothing if you don't have a phone. Like I told you, I'll call soon's I get to town."

Jonathan wondered why he hadn't seen a telephone. He had assumed it was in Leon's bedroom. "You mean you don't have one? You don't have a phone?"

"That's right. Costs too much nowadays." Leon began to eat the scrambled eggs Maria had placed in front of him.

Jonathan felt a sudden tightening in his throat. "When will you go to town?"

"Tomorrow or the next day, I don't know."

"Can I go with you?"

Leon looked up from his eggs. "Not if I'm on business. Now don't be bothering me all the time about things that don't matter. I got enough worries now that I have another mouth to feed."

Jonathan tasted the eggs Maria had scrambled. They didn't taste like eggs. They didn't taste like anything. He swallowed the slippery yellow lumps without chewing.

Maria refilled Leon's coffee cup. "Maybe when you go to the store, you could take me and Jonathan along?" she said. "We'll be needing eggs and some other things tomorrow."

Leon glared at her. "Maybe."

As soon as he finished his coffee, Leon went outside. Maria washed the breakfast dishes and Jonathan dried.

"I've never seen a black sink before," Jonathan said. "I thought all kitchen sinks were white."

Maria wiped the edge of the sink with a towel, then dried her hands. "My mother used to have a stainless steel sink."

"Oh, yeah," Jonathan said, remembering, "I've seen those, but not a black one like this."

"It's old," Maria explained. "Everything around here is old."

Jonathan nodded, looking out the window at the heaps of junked auto parts. "Does Leon work on cars every day?"

Maria shrugged. "Just when someone he knows has one that's busted."

"Do you ever watch?"

Maria's eyes grew serious. "No."

Jonathan thought Maria looked brittle, like the spun-glass angel his dad used to fasten to the top of their Christmas tree. Her skin was too white, too pale for a kid, and she certainly didn't look very happy. He wondered if she ever smiled.

"What do you do all day?"

"I mostly watch TV while he's working," she said, "but sometimes I play in the old Chevy. It doesn't have a motor, but the inside's still real nice."

"Can we play in the woods?" Jonathan asked.

"When Leon goes away we can. He never used to let me out of his sight, but now he sometimes leaves me here alone or with Judy Mae."

"They're going to get married?"

"Yeah, she wants to marry him. I heard her say it. I'd never want to marry someone like Leon."

"Was your mom married to Leon? Is he your step-father?"

"My mom wouldn't have married him either. He's my legal guardian. That's all."

"Oh," Jonathan said, wondering exactly what legal guardian meant. He had friends with stepparents, but he didn't think that was the same as a legal guardian.

Leon clumped back into the house with a cardboard box full of tools. He looked at Maria, then shifted his eyes to Jonathan. "I'd better fix the TV first," he said.

"What's wrong with it?" Maria asked, following him into the living room. "It was okay yesterday."

"You have to change the tubes and things every now and then. They go bad and you have to change them."

"But there's a movie on today. I wanted to see it."

"Stop whining, girl. You watch too damned much TV anyway. If I don't fix the set now, it'll cost me twice as much if the thing blows up."

Maria looked at the floor, trying not to show how upset she was. "TVs don't blow up," she said weakly.

Leon's face colored with blotches of red. "I say they do, so go find something else to do. Both of you."

Jonathan watched from the doorway as Leon unplugged the television set from the wall and unscrewed the little screws on the back cover. He removed several bulblike things and a little board and dropped them into a clear plastic bag. "These are the parts that go bad," he said. "I'll order a set of new ones when I get to town."

"How long will that take?" Maria asked.

"I don't know. Maybe a long time."

Leaving the back panel off the television set, Leon walked by them and into the bathroom. Within minutes the sounds of clanking pipes and the swoosh of a bathroom plunger echoed into the living room.

"What do we do now?" Jonathan asked.

"You want to go outside?" Maria said, her lower lip still drooping.

"Sure."

"What do you want to do?"

"I don't know."

"C'mon, I'll show you Leon's garage."

He followed Maria into the yard, walking directly behind her as she forged a path between the mounds of fenders and grills. She pointed out the Chevy that didn't have an engine. It sat, leaning to one side because of two flat tires, in a patch of tall weeds.

The garage doors were wide open, swinging on large hinges rather than rising up out of the way like the garage doors Jonathan remembered from his old neighborhood. He peered inside and saw a dirty, cavelike room filled with junk. An open loft at the far end of the cluttered space suggested at one time the garage might have been a small barn. The floor was littered with more automobile parts, and several workbenches along two of the walls were also heaped with rings and gaskets and broken rubber belts. All sorts of tools hung from the walls, along with several rifles and a handgun.

"Can I look at the guns?" Jonathan asked.

"No, don't mess with any of his stuff," Maria warned.

"How could we hurt anything? The place is already a mess."

"He'll know if you take any of his stuff."

"Well, I wasn't going to take anything," Jonathan said, backing out of the doorway. "I just wanted to look."

"I have a jump rope," Maria said. She retrieved a length of white clothesline from a nail behind the garage door. "Now that you're here, we could tie one end to a tree and you could turn for me."

"Aw," Jonathan began. Jump rope was a girls' game, but he saw the look on her face. He figured none of the boys from school, or anyplace else for that matter, would ever know. "Sure, maybe later," he added.

Maria stiffened. "I hear a car. Do you hear it?"

Jonathan strained his ears. It did sound like a car was approaching.

"I'd better tell Leon," she said, and ran back into the house.

An old Ford pickup bounced around the last bend just as Leon came outside. The old man driving the truck pulled past Leon's van and parked close to the garage.

"Howdy," he called. "She's acting up again. Can you take a look at her?"

"Sure. Just let me wash my hands and I'll drive you back into town."

"Can I go along? To use the phone?" Jonathan asked.

"Not this time. William here is a customer. We have to talk business."

Jonathan raced inside and wrote his grandmother's phone number, nice and big, on a piece of paper. He waited, smiling, right next to the man named William. As soon as Leon returned, Jonathan thrust the paper into his hand.

"Please call my grandma. Ask her how long before I can go live with her."

William raised his eyebrows, looking at Leon.

"This here is the son of an old army buddy of mine. The two of us were like brothers. I'm looking after the boy for a while."

William smiled. "That's nice. That's real nice."

Leon grabbed the scrap of paper and wadded it into his pocket. "Sure, kid, I'll see what I can do. You two see that you stay out of trouble till I get back. I won't be long."

As the two men drove away in the van, Jonathan realized Maria was back in the house, watching him through the screen door. "You want a cracker with jelly on it?" she asked. "Then maybe we can play jump rope, just for a little while."

"Okay." Jonathan felt good for the first time in two days. He knew his grandmother wouldn't make him wait too long. He just knew it. He smiled to himself as he watched Maria layer grape jelly on two Saltine squares.

"I'll be going to live with my grandma soon. Leon's going to call her for me."

Maria did not look up. "He used to call my aunt, but she was sick a lot."

"What happened?"

"I thought maybe I could live with my aunt. She really liked me and my sister."

"Where's your sister?" Jonathan asked.

"She died," Maria said flatly, "same time my parents died in an automobile accident."

"So why didn't you live with your aunt?"

Maria's face went blank, and suddenly she seemed to be looking at some faraway place only she could see. After a few moments she said, "Leon kept calling her for me, but then one day he told me my aunt died, too."

Jonathan immediately wished he hadn't asked. Her eyes reflected the same pain he was feeling, but at least he still had his grandmother. "That's rough," he said, "losing your whole family like that."

"Yeah," Maria said, nodding. "It all happened so fast. It was only three weeks after the accident when Aunt Alisa died."

Chapter 8

LEON drove into the little town of Reinholds and dropped off old William before he pulled into the parking lot shared by the Reinholds General Store and the Cacoosing Dairy. The dairy would be closed, but the general store was open until three on Sundays. Leon guessed they had to do something to compete with the big shopping centers that had sprung up like concrete mushrooms all over the county.

The lines on the parking lot had been freshly painted since his last trip to town. He parked squarely in the middle of two spaces and shut off the engine. He sat there for a moment, thinking how tired he was. A tightness crept across his shoulders; his eyes wanted to water. During the night, he had been awakened again by his nightmare. After the nightmare came the headache. Always at the same screaming pitch, never letting him forget, and because of the pain, he hadn't been able to go back to sleep until the first light of dawn. He wished the goddamn dream and the pain would go away, but he also knew wishing alone would not make it happen. The only thing that would stop his torment was for him to get even. He reached into his glove compartment and searched for a wrinkled scrap of paper he had been saving for almost two years.

He walked over to the phone booth near the entrance to the dairy. If he was going to follow through with his plan, he had to check out Cozelli's address. Leon dropped a quarter into the slot and punched out the number he had scribbled on the scrap of paper, right next to Cozelli's address in Harrisburg.

"Please deposit one dollar and seventy-five cents for the first three minutes," a hollow voice said.

He slid the coins into the silver opening and waited. The phone began to ring.

"Hello," a child's voice answered.

"This is Harry Cohen," Leon said. "I'd like to speak to Tony Cozelli."

"Hold on," the child said, then, "Dad, it's for you!"

"Hello."

"Tony, this is Harry Cohen, I don't know if you remember me, I was in your unit in 'Nam, assistant to the chaplain."

"Oh, yeah," Tony said after a pause, "what a surprise. How are you?"

"Fine, I'm in Harrisburg for a few days, and I thought I'd look you up. You're probably too busy to get together."

"Gee, I'm sorry, but today my wife and I are going to be painting the kitchen in our new house. We're moving into a new place on Friday."

"Yeah? Where's the new place?"

"Winston Road, it's on the other side of town."

"No fooling?" Leon said. "I have a cousin on Winston Road. What's the address?"

"It's 2166. Is that near your cousin?"

"Nah, he must be a couple of miles away. Listen, next time I'm in Harrisburg I'll give you a call. Will your number be the same?"

"No, we don't have the new number yet. We have to set up an appointment with the phone company. There's so goddamn much to do when you move. Excuse my French."

Leon laughed. "Hey, how's that little boy of yours? What's his name again?"

"Billy, he's fine, growing like a weed."

"Yeah, I'll bet. Listen, it was nice talking to you. I'll look up your number when I come back in about six months."

"Hey, that would be great. Thanks for calling."

Leon grinned to himself as he walked away from the phone. What luck. He had Cozelli's new address before the guy even moved. He was now much closer to getting even than he had been. Friday, he'd said. Maybe in the confusion of moving, the kid might go outside to play? Billy Cozelli might be the easiest one of all.

Leon wrote the new information on the same scrap of paper and put it back in his glove compartment. With Cozelli's address safely tucked away, he would concentrate on Jonathan. He had a nagging feeling he would never be able to let down his guard with this kid. Jonathan was clever, a thinker. He had always felt pretty uncomfortable around thinkers, but he would show the kid that he was getting to be a pretty good thinker himself.

Leon felt good about the way he had handled the kid so far, but now he had to think of some way to soften the news about the grandmother, because Jonathan was not going to be as easy to fool as Maria. A thinker like Jonathan might open his mouth at the wrong time. He had to be a little extravagant with the kid, at least in the beginning.

He went inside the general store and browsed. Comic books were always good. Leon had read tons of them when he was a kid, especially the Marvel superheroes. He thumbed through a few paperbacks, also, but this kind of reading always gave him a headache. Too many words too close together. It was hard to focus. He picked up several paperbacks, all with pictures of teenage boys on the cover, along with a dozen or so comic books. No reason why these wouldn't do.

At one end of the candy counter stood a rack of plastic toys. No good. Jonathan was too old for that kind of stuff. Near the floor, on the same rack, he found a stack of boxed games. The games were sealed, but the outsides of the boxes had confusing descriptions about how the game was played and how many could play it. If he was as smart as he acted, the kid could figure it out for himself. The kid could teach Maria, too, give them something to do when he had to be away from the house. Now that the TV was out of commission, he guessed they had to have something to do on rainy days. He added two games to the pile of books under his arm. On his way to the cash register, he looked for aspirin, but he spotted instead a new, extra-strength painkiller in a bright yellow box. He picked out the largest bottle they had.

"That'll be fifty sixty-two," the woman at the register said after she had punched in the individual amounts for each item.

Leon looked at the green digital figures displayed at the top of the cash register: 50.62. "Fifty bucks! How can it be that much?"

The woman's lips tightened into a thin line. "Everything's marked. You can add it up yourself, plus tax."

"Yeah, the tax," Leon said, thrusting his hands into his pockets. "I forgot about the tax."

"It adds up, but we have to send our share to the governor, don't we?" she said.

Leon hurried back to his van. That bitch had made him mad. What was he supposed to have? A calculator in his brain? He revved the engine and squealed out of the parking lot onto the main street of Reinholds. It never failed. Whenever he drove into this goddamn town, someone made him mad.

He headed home. The bright glare of the morning sun hurt his eyes. Damn, he had forgotten his sunglasses. He floored the gas pedal, sending the plastic bag of books and games flying across the seat almost to the floor. After spending fifty bucks on the kids, he had to get to work on William's truck and earn some money. He was tired and now angry, but getting under the hood of the pickup would calm him down a little.

He knew it was the carburetor; any fool could hear it was the carburetor. Cleaning out the gunk inside it, and maybe gapping a new set of plugs, would give William another couple of months before something else went wrong. Leon enjoyed the challenge of putting a car or truck back on the road with the least possible expense to the owner. Not like those fancy mechanics who charged an arm and a leg, turning every little adjustment into a major overhaul.

The minute the kids heard the van, they ran to greet him. He kind of liked that. The two of them seemed to be getting along all right. Maybe Jonathan would help Maria loosen up a little. She was such a little scaredy-cat, always had been.

"Did you call my grandma? What did she say?" Jonathan yanked open the door of the van even before Leon had turned off the motor.

"Yeah," Leon lied, "I called. Let me get out of the car, will you?"

"What did she say?"

"Wait till you see what I brought for you and Maria. Some games you can play together, and books." Leon saw the kid's face fall.

"Tell me about my grandma first," Jonathan said. Leon thought the kid was going to cry.

Leon wasn't used to showing affection to anyone except a woman he was trying to come on to, but he knew he would have to be gentle, give the kid something besides comic books and games until he got over the news about his family. He placed his hands squarely on the boy's bony shoulders and leaned over so he could look him in the eye.

"I didn't get a chance to talk directly to your grandma. I talked to her nurse."

"What nurse? She doesn't have a nurse," Jonathan insisted as the tears puddled in his eyes.

"She does now. She's not feeling very well. I told you this would be hard for an old lady to take. Come on, look at the games." Leon awkwardly hugged the boy to his big stomach. There was nothing to this kid but skin and bones.

For a moment the boy threw his arms around Leon and held on, trembling slightly. Then he pushed himself away and ran inside the house.

Let him cry it out, Leon thought. He'll be okay. We'll have more tears when his grandmother dies of a heart attack in a day or two, but by then he'll be used to the place. When Jonathan calmed down, then he could head over to Harrisburg and grab Cozelli's kid. This one wouldn't take him three years, he'd do it fast. Once he had all three of them right here where he wanted them, the score would be settled. Finally, he would be even, and then the goddamn dream would stop torturing him for good.

Leon spotted Maria hovering just inside the screen door, watching him with those dark, accusing eyes. A smile worked its way across his face and he laughed out loud. Meanwhile, until Jonathan got over feeling sorry for himself, he could always depend on the company of his little girl.

Chapter 9

Ed Grady put down the phone and sighed to himself. A steady ache throbbed behind his eyes. Saturday, Sunday, and Monday had been the longest days of his life. He was weary from lack of sleep, but the exhaustion also stemmed from the slow, methodical process the local police department had devised for tracking down missing children. He wanted them to be thorough, but dammit, nothing was happening. It was Tuesday, the fourth day, and they were still looking in shopping malls and parks. Jonathan would not hang out in a mall or a playground for four days. He still slept with a stuffed Garfield in his bed, for God's sake, and he had wanted a night-light last December when he had the flu. He was not a teenage druggie prone to staying out by himself or running away. Jonathan was still very much a little boy.

"Anything?" Susan asked when she walked into the room.

"No. Fernandez is now consulting with the police in downtown Atlanta, but neither one of them is saying what they're going to do next. It's still wait and see."

Outside, the afternoon sky had turned cloudy and the wind rustled the leaves of the huge tree on their front lawn. Ed could hear the wind chime on their back patio hammering out a restless tattoo unlike its usual annoying, but gentle tinkle.

Susan sat down on the sofa next to him and cuddled into his arm. "Ed, he's hurt. Somehow he got hurt, or—"

"They've checked the hospitals. I've been to ten hospitals myself."

"But what if he's hurt, lying in a ditch somewhere? What if he's unconscious? What if it starts to rain? I've been terrified that we're going to get a downpour. Did you see the dark clouds to the east?"

He kissed her lightly on the top of her head. "Fernandez is on his way over here. We'll ask him what he thinks. They've been through this before."

"Not with our son, they haven't. Ed, what if some child molester . . . What if he's . . ."

He wrapped both arms around her and held her while she leaned her head against his shoulder. She couldn't bring herself to say the words, What if he's dead? Neither of them could say it out loud. What if their Jonathan has been killed by some crazed lunatic?

Things like this just didn't happen in clean, upper-class neighborhoods. He had sold a hell of a lot of houses to earn enough for a move into this section of Dunwoody, and he had kept on selling until he was able to set up his own real estate agency with a half-dozen salespeople working for him. Now it all seemed so ludicrous. He owned a profitable company, a house in the finest part of town, and a bank account that would guarantee their son a college education, that is, if they still had a son. God, he prayed, please help us find Jonathan.

"Susan!" A scream penetrated into the room from outside. They both rushed to the door, but it burst open before they reached it. Without explaining her rude entry, Claudia thrust a slightly bent postcard toward them.

"This just came in the mail. It's addressed to Brian from Jonathan."

Ed couldn't stop the tremble in his hand as he reached for the card.

"Oh, my God," Susan said. "Look, Ed, it's Jonathan's handwriting."

Brian's address was neatly printed under a name that had been crossed out. The message was written in tiny, cramped words, but there was no question in his mind it was Jonathan's message.

Dear Brian,

I'm sorry I didn't get to see you before I left. Could you and your dad try to find Ginger for me? Please take care of her until my dad's friend can bring me back to get her. I guess Ginger got real scared from the explosion. I guess you did, too.

I wish we could still be best friends even if I have to live in Columbus with my grandma after she feels better. Something this awful is pretty hard on someone that old. I'll try to call you from my dad's friend's house when we get there.

Your best friend,
Jonathan

"What friend? What's he talking about?" Susan screamed. "Where is he?"

Ed flipped the card over several times. "It's postmarked Virginia. This is the Glade Spring Motel, Glade Spring, Virginia."

"But it doesn't make sense; I've never even heard of Glade Spring," Susan said.

71

"I'll check the map in my car. I'd better call Fernandez," he answered.

"Where in your car?" Claudia said. "I'll get it."

"Right on the door, in that little pocket."

Claudia was out the door. Ed picked up the phone, but Susan touched his arm before he dialed.

"Someone, a man, told Jonathan he was your friend," she said slowly. "He said that to trick Jonathan into getting into his car, isn't that right?"

"I don't know, honey. It looks that way."

"What does he mean about an explosion? Why does he think he has to live with Mother?"

Ed wanted the answers to those questions as badly as Susan did. He punched out the numbers for the now familiar direct line to Detective Fernandez.

The doorbell rang. Susan ran to get it and called back to him. "Never mind calling. He's here."

Fernandez entered, followed by Claudia, who had retrieved the map from Ed's car. She carried it as if it were the Holy Grail.

Fernandez handled the postcard by the edges, his face darkened by a foxlike frown that somehow seemed to suit his slight frame. He turned it over as Ed had and read it several times. "I guess you've all handled it."

"You told us not to open any letters addressed to us that might be a ransom note," Ed answered. "This is a postcard to Brian."

"Just the same."

"You think there're fingerprints on the card?" Ed asked.

"None that'll do us any good."

Ed turned away from the cold, hard glare in Fernandez's eyes. He fully expected him to suggest that the Gradys had somehow kidnapped their own son for whatever perverted reasons people did things like that. The insinuation in Fernandez's eyes was eating him alive.

"What's this explosion he mentioned?" Fernandez asked.

"We have no idea. He talks about his dog being scared, but there hasn't been any explosion that we know about."

"How about firecrackers or some homemade thing the kids could have made themselves?"

"Jonathan doesn't play with firecrackers."

"Does he have a chemistry set?"

Ed felt his lungs tightening, as if he had just finished running a very long distance. "No," he said. "He's been wanting one, but we thought he was too young. We thought we'd buy him one next Christmas." Ed tried to imagine what next Christmas would be like if they hadn't found Jonathan.

Fernandez turned to Claudia. "How about your son? Does he have the chemistry set we're looking for?"

"How do you know the explosion came from a chemistry set? Jonathan didn't say it did," Claudia answered.

The detective cleared his throat and studied Claudia's nervous grip on the road map. "Then your son has one?"

Claudia flushed. "No, he doesn't. I just wondered how you came to that conclusion."

"Listen, ma'am, I'm just trying to make sense of the boy's postcard. So far it's our only connection to what happened to him."

"Since when would a kidnapper permit his victim to mail out postcards?" Ed finally asked.

Fernandez shook his head. "Says he's with a friend. You know which one?"

"No friend of mine would take my kid to Virginia

without even telling me. Someone just said he was a friend. That guy in the van on Friday night."

Fernandez nodded. "Perhaps. You're certain it's your son's handwriting?"

"Yes, we're sure," Susan said.

"Do you have any other handwriting samples we could check it against?"

"Yes, I'll get something from his room," Susan said, then hurried up the stairs.

Fernandez turned the postcard over one more time. "Card like this doesn't sound like a kidnapping. He says he's sorry he didn't get to see Brian before he left. It doesn't sound as if his departure was against his will. Your son doesn't mention anything that sounds suspicious."

"Everything about it is suspicious because none of it makes any sense. Jonathan was kidnapped. Can you think of any other explanation? I can't," Ed shot back.

"Have you checked with the boy's grandmother?"

"Of course. She's worried sick just like we are."

"Then the boy's not with her?"

Ed gritted his teeth. "No, definitely not."

"Strange. He mentions something awful. Do you think he means running away? That would be something awful from a kid's point of view."

Ed was losing all patience. "He didn't run away and check into a motel in Virginia. He probably didn't have more than ten cents in his pocket. Somebody, that guy in the van, lured him into the van and took him there."

"That's one possibility."

Ed could feel the heat rising up the back of his neck. "Listen, instead of sitting here, get somebody up to that motel to check it out."

"First, I'll have someone in Atlanta check out the handwriting, then if the writing experts agree your son wrote this, I'm going to have to bow out of the case."

"What are you talking about?"

"If this is an abduction, he's crossed state lines, and that goes under the federal kidnapping statute. We'll have to turn the case over to the FBI."

Chapter 10

"**I** HAVE to wash clothes. You wanna help?" Maria asked.

Jonathan finished wiping the last of the breakfast dishes and hung the towel over the refrigerator door handle. "Okay. Where's the washing machine?"

Maria shook her head. "No machine. I scrub the stuff here in the sink, then we have to hang it outside on the line."

"Oh," Jonathan said. He was trying, but he still had not gotten used to the primitive routines of this isolated little household. Everything was strange to him, but he didn't mind helping Maria with the cooking and cleaning up. In fact, the cooking and chores helped to break up the long, tedious days with nothing to do. Today was Tuesday, and right about now Mrs. Montgomery would be dictating the words for the weekly spelling test. Even though he hadn't studied one word, he wished he could be sitting in his usual seat in the second row taking that test. He sure never thought he would miss going to school.

"Get your dirty clothes," Maria said. "I'll be right back."

Jonathan returned to the kitchen with twice the amount of laundry that Maria carried. He realized he had foolishly changed into clean clothes every morning, and they were without a washing machine.

"You changed into jeans," Jonathan said, noticing Maria had taken off the dress she had worn for the last three days since his arrival.

"I have to wash my dress," she said, matter-of-factly.

"How come you wear that same dress all the time? Jeans look more comfortable."

Maria did not look at him when she answered, but seemed to be watching that faraway spot again. "I guess the jeans fit me better, but I like my dress. My mother bought it for me. It's the only thing I have from before."

"Why didn't you bring your stuff? I would've brought my stuff if it hadn't all burned up."

Maria plugged up the sink, added some detergent, and began to run the hot water. "There wasn't time. They had to sell our house in a hurry to pay for three funerals, and Leon couldn't get inside to get my clothes or anything."

"Where was your house?"

"Los Angeles. I liked it there."

Jonathan watched Maria divide the clothes into two piles; one for light-colored items, the other for jeans and dark colors. He separated his things into similar piles. "Is this the way?" he asked.

"Yeah," she answered. "There's a lot of stuff here. The sink doesn't hold too much."

Jonathan felt his face redden. "From now on I'll wear my clothes for a couple of days. I didn't know about not having a washer."

"Okay," she answered. The sink had filled and Maria began to place the light colors into the sudsy water. "You want to play Monopoly later, when we're done with the clothes?"

"We played it all day yesterday."

Maria worked the sudsy shirts and underwear back and forth between her hands. "There's nothing else to do. I wish we could watch TV. I like "Laverne and Shirley" and the old "Gilligan's Island" shows. I know Gilligan's theme song by heart."

"Did Leon say how long it'll take to get new parts for the TV?" Jonathan wondered. "I used to watch the Hawks' games with my dad, and the Atlanta Braves."

"No," she said, trying to rub an itchy spot on her nose with the back of her wrist. "He said the store was out of the parts; they have to order them."

"I'll teach you the other game if you want."

"Okay, but if I don't like it, can we go back to Monopoly?"

"Sure," Jonathan answered. He didn't know why, but he felt older than Maria. Sometimes she acted as if she, too, were only ten years old, maybe even younger.

Suddenly Jonathan heard the spray of loose gravel as a car drove up to the house. He looked through the dirty pane of glass expecting to see the van, but instead Judy Mae's beetle came to a stop right outside the kitchen door.

Judy Mae pushed open the door, balancing two small paper bags in one hand. "Well, aren't you two the busy bees? Where's Leon?"

"He went into town," Maria answered.

"Already? What for?"

"He's fixing a car for somebody. He had to buy some new parts."

"Shoot, I was hoping to get here before he left. I brought the leftover doughnuts from yesterday."

"Wow, thanks," Maria said, coming as close to smiling as Jonathan had seen so far.

Judy Mae walked over to Maria and put an arm

around her shoulders. She hugged Maria hard, pulling the girl away from the sink until her reddened hands could no longer reach the soapy water. Pearls of soapsuds dripped from Maria's fingertips onto the floor.

"I figured you kids might as well enjoy these doughnuts; Jake just throws them away. He won't sell day-old doughnuts, even though he'll heat up chili that's three days old. That's crazy if you ask me."

Judy Mae poked through the pile of dirty laundry on the floor with the toe of her white shoe. "I don't know how you can get Leon's work pants clean. He needs a washing machine."

Maria looked at Judy Mae and this time actually smiled. Judy Mae smiled back, her face warm and friendly. Jonathan liked the way Judy Mae smiled a lot, and he also liked the way she was willing to talk to Maria and him almost as if they were grown-ups. Leon didn't talk to either one of them very much, unless he was barking orders or telling them how much things cost nowadays. If he had to stay here in the woods until his grandmother got well, he wished Judy Mae could spend more time with them.

"I brought you a carton of milk, too," Judy Mae said. "Leon's always running out of stuff, and kids should have plenty of milk."

Jonathan looked inside the greasy paper bag Judy Mae had placed on the table. The sugary, sweet smell made his mouth water. "Can I have one?"

"Sure, honey. You don't even have to ask. You're a part of this family now, so you just help yourself."

Maria dried her hands and took one of the doughnuts.

Judy Mae smiled. "I think having Jonathan here with you has made you come out of your shell."

Maria made a face, forcing her lips into a pout. "I wasn't in no shell."

Judy Mae laughed. "That's just an expression, honey. It just means you seem happier. You needed a friend, someone to talk to. You two gettin' along all right?"

Maria nodded, but Jonathan spoke up. "We get along fine, but I wish we could go to school."

Judy Mae frowned. "Leon doesn't believe in schools, but I'll ask him if there's some way he could get you kids into one. I went to high school, and I would've graduated except some of the teachers didn't like me too much."

"Was the school nearby?" Jonathan asked.

"My school? No, it was over in Sinking Spring where my folks used to live."

Jonathan said, "Did Leon go to your high school?"

Judy Mae fluffed her hair with one hand. "Heavens no, honey."

"Where did he go?"

Suddenly Judy Mae looked perplexed. "Well, I don't think he ever mentioned the name of his school, but I know he didn't like it. Got into trouble, I guess, like boys do. I just know it wasn't the school I went to."

"My teacher, back in Georgia, said we have a responsibility to become educated, a responsibility to society," Jonathan said solemnly.

Judy Mae looked at Jonathan out of the corner of one eye. "She must have been a smart lady, your teacher."

Now Jonathan really wished he could be taking his spelling test, even if he flunked. "Yeah, I guess she was." He paused, wondering if it was okay to ask a brand-new friend a favor, then said, "Judy Mae, I have a letter I want to mail."

"I go right by a mailbox, I'll mail it for you. Why didn't you give it to Leon?"

"Well, I don't have a stamp, and I didn't want to ask Leon for one. I don't even have an envelope, but I printed Brian's name and address on the back of the letter. I'll show you." Jonathan ran into the bedroom and quickly yanked his letter to Brian from his notebook. He had folded the single sheet into thirds and used the back of the center fold for the address.

"Who's Brian?" she called after him.

He returned and handed her the letter. "He's my best friend. He lived next door to me."

"I hate to write letters," she said, studying the address. "You print real nice."

"Thanks," he said. "Do you think the post office would let me mail it like that, without an envelope?"

Judy Mae thought for a moment. "Honey, I don't know. Why don't I take it home with me and put it in a real envelope? I can copy the address and put a stamp on it. That'll be much better."

Jonathan smiled gratefully.

"I'll get you some envelopes and stamps and bring them over. Shoot, if you have a best friend, you should be able to write to him."

"Thanks, Judy Mae."

"Sure, honey," she answered. "What kind of best friend would you be if you didn't write once in a while?"

Jonathan nodded, afraid he was going to cry again. He had cried himself to sleep every night since he arrived in Pennsylvania, but the daytime was becoming easier. He tried not to think about his parents, but now, for the first time, he was feeling the pain of his separation from Brian. It wasn't fair that he had to move so far away from his friends, but he was glad at least Judy Mae understood.

"Well, I gotta get back to the diner," Judy Mae said. "Tell Leon hello for me."

"When will you be back?" Jonathan asked.

"Here? Let me think. I probably won't have a day off until Friday because Jake's making such a fuss about all the time I took off last week. I'm gonna be real happy to tell him what he can do with that job after Leon and me get married."

"Will you come over on Friday?" Maria asked.

"Sure, honey. I'll help you clean the place a little, and then we'll cook something real special for supper. Would you like that?"

"Yeah." Maria beamed.

"I can help, too," Jonathan said.

Judy Mae laughed her infectious giggle and tousled Jonathan's hair. "You bet you can. And don't you worry. Now that Leon doesn't have all those court dates on his mind day and night, maybe he can find time to see if there's a good school around here."

Judy Mae gave Maria another squeeze and turned to Jonathan. She hesitated for just a second, then gave him a big hug, too. His face pressed against her soft, white uniform and a whiff of perfume tickled his nose. The scent was strong, like flowers and cinnamon, reminding him of a candle his mom used to burn in the bathroom when company came. She let go of Jonathan and fished her car keys out of her pocket.

"'Bye," she called. Judy Mae let the screen door slam and hurried to her car.

Maria returned to the sink and began to scrub the clothes back and forth between her knuckles.

"What did she mean about court dates?" Jonathan asked.

"You know, all the times he had to go south, to appear in the court."

"Why?"

Maria arched one eyebrow. "I don't know. You were there, weren't you?"

"Why would I be there? I've never been in a court."

"Well, I don't know. It had something to do with you. I heard Judy Mae and Leon talking about it for a long time. They think I can't hear if they go outside to talk."

"But you heard them talking about me?"

"Sure. If I know Judy Mae's coming over, I open the parlor window, just a crack. They always went outside to talk about getting married and about you."

A sudden surge of gooseflesh rippled up Jonathan's arms. "How could they talk about me? Leon didn't even know me until last Friday, until after my house burned down."

"He knew you. He talked about you."

The last bite of doughnut wedged in his throat. How could he have been so dumb? How had Leon known where to find him as he walked home from school that day? How much of Leon's story about his parents had been a lie? He suddenly remembered the time Kevin, a boy at school, had convinced him that he had a snake in his lunch box. Kevin boasted that his uncle had trapped a live baby diamondback rattler up in the hills and had given it to him. He was going to feed it mice and raise it to be the biggest rattler in Georgia. Jonathan had fallen for every word of Kevin's tale, to the point that he was sure he could hear a faint rattling sound inside the lunch box. He was now feeling just as foolish as he had when Kevin, with a melodramatic flair, had sprung open the lid to reveal a peanut butter sandwich and a plastic bag of celery sticks. Only this time was different. Leon wasn't just playing a little joke, was he?

"When did they start talking about me? How long ago?" Jonathan asked.

Maria thought for a moment. "I don't know. About a year ago, I guess. Right after he met Judy Mae."

Jonathan's mouth went dry. There wasn't even one drop of spit on his tongue. "When did your parents die? How long ago?"

Maria's face closed up; again she was somewhere far away. "Long ago. Three years, I think."

"So how come you came here, to Leon's house?"

"Leon knew my dad. He promised my dad he'd take care of me if anything ever happened to him or my mom."

"So he was like a neighbor or somebody you knew real well?"

Maria shrugged, screwing her face into little twists, trying to remember. "No, it wasn't like that. He knew my dad, not me."

Jonathan kept pushing. "But you came to live with him; who decided you'd live here?"

"Leon just happened to be in California the day of the accident. He said he'd take care of me 'cause I had nobody left. Leon says it was real luck, the way he was right there the exact moment I needed him."

Chapter 11

SPECIAL FBI Agent Kira Thomasian rolled her head from side to side, trying to release a kink in the back of her neck. It wasn't just the result of the hours she had been behind the wheel, but probably the toll of the stress that had been building gradually all day long. The volume of active cases in the Atlanta FBI Field Office was off the charts, as usual, so Kira drove alone. She was slightly miffed that she was still doing grunt work to begin with, but the fact that she had not been assigned a partner only confirmed her assumption that her first case would be nothing more than routine questioning. This translated to mean the agency had nothing to go on except the report of a missing and a postcard of suspicious origin received by the family earlier today. She figured this side trip to a lonely little motel was part of the package; low man on the totem pole gets to check out the abduction that may not even be an abduction, while everyone else in the Atlanta Criminal Section investigates real crime. It was the bureau's way of making a new agent pay her dues.

She had been assigned to the Baltimore Field Office after completing her training at the FBI National Academy in Quantico. They had loaded her down with paperwork to the point where she never even had a chance to visit the newly redesigned Baltimore harbor everyone talked about. After six months she jumped at a transfer to Atlanta, only to find more of the same when she got there. She saw no way to get around the Mickey Mouse stuff, and she certainly hadn't struggled through all those years to get her degree in criminology followed by a grueling thirteen and a half weeks at the academy to give up now.

The traffic out of Atlanta had been heavy, followed by several slowdowns along the interstate in Tennessee because of patches of construction. It was five-thirty Tuesday afternoon before she crossed the border into Virginia. This was a sleepy part of the South with small, friendly towns nestled here and there in the rolling green valleys that eased lazily between the mountain peaks of the Appalachians. Names like Cripple Creek and Buck Mountain imparted a feeling of remoteness from the busy streets of Atlanta where most of her agency work had taken her so far. In the distance she heard the mournful whistle of a train, but the only other signs of an advanced civilization were the cars whizzing by in both directions on the long stretch of highway.

According to her map, another twenty or twenty-five miles would bring her to Glade Spring, Virginia. The miles passed slowly, but finally she pulled the Plymouth from the FBI motor pool off Interstate 81 and drove a few hundred feet to the entrance of the Glade Spring Motel. The desk clerk looked up from a slick magazine with a picture of a baseball player on the cover and smiled when she walked into the office. Judging by the number of cars in front of the rooms, business was slow.

"Hello," he said, still grinning.

She pulled her ID from her shoulder bag. "Hi. I'm

Kira Thomasian, Federal Bureau of Investigation. I'd like to ask you a few questions."

The clerk's face froze midway between his grin and an expression of sheer disbelief. "I've never seen a federal ID before, let me take a look at that."

She waited patiently while he scrutinized every detail. She knew, of course, that aside from her gender, her youthful appearance did not make her a ringer for an Eliot Ness lookalike contest. Kira's mother had always complained that any young woman who looked as good as Kira did had no business hiding those looks behind a badge.

"You could be a fashion model, with your height and figure," her mother had said. "You could land a husband in a minute if you didn't act so tough and know-it-all."

Poor Mom, Kira had thought. The twentieth century was just a bit too much for her.

The clerk's eyes slowly traveled from Kira's face down to her shoes. After this visual excursion, he was willing to relinquish his hold on the leather case that held her ID card and badge.

Kira tucked her ID back into her bag. "I'm checking on a ten-year-old boy missing since Friday, April seventh. His name is Jonathan Grady." She held up an enlarged photograph of Jonathan. "This postcard from your motel was written by the boy. It's postmarked yesterday, Monday the tenth. It arrived in Atlanta this morning."

The clerk examined the copy of both sides of the postcard. The original was still in the lab, but Kira doubted latent prints would find anything usable.

His face lit up. "Sure, I remember. I don't know who wrote it, but I mailed it myself on Saturday."

"You mailed it?" Kira straightened her shoulders. Maybe this case had some substance after all.

"Ada, that's my sister-in-law, was cleaning and

found this and another card in Mr. Kirby's room after he and his boy checked out. Cards had stamps on them, so Ada brought them to the desk. Funny, though."

"What was funny?"

"We ran out of those cards a while back. I didn't think there were any around. I have to get some more printed up one of these days. Good advertising."

"I'm going to need your name, Mister . . ."

"Jenson. Ralph Jenson."

"Mr. Jenson, did you notice who the other card was addressed to?"

"It didn't seem to be the same handwriting on the two cards, but then I'm not certain. I just mailed them as a courtesy. I don't read other people's mail."

Kira pointed to the photograph lying on the desk. "Was Jonathan Grady with Mr. Kirby?"

"No, I told you he had his son."

"Then you know his son? You saw him?"

Jenson hesitated. "No, come to think of it, the boy waited in the car for his father, but Mr. Kirby called his wife and they talked about the kid. Called her right here in front of me when he checked in."

"You have a home address, phone number, for Mr. Kirby?"

He tucked in his shirt, puffing out his chest. "Certainly, on his registration cards. We do everything according to the books. Hold on just a second."

Kira studied the profile of the nervous little man as he searched through a card index in the top drawer of a battered file cabinet. One would say he was not the criminal type, but then she had also learned there was no such thing as a criminal type. He pulled out a handful of registration cards and placed them in front of her.

"These were all filled out by the same Mr. Kirby?" she asked.

"Sure. He's been kind of a regular customer, but he said his work down this way was over for a while. Nice fellow, a family man."

Kira flipped through a stack of cards, handling them only by the edges. "What kind of work does Mr. Kirby do?"

"Mechanic, airplane engines. Works at airports. Last job was at Knoxville. He said the regular guy broke his arm."

"The license number for the Ford van is not the same on all these cards."

"What?" Jenson eyed the discrepancies. "Oh, you know how that is. You know your license number like the back of your hand until somebody asks you what it is, then you forget. The address and phone number are the same."

"Mind if I call this number? I'll pay for the call."

"No need. You go right ahead."

Kira dialed the Pennsylvania number.

"Doctors' office." A woman's voice came over the phone.

"Yes, I'm with the Federal Bureau of Investigation, and I'm checking on the residence of a Mr. Lee Kirby. He gave this number as his home phone."

"No, I'm afraid there's a mistake somewhere. This is a medical center, the Galworthy Medical Center, and I don't know anyone by that name."

"Would you mind giving me the address of the medical center?" Kira checked the address against the one Kirby had written on the card. Identical. "And there wouldn't be any private residences in your building?"

"Heavens no. We have the four doctors' offices and the waiting room, and there's also our emergency room. That's it. I'm afraid someone has been pulling your leg."

"Indeed," Kira said calmly. "Thank you so much for your help."

Jenson looked somewhat paler than he had a few moments earlier. "There was some problem?"

"Yes. Mr. Kirby gave you the address and phone number of a medical center in Altoona. Do you have any credit card vouchers for him?"

"He paid cash. Always."

"The car he drove was a Ford van?"

"Sure, it was a van. That I saw with my own eyes."

"Our eyes can deceive us. Are you certain it was a *Ford* van?"

His face fell. "Those vans all look alike. I think it was a Ford, but I'm not certain."

"What year? Late model?"

"No, not too new. Kind of beat-up."

"What color was it?"

He wiped his hand across his mouth, clearing his throat in the process. "I think it was a light color. Maybe beige or a cream color."

Kira wrote down the colors. "Not white?"

"No, not white. More a light yellow or cream color, I'd say."

"Okay, thanks." Kira slipped her notebook back into her purse and removed a printed form and a clean plastic bag. She carefully slipped the registration cards into the bag and began filling out the first few lines of the double-sided FBI witness report.

"Let me explain what happens next, Mr. Jenson. I'm going to need some personal data on you as a witness, and I'll have to borrow these registration cards from you. We'll also be checking into your telephone company records regarding the last phone call he made to his wife. When exactly was that?"

"Let's see, Friday night about six—no, maybe it was closer to seven."

"What room did he use?"

Jenson was now showing signs of perspiration on his forehead. Make them sweat, she had heard over and over again in her "unofficial" rap sessions at the academy in Quantico.

Without actually touching the bag holding the Kirby registration cards, he looked through the plastic and studied the top card from Kirby's most recent visit. "He was in five."

"Has the room been occupied since Kirby and the boy left?"

She noticed more beads of sweat, this time on his upper lip. "What exactly do you think Mr. Kirby has done?" he asked.

"He's wanted for questioning in a possible kidnapping. Has the room been occupied since they left?" she repeated.

"No, yes, I think we used it last night." He went back to his file drawer. "Here it is; young couple from Tennessee last night."

"So the room's been cleaned twice?"

"Yes," he said weakly.

"I don't want anyone else to go in there. I'm going to send for a lab unit. As soon as they get here, they'll dust for prints and go over the room for other evidence. I'll also send for an artist."

Jenson's face had blanched to a pasty-gray color. She had heard it wouldn't be as easy for a woman to bring out that sort of panic in a witness, not the way her male counterparts could, but according to the face of this guy, she was right on target.

"An artist?" he said.

"Yes," she answered, softening her tone a bit. "Do you think you could work with one of our artists to come up with a composite sketch of Mr. Kirby?"

His lips now looked blue. "Yes, I think so."

"Good, we'd appreciate your help."

Slowly, she led Jenson through the remaining questions on the form. She had most of the answers in her notes already, but repetition was a good way to check his memory. His story remained consistent. When she got to Kirby's physical description, she repeated every question twice. As nervous as he was, Jenson insisted he could describe the man named Kirby to a T, and he did.

Kira handed him her card. "Thank you for your cooperation, Mr. Jenson. I'll be getting back to you, but in the meantime, if Mr. Kirby shows up again, please call me at this number. Give him a room and treat him as you would any customer, but then call me the first chance you get. We need to have a little chat with this man."

Kira had a hunch that certainly couldn't be backed by any evidence she had collected so far, but she somehow knew this wasn't a case of the parents getting their wires crossed with a friend or relative who had promised the boy a weekend in the country. She was equally certain Jonathan Grady had not been taken away by a babysitter who had forgotten to inform the parents where they were going.

Mr. Kirby, whoever he was, had done a fair share of planning in order to establish an identity with the motel clerk. Even if Jenson had seen pictures of Jonathan on the evening news, he never would have made the connection. Kirby had made sure Jenson "knew" him and his alleged son, and Kirby had taken the trouble to carefully lay a trail of false evidence to screw up her investigation.

Thank God the boy had somehow managed to write the postcard. She didn't know how he had slipped it by Kirby, but she was certainly glad he had. She was hoping in this, her first case, she had stumbled upon a crime that required real police work. Without a doubt, finding Lee Kirby and Jonathan Grady would put her name on the agency map.

Chapter 12

Aᴛᴇʀ he had returned from his trip to the auto parts store in town, Leon spent the rest of the day tearing down the motor on Chuck Weaver's dilapidated Pontiac. He put in a hard day's work, but he wasn't complaining, even though it was after six when he finally left the house for Judy Mae's apartment in Reinholds. Today's job would net him at least eight hundred, and he had picked up ninety bucks yesterday for the work he had done on old William's pickup.

He had almost forgotten the feel of having extra cash in his pockets. So much of his time during the last year had been spent on his efforts to locate Jonathan that business had suffered. He had to keep working steady, get folks used to the idea that he was available to do an honest job a helluva lot cheaper than those rip-off artists who called themselves certified mechanics. Hell, certification didn't mean a thing if you didn't have a way with engines. Leon knew he had the touch, right here in his fingertips. He could do anything those certified guys could do.

Leon settled behind the wheel of the van and drove away from the house. Jonathan had acted strange all day while he'd been working on the Pontiac. The kid stayed away from him, keeping to himself and talking only to Maria, but Leon knew it was just a temporary mood. The kid would come around sooner or later, and he would have his chance to put Grady's only kid through his paces. Grady might never put two and two together, but that didn't even matter. The fact that he would finally get even was all that was important. No, he wouldn't let Jonathan's little phases bother him. Except for finding the empty milk carton Judy Mae had given to the kids, nothing had bothered Leon today.

He would never forget the time, about two years ago, when he had picked up a carton of milk at the grocery store, and there, plain as life, was a picture of Maria on the box. His hand had begun to tremble right there in the store, but somehow he managed to put the carton back on the shelf without dropping it. Ever since, he bought milk only in plastic bottles. The kind without pictures of missing kids. Dairies should stick to milk and butter, he thought, and Judy Mae should learn to mind her own business.

Who was he trying to kid? Judy Mae would never learn to mind her own business. He planned to talk to her about the milk carton, but she'd surely find something else to poke her nose into. She was just that kind, and he knew now he had to break off with her. Marrying her might tend to complicate things, and certainly he was better off without her and her snooping.

The wind was still full of winter, chasing gray clouds into circular patterns in the distance. Through the clouds, the slanting rays of the setting sun cast narrow shadows of the trees across the road to the east. It looked like rain.

He pulled into the driveway and maneuvered the van between a border of overgrown hedges leading to Judy Mae's apartment. Actually, it was a portion of the bottom floor of a rambling old house that had been divided into four rather haphazard living units back in the fifties. Once the grand residence of a prominent family, the house now desperately needed paint and the front porch sagged. The lawn hadn't been properly tended in years, and, to the rear of the house, the backyard and a garden had evolved into muddy parking spaces for the tenants.

Since no one had ever thought to redesign the front entrance, Judy Mae had to enter her place through a rear door that probably once served the hired help. The floor plan was an accidental collection of rooms featuring a closet door that opened onto a blank wall. This sloppy kind of remodeling gave her almost no closet space and a kitchen that adjoined the bedroom.

Judy Mae was standing in front of the living room mirror, fussing with her hair, when he let himself in.

"You're late," she said, walking over to greet him.

"I was working."

"So the kids told me. Did you get any of the doughnuts?" She kissed him playfully on the lips.

"Yeah, I got one, but I don't like the kind of milk you gave the kids. I thought I told you to buy plastic bottles or glass?"

Judy Mae tossed her head. "Well, I wasn't at the market or the dairy, I was at the diner. I had to buy what Jake uses to water down the cream for the coffee, which is low-fat milk in cartons like that. It didn't kill them."

"I told you I don't like to taste little bits of wax floating in the milk."

"I've never tasted any wax, and since when do you drink milk?"

Leon's fingers tightened into fists. "Goddamn it, do you have to argue about everything? Just once couldn't you do what I ask?"

Judy Mae put her arms around his waist and rested her head against his chest. "Sorry, sweetie. Don't.be mad. You want a beer?"

"Yeah, okay," Leon said. He relaxed his knotted fists and flexed his fingers slowly. He pulled off his jacket and sat down on the couch, rumpling the blanket Judy Mae always kept spread out over the back and seat cushions.

Judy Mae placed two opened cans of beer on the table in front of the couch, then immediately smoothed out the wrinkles in the blanket. He noticed puffy bubbles of foam oozing from the triangular-shaped holes in the tops of the cans. She shook the beer too much when she opened it. Christ, she couldn't even open a can of beer the way he liked it.

"Don't fuss so much, Judy Mae. You're always fussing."

She stopped adjusting the blanket and sat next to him, wiggling as close as she could get. The heavy scent of her perfume filled the room. The top button of her blouse was open. "I missed you," she said.

He kissed her savagely, picturing in his mind her naked body upon her bed. They always had sex at her place—because of Maria and now Jonathan—and they always had it first, before they talked or watched TV. That way, he was relaxed when she started all her chattering. He liked Judy Mae well enough until she started to talk.

He forced his hand down inside the tight fit of her bra, awkwardly pulling her left breast up toward his lips. She groaned a little, clutching at his shoulder with one hand, and opened the remaining buttons on her blouse with the other.

"You wanna go into the bedroom?" she purred in his ear.

He nuzzled her breast, his lips hot and sticky. He drooled, dripping saliva on a little lace flower sewn onto the exact center of her bra, then he grabbed at her shoulder straps.

"Easy, sweetie, this is a new bra," she said. "I'll help you."

Judy Mae slipped out of her blouse and unhooked her bra. His eyes focused on the smooth, white fullness of her breasts rising and lowering as she breathed. She had a great set of tits, all right, big and firm, just the way he liked them. He could envision her, thighs spread, under him, but he wasn't getting an erection. Judy Mae had a way of ruining things for him. He had been so upset with her because of the milk carton that he just wasn't getting hard. Usually he walked in the door with a hard-on.

She leaned back to one end of the couch and pulled him toward her. Greedily he sucked at her nipples and pawed at her crotch through her denim jeans, his hand working compulsively between her thighs. He started to breathe heavier.

"You want me now, sweetie?" she teased.

"Yeah," he groaned. "Take off them goddamn pants."

"Don't you want to go into the bedroom?"

"Let's do it here." Leon pulled down his zipper. Finally he was hard enough, but he didn't think it was going to last. What the hell was the matter with him tonight? It was Judy Mae. She had upset him with that milk carton, that's what. It was her fault.

"You can't wait, can you?" Judy Mae giggled, apparently delighted with his pressing need to make love to her right there on the couch. She slipped out of her jeans and panties and tossed them on the floor.

Judy Mae was ready. He could tell by the way she arched her back, pressing against him tighter and tighter. Leon did not remove his shirt. He shoved his pants down only a matter of inches and mounted her.

He heaved forward and thrust himself deep inside her, sighing when he realized it was going to be fast. A few powerful bursts of energy and it was all over. Judy Mae had barely gotten warmed up.

"That was too quick," he said. "I just couldn't get you fast enough." He saw the puzzled look in her eyes. "What say we do it again? Just give me time to drink my beer and we'll do it again."

Judy Mae smiled as she pulled herself to her elbows. "You were crazy for me tonight, weren't you?"

"Yeah, I guess I was."

"When a man needs a woman that much, it's time to get married, wouldn't you say?"

"You said June." Leon pulled up his pants and buckled his belt.

She laughed out loud. "What'd you think I meant, right this minute?" She gathered up her clothes and strutted naked through the kitchen toward her bedroom. "I'll be right back, sweetie," she called to him. "Don't go 'way now, you hear?" Leon could hear her giggling to herself all the way.

He pulled a long draft from his beer and settled back against the couch. His fingertips brushed against a wet spot on the now hopelessly rumpled blanket, and he quickly jerked his hand away from it. Judy Mae returned, dressed in a fuzzy blue robe. She smiled and sat down next to him, right on top of the wet spot.

"You wanna talk?" she asked.

"What about?"

"Oh, just something I wanted to talk about."

"Okay, go ahead," he said.

She snuggled closer. "Honey, I know how you feel about schools, but not everybody thinks they're a waste of time. Getting an education is a responsibility."

He squinted at her, not sure he had heard her correctly. "What the hell are you talking about?"

"We have a responsibility to society to send Jonathan and Maria to school."

Leon's mouth went dry. "Who've you been talking to?" he demanded.

Judy Mae blushed. "Well, it's what I think, too. School is important for kids."

"Who told you that?"

"Jonathan."

"Jonathan? He's just a little kid."

"But he's a smart little kid, and he's right. They both should go to school."

Leon lurched to his feet. "What else did you and Jonathan discuss when I wasn't around?" He spun around to face her.

"Nothing, just talk," she answered.

"What kind of talk?"

"Sit down and relax, Leon. Shoot, if I'm going to be their mama, I have to talk to them, don't I?"

Leon sat, wondering how he was going to handle this. The kid was even smarter than he had thought if he was able to con Judy Mae into working for him in such a short time. The two of them together spelled trouble, no matter which way he figured it. He had to have time to think about this.

Judy Mae instantly locked arms with him and twined her fingers through his. "Don't you want the kids to learn how to get a good job when they get older?"

"I hadn't thought about it."

"They're not going to be kids for long. I already told you how Maria was all grown-up with her first period."

"Yeah, you told me."

"And Jonathan, he's smart. You should've seen the nice little letter he wrote to his friend. He prints real careful, every A, every B, just right."

Leon felt the color draining from his face. "What letter? What are you talking about?"

Judy Mae got up and walked to a table crowded into a little alcove between the living room and the kitchen. She rummaged through her purse and produced a long white envelope. "Here it is. I think it's sweet he has a best friend back home in Georgia."

"What are you doing with this?" Leon thundered.

"Nothing, sweetie. I'm going to mail it for Jonathan tomorrow."

Leon jumped up and grabbed the envelope from her hands. The address was Dunwoody. Brian Nowlin. Must be the kid next door Jonathan talked about, his friend. "Jonathan wrote this?"

"Well, I addressed it for him 'cause he didn't have any envelopes, but he wrote the letter."

Leon tore open the envelope and let it drop to the floor. He concentrated on the first few sentences. He saw his name, Leon Hoffman. The kid even spelled it right.

"You can't do that." Judy Mae ripped the letter from his hand. "You shouldn't be reading somebody else's mail."

Leon felt a jolt of pain penetrate his skull. He arced the back of his hand toward her, connecting squarely with her jaw. His head now throbbing with rage, he watched her fly backward, falling against the table. A tiny stream of blood trickled from the corner of her mouth.

Stunned for a moment, she lay there with her head resting against one leg of the table. She felt the back of her head and winced a little, then, trembling, pulled herself to her feet and faced him. She must have become aware of the blood running to her chin because she touched it daintily and then examined the red smear on her fingertips. Suddenly she began to holler and cry.

"Christ, nobody slaps me around, not anymore. I thought you were different from all the others. God-damn men, you're all alike. Nobody slaps me, you understand?"

She was hysterical, shrieking like a crazy woman, and each shriek was like the blow of an axe to his brain. Leon had to quiet her, to stop the thudding in his head.

"Shut up, Judy Mae. You'll have the neighbors running down here."

"I don't give a damn," she screamed. "I want wit-nesses if I'm going to get bashed around by a big lug like you. You have no right!"

Her shrill words no longer made any sense. He just wanted her to stop. "Shut up," he yelled, clamp-ing his hand over her mouth. She brought up her knee, ramming it into his groin. Instantly, pain shot up his spine; color washed out of his line of vision. He grabbed two fistfuls of her hair so she couldn't get away.

"Goddamn you," he cried. His hands slipped to her throat. If he could just squeeze off her air for a moment, maybe she'd stop her hideous screaming. His thumbs pressed harder, pushing against her windpipe. He had to think, but she was kicking and thrashing against him, completely out of control. "Stop it," he hissed through clenched teeth. "Stop it!"

He saw the letter fall from her hand to the floor, but he did not release his grip on her throat. Good, he thought, she was coming to her senses. Her head rolled backward, her weight pulled against his hands. He let go, and Judy Mae slumped to the car-pet.

For a moment he just looked at her lying there, relieved she had finally stopped yelling. The strength flowed out of his arms, replaced by a weakness seeping all the way down to his fingers. "Man, you sure can holler. Why'd you want to scream like that, anyway?"

Judy Mae did not respond.

He bent over and grabbed her arm, pulling her toward him. Her bathrobe gaped open in front. She hadn't put on her underwear again; she was stark naked underneath. He held her hand, but it didn't feel right. Something was wrong. He let go and her hand plopped limply to the floor. Christ, had he killed her? He grabbed her wrist and felt for a pulse, but his fingers were too big to fit between her little bones. He touched the side of her throat. Nothing. She wasn't breathing. He couldn't feel a pulse in her neck.

Judy Mae was dead.

Chapter 13

Leon sat on the floor next to Judy Mae. He thought about all the dead men he had seen in 'Nam. Covered with sweat and blood, and sometimes mud, there had never been any question that they were dead. Judy Mae didn't look dead. She wasn't even dirty. Except for the little bit of blood beginning to dry upon her chin, she simply looked as if she were sleeping.

Her breasts were still, but he liked the way they were pointy yet supple when he ran his fingers around the darkened circles of her nipples. He could feel a stiffness growing within his pants in spite of the pain lingering in his groin. He thought about having Judy Mae one last time, but decided it might not be right. It might feel weird if she couldn't move with him, but there was a stronger reason for him to repress the urge. He remembered hearing a story when he was just a kid about a man who had fucked his wife after she died, and his dick got stuck in there. Leon wasn't going to risk anything like that. He pulled Judy Mae's bathrobe closed, covering her completely.

It was still early, but it was now dark outside. Leon listened at the door, but he heard only wind howling through the trees. He had to think. Had anyone seen his van parked in the driveway? If he left now, sooner or later someone would discover Judy Mae lying here on the floor. A neighbor might remember seeing the van, and they would know he had been inside her apartment. Everyone would say he killed her.

Leon wiped the sweat from his forehead with the back of his hand. Now what? Hell, he could go to jail for this even if it was an accident. Accident? Shit, who'd believe him? Certainly not any cop he had ever met. He had to get rid of her body, hide it somewhere. Somewhere where no one would ever connect him to her death. Maybe if he threw her into the creek? No, it wasn't deep enough. Even though Jonathan had mistaken it for a river, it was still just a creek. He'd have to find a place to dig a hole and bury her.

The bunched-up blanket on the couch caught his eye. He pulled it free and spread it out on the floor next to Judy Mae. A slightly purplish-blue cast colored her fingers. Her hands weren't real cold, but when he touched her, a white spot the same size as his fingertip remained on her skin after he let go. White spots on her blue hands definitely made her look dead. Then, right before his eyes, the purple suddenly began to fade and her fingers blanched to a chalky white. Leon shuddered, not wanting to see what other changes were going to occur.

Carefully, he rolled her onto the blanket and wrapped her up like a big sausage. The kid's letter stuck out from beneath the blanket. He quickly stuffed it into his pocket, remembering he would have to deal with Jonathan later.

Leon turned off the light near the door and peered through the window. No one was around; he couldn't hear any footsteps or car engines, but he didn't want to take any chances either. He would wait until later, just to be certain all of Judy Mae's nosy neighbors were home for the evening, then he would find a safe place to bury her. He didn't see any other choice.

As quiet as it was outside, it was even quieter in the apartment. He had finally silenced Judy Mae once and for all, but the absence of her constant chattering and giggling was driving him crazy. Noise. Now he needed noise. He flicked on Judy Mae's TV set, not too loud, and turned on a little light over the stove in the kitchen. Next, he turned off all the other lights in the apartment. If any of her nosy neighbors listened at her door, they would think Judy Mae had fallen asleep on the couch watching TV.

He sat on the couch, one eye on the TV, the other on the rolled blanket a few feet away. Judy Mae wasn't going anywhere, so he settled back to watch the last half of a comedy show that obviously was intended for kids. Once he got the hang of what they were laughing about, he got a kick out of the little kids saying funny things to each other.

A little wisp of a girl with great big eyes was talking to a pudgy, round-faced boy who was wolfing down a piece of cake. "Your idea of a well-balanced meal is a Twinkie in each hand," she said.

The girl reminded Leon of Maria.

The boy gulped a big swipe of milk and said, "Alert the media . . . Susie made a funny." He stuck out his tongue.

"I'm going to call a carpenter," the girl wailed. "In another hour you won't be able to fit through the door."

Leon laughed. He didn't remember kids talking like that when he was their age, but then maybe he just forgot. He held out his wrist, to catch the glow from the TV, and checked his watch. The second hand pounced forward a few times before his eyes actually focused on the hour. He decided to wait until the TV show was over.

At the end of the half hour a news brief flashed on the screen. A woman said something about the president visiting Japan and the United Auto Workers threatening to strike General Motors. Leon hated watching the news, especially when they mentioned kidnappings and the manhunts that followed.

He had never heard one word about Maria on the news, but just the thought of it had left him feeling nervous for months. Naturally, he had disconnected the TV at home after he took Maria, the same way he had taken care of it after Jonathan's arrival. That was one really smart thing he had done. He had waited six months until he hooked it up again, although it probably would have been safe after just a few weeks. The TV reporters always found something new to talk about, and the old stuff was soon forgotten.

Leon grinned to himself. He had covered his tracks pretty good, he thought. The cops, even the FBI, could search away; they'd never be able to connect the sudden disappearance of Grady's kid to him.

The last few sips of his beer had grown warm, but he drained the can anyway, then let out a loud belch. He had waited long enough. He slipped on his jacket and pulled up the zipper before he opened the door to check outside. The wind whipped through the darkness, violently lashing against the trees. A big storm was moving in. The wind, colder now than it had been, even smelled like rain. Not a good night for digging a grave, he thought, but a storm meant clouds, and clouds meant there would be no moonlight to give him away.

The van was parked near the door, but he moved it closer, just in case. He left the motor running but did not turn on his headlights. Except for the hissing of the wind, it was quiet; too quiet. Had the neighbors heard? Maybe they were watching him through the windows even now. He had to be careful and not act suspiciously.

He let the rear doors to the van remain open as well as the door to Judy Mae's apartment. There wasn't a sound coming from anywhere in the building.

Then he remembered, his fingerprints would be on the TV. He wiped the TV controls with his handkerchief, wondering if he should turn off the set. The noise was good, he thought, and he liked the warm glow of light. He'd let it play. Finally he picked up Judy Mae and carried her outside.

The rolled-up blanket sagged in the middle, Judy Mae's tail end slipping almost to his knees. Something had happened to her body while he waited. She smelled funny. He thought dead people didn't smell bad until they started to decay. It was time to hurry.

He dumped her into the back of the van, trying to toss aside his hydraulic jack with one hand while he manipulated Judy Mae with the other. The blanket snagged on the spare tire. He hauled around too much junk in the van, that was for sure, but at least there were no rear seats to get in his way. He tugged and shoved until he could close both doors.

Still no sign of neighbors. He closed Judy Mae's apartment door, wiping the doorknob with his handkerchief, and hurried to the driver's seat.

He listened before he moved the van. Somewhere in the distance he thought he heard a stereo or radio playing country music, but no cars were approaching, as far as he could tell. A bead of sweat trickled down his forehead. He wiped it with his sleeve and shifted into reverse.

Backing the van slowly into the street, he switched on his headlights and headed out of Reinholds toward Adamstown. There were plenty of wooded stretches along the little country roads in that area where he wouldn't run into any other cars at this time of night. Hell, on a miserable windy night like this, people rushed home from work, content to spend the evening in front of the TV. Only a damned fool would be out for a drive. He was certain it would be safe; no one would take notice of a van parked along the road for the fifteen or twenty minutes it would take to bury Judy Mae.

He sped away from Judy Mae's apartment for a few miles, then slowed down. No one had seen him leave her place. So far so good. He concentrated on finding a suitable spot for the grave, and soon his headlights picked up a clump of trees on the left. Hitting the brakes, Leon looked closer and quickly made a U-turn, stopping only after he had driven into the woods a good twenty feet from the road. He got out and took a few steps. Plenty of scruffy, low-growing pine grew close to the road. Beyond, Leon thought he saw a denser woodland. The earth was several inches thick with pine needles, which he scraped away with the side of one shoe. Perfect. The ground was soft; the night was pitch-black. No one was around, and the only sounds he could hear were the hum of the van's engine and the relentless wailing of the icy wind.

He wished he had a regular shovel, but all he carried was a little camp shovel with a folding handle he used to dig out of snowbanks in the winter. It would have to do. The headlights might draw attention, so, dropping to his knees, he worked in the dim shadows cast by the light from the interior of the van.

How had all this happened? he wondered. Judy Mae brought it on herself, meddling where she had no business. And that damned Jonathan had to stir things up by writing a letter. He'd figure some way to get the kid to calm down when he had a chance to think. Right now he had to dig.

The grave was shallow, barely two feet deep, when giant, sluggish raindrops began to hit the back of his neck. The rain pelted the trees above his head. The branches seemed to shiver and groan, releasing a cascade of rain into the narrow opening he had dug in the ground. Shit, he wasn't going to be able to dig much deeper if the earth turned to mud. Maybe it was deep enough.

He carried Judy Mae to the grave and dropped her in. The blanket came undone and he saw her face, stark white in the eerie glow from the van's light. Her bright red lips opened slightly, as if in a sigh, and he was certain she was trying to open her eyes. He covered her quickly and began to shovel the heaps of wet dirt down over her.

Now the wind slapped the cold rain against his face. Water ran down the back of his neck. What a downpour, he thought. Just like the frigging drenchers in the jungles of Vietnam. He hurried inside the van and mopped the rain from his head. This was no night to be out. He'd better hurry home to the kids.

Chapter 14

DRIVEN sideways by the wind, the cold rain flew against the windows and hammered noisily on the tin roof of the little house. Jonathan couldn't remember ever being this frightened during a storm when he had been safe at home with his parents. He was caught up with the terror of the storm, but at the same time he had an urgent need to make Maria understand his growing fear of Leon, his fear of what Leon might do next.

"Maria, how would you like to go to Georgia?"

Maria sat cross-legged on the floor with her back against the old couch. She was arranging the Monopoly money into neat little piles. "I've been there. At least I think it was Georgia."

"When? When did you go there?"

"When Leon took me, when I was little."

Jonathan leaned closer. "Why'd you go to Georgia with Leon?"

Maria shrugged. "I don't remember. He just took me. I hated the long drive. We mostly sat in the van, but sometimes we ate in little restaurants, which was fun, but then he just stopped taking me."

"Why didn't you tell me before?" Jonathan asked. "Why didn't you tell me about going to Georgia?"

Her eyes widened, but Jonathan knew she didn't

understand. She could not have guessed what Leon had been up to. Jonathan wasn't even sure he believed all the unthinkable thoughts that kept popping into his head.

"I don't know," she answered. "I didn't think it mattered. They were just dumb trips in the van. I was glad when he let me stay here with Judy Mae and he started going away all by himself. Besides, he told me not to tell anybody."

"Maria," Jonathan said firmly, "I'm going to run away. I think we both should get away from here, away from Leon. Come with me. I want to go home, to Georgia."

"Why do you want to go there? Your house burned up, didn't it?"

"Leon said it did, but I want to see for myself. I don't think he's telling us the truth."

"Yeah, but what if he is?"

Jonathan ignored that possibility. "I'm going to go back and look for my dog. You want to come along?"

Maria finished sorting the Monopoly five-hundred-dollar bills into two equal stacks before she looked at him. "How're we gonna get there? It's too far to walk."

"Maybe we could hitchhike? I think I know the way. I wrote down the roads and all the bridges and stuff when Leon drove me here, and all we have to do is go back the same way."

"It's too far."

The wind howled, rattling the windowpanes. The din of the pouring rain reminded Jonathan that running away would not be easy. Maybe people wouldn't want to give a lift to two kids hitching by themselves, but walking all the way to Georgia in the rain would be better than staying here with Leon. Besides, if they could get to a phone, he could call the police. They could help him get home.

"I wish we had some money," he said, fingering the brightly colored Monopoly currency. "Some real money."

Maria stood up. "I got some."

"Where? How much?"

Maria forced her hand down between the cushions of the couch and produced a rumpled blue wad of cloth. She extended her hand to Jonathan. "It's in here. More than twenty dollars."

Jonathan untied the knot which held the money in place and studied the pile of coins and six or seven crumpled one-dollar bills.

"I've been saving that for a long time," she said proudly.

"How'd you get it? Did Leon give it to you?"

She shook her head. "He throws his money on his dresser at night. I take a little every now and then. He doesn't know I have it."

He retied the bundle and handed it back to her. "Keep it hidden, until we're ready to go. It might be enough for bus tickets."

"Where would we get on a bus?"

Jonathan shook his head. "I don't know exactly, but there's got to be buses going to Georgia."

Maria sat down on the couch. She reached way down into its dusty innards and replaced her hoard. "What if Leon catches us? He'll whip us good."

"Has he whipped you before?" Jonathan asked.

Maria flushed. "Yeah, plenty of times," she answered, half to herself.

"Then that's another reason why we should go. Why should we stay here with a guy who's gonna whip us?"

"Leon says he'll beat me bloody if I ever go anywhere he don't want me to go. Maybe you should go alone. You can take the money."

Jonathan felt tears sting the corners of his eyes.

Somehow he had to convince Maria to go with him. He couldn't just leave her here alone with Leon. "No, we'll both go, and he won't catch us. We'll wait until we can get a good head start without him knowing."

"All right, but I'm not going tonight in all this rain," Maria said flatly. "Tonight I get to sleep on the couch, so I want to sleep here rather than on a bus."

Here was another searing question Jonathan had worried about. Maria had gotten up very early every morning since he arrived, but today he was certain she'd emerged from the bathroom without ever having crossed through his bedroom. That could only mean she had slept in the big bedroom with Leon. But where? As far as Jonathan was able to tell when he had peeked into the room, there was only one bed, a double bed covered with the faded squares of an ancient quilt.

"How come you get to sleep on the couch tonight?" he asked.

"Because Leon went to visit Judy Mae."

Not seeing any connection between the two, Jonathan asked, "Where do you sleep if you don't sleep on the couch?"

Maria's face went crimson and tears came to her eyes. Her lower lip trembled but no words came forth. Jonathan was immediately sorry he had asked. Something very wrong was going on, and he was ashamed he had embarrassed her. He'd heard about grown men doing terrible things to little girls, and he was pretty sure he understood what those things were. At least he thought he knew.

"It's okay," Jonathan said quickly. "Let's not talk about it. Let's just decide what we need to take when we leave. We can carry stuff in my backpack."

The tortured look on Maria's face softened a little. She wiped her eyes, but just then the screen door in the kitchen crashed against the outside wall with a thud. Jonathan looked up as the inner door swung open. A dripping wet Leon filled the doorway; the rain followed him inside.

"Don't just sit there," he thundered. "Help me get these muddy shoes off my feet."

Maria scrambled from the couch into the kitchen and helped Leon with his shoes while he blotted his face and the top of his bald head with the kitchen towel.

"That's better," he said. "What a night."

Maria stared at him, her eyes wide, unblinking saucers. She grabbed an old rag from under the sink and wiped up the puddle of rain and mud on the floor under Leon's feet.

"Come into my room, girl," Leon said. "You can help me get out of these wet pants."

Maria's face went crimson. "Couldn't I stay with him?" She gestured toward Jonathan. "We've been playing a game."

Leon grinned, showing his teeth. His eyes narrowed, burning into little black holes in his face. "I bet you'd like that, wouldn't you?" His smile faded. "Get into my room before I get the strap."

Slowly cringing back against the wall, Jonathan tried to melt into the shadows of the doorway leading to the living room. He wanted to dash outside in spite of the terror of the storm and the cold blackness of the night, but his trembling knees had somehow become disconnected from his brain. His feet were powerless to move. Leon turned and spotted him.

"What're you doing, boy?"

"Nothing," Jonathan squeaked. "Just standing here."

Leon grinned again. "Maybe you'd better get on into my room, too. It's time you learned a little bit about the facts of life."

Something grabbed hold of Jonathan's insides and twisted so hard he thought he was going to wet his pants. He tried to speak, but all he heard was a choked rush of air from his own lips.

Outside, the wind shrieked, exploding torrents of rain against the windows. The glass shuddered, sending wispy drafts of cold air creeping into the house. Maria and Jonathan walked through the bathroom without turning on the light. Leon pushed them into his dark, musty bedroom.

Chapter 15

ED Grady tried to calm the trembling that had crept into his voice during the last six days. He took a deep breath and said, "Let me see if I have this straight. You're certain Jonathan was at the motel in Virginia with a guy named Kirby, but then all traces of him disappear."

Special FBI Agent Kira Thomasian looked as if she hated this part of her job, but she spoke reassuringly. "Remember, I was assigned to Jonathan's case less than forty-eight hours ago. We've lost the trail of this Lee Kirby, but don't worry, we'll pick it up again."

Ed fidgeted, shifting his feet, folding and unfolding his arms across his chest. He still had a solid lump in his gut from their encounters with Detective Fernandez. With all his barbed questions, Fernandez had implied that Ed and Susan were somehow to blame or possibly even responsible for Jonathan's sudden disappearance. Susan had been devastated by Fernandez's attitude; Ed just got pissed off.

He was hoping for some real action when the FBI was called in, and instead he saw this woman as too young, too inexperienced, even too beautiful to be capable of doing them any good. Kira Thomasian's hair fell softly in gentle waves to her shoulders; her nails were perfectly manicured, her makeup flawless. All of this, Ed was certain, did not come about without a certain amount of time spent in beauty and nail salons.

He knew it was wrong and sickly male chauvinistic to think a woman couldn't do the job simply because she was attractive and took excellent care of herself. After all, every day in his business dealings he was surrounded by competent women who were also good-looking. But goddammit, this was his son. He wanted some tough son of a bitch, a real he-man, to find and crucify the bastard who had taken Jonathan.

The phone jangled, startling Susan upright from her slouched position on the sofa. She reached for the portable phone she now carried with her no matter where she went in the house. After one ring Susan was speaking.

"Hello. Yes . . . No, we have nothing new to tell you. You're supposed to check in with the local police or call the Atlanta Field Office of the FBI. Please, we have to keep the line open . . . in case . . . there's a call."

She put the phone down. "Another TV reporter, Channel Five this time," she explained. "Why can't they let us alone?"

Ed watched the torment recoil in Susan's eyes. More than anything, he wanted to erase this week of agony from their lives, to bring Jonathan safely home where he belonged, and instead here he sat, helpless. He couldn't even prevent the local TV reporters from hounding them to death.

Susan leaned back into the thick, cushy pillows that lined the sofa, her shoulder brushing Ed's. She had grown painfully quiet when the two of them were alone, talking only in whispers, but mostly not talking at all. Ed listened as she cried herself to sleep every night, all the while his own tears soaked into his pillow.

"So what are you doing?" Susan asked Agent Thomasian. Her voice sounded hollow to Ed, not like the Susan he knew so well. "Tomorrow it will be one week since Jonathan disappeared."

"Believe me, we've been busy," Thomasian said. "After the lab people went over the motel room, we had an artist work up a composite sketch based on the clerk's recollections." She placed a copy of the drawing on the coffee table in front of them.

Ed studied it for a moment. "So this is what he looks like?"

"We ran the name Lee Kirby through our computers, just in case it's not an alias."

"And?" Ed asked cautiously.

Agent Thomasian flipped through a notebook, stopping at a page that was entirely covered with writing. "Our various data banks came up with a couple hundred Lee Kirbys. We then defaulted the list, eliminating the ones who were in prison, mental institutions, retirement homes, and so on."

"So how many Lee Kirbys does that leave us?" Ed asked.

"About forty, scattered across the country. We also eliminated two who are currently residing in foreign countries."

"Great," Ed said, shaking his head wearily. "What next?"

"Well, one by one, all the men named Lee Kirby will be checked out. We also have the lab going over everything they picked up at the motel yesterday. Unfortunately, there isn't much to go on. Whatever evidence there might have been has probably been compromised by the motel's cleaning and the guest who occupied the room after Kirby."

Susan looked distant, anguished, as if it took

great effort for her mind to cull fragments of sense from the conversation. "Is it true that the longer he's gone, the less likely it is you'll ever find him?" she asked.

Now Agent Thomasian looked pained. "No, that's not true at all," she said, but Ed noticed the flush that crept up her neck. What she said, apparently, was not what she really believed.

Susan went on, "I heard that if they don't have a lead in seventy-two hours, the police are ready to close the case."

Thomasian opened her mouth to speak, but Susan raised her voice and continued.

"Don't deny it, I know it's true. You're not ready to give up on Jonathan, are you?"

The FBI agent's eyes grew moist. She blinked several times and then reached out and placed her hand on top of Susan's. "Please, don't torture yourself like this, Mrs. Grady. I have access to the most sophisticated criminal investigation techniques in the world, and I intend to do everything in my power to find your son. It just takes time."

"How much time do you think we have?" Ed asked. At least the young woman in charge of the case had some compassion for them as parents.

Thomasian looked at the floor. "Naturally, you don't have any guarantees when you're dealing with someone who's sick enough to abduct a child, but statistically speaking, if they're going to kill the child, they generally do it pretty fast and usually not too far from the point where the child was seized. Since he took the boy all the way to Virginia, we think there's a very good chance your son is still alive."

"What about the license numbers he gave to the motel?" Ed asked.

Thomasian shook her head. "All phony, just like his address and phone number."

"You checked out that address in person?"

"Not me personally, but someone out of the Pittsburgh office went there. It's a suite of doctors' offices, all right. The mere fact that he covered his ass —his trail, with the repeated use of that same address and phone number, indicates definite premeditation. He did some planning on this, but he'll slip up again. They always do."

"But why Jonathan?" Ed asked. "Why'd he pick on Jonathan? If he's been planning to kidnap Jonathan all along, he must have a reason besides ransom. We're not millionaires."

"He may have planned to kidnap a child for months, even years, and your son could have been a random selection. Then again, as you say, he may have had a reason to zero in on Jonathan."

"But who would do such a thing to a little boy? Jonathan's probably scared half to death."

Thomasian again indicated the copy of the composite sketch lying on the table in front of them. "That's why you have to study this sketch. Maybe it'll come to you. Perhaps some guy you did business with? Maybe a deal that went sour?"

"Ed doesn't give his customers a raw deal," Susan said defensively. "He's very well-respected in the real estate business."

Ed squeezed Susan's hand. He had never loved her more than he did this minute, but he understood what the agent was getting at. Nowadays it didn't take much for a disgruntled client to run screaming "lawsuit" to the nearest attorney, but what if that client were slightly unbalanced or deranged, perhaps even psychotic? He guessed that under certain circumstances anything could happen.

"I understand that," Thomasian said, "but please try to think. Does this picture look like anyone you have ever known?"

"I don't know," Ed answered. "He looks like no one I know, yet he might be a dozen guys I've met in my lifetime."

"Try to think of this face with more hair, perhaps when he was younger. Remember, hair would make his appearance change considerably."

"Yeah, you're right."

"What about with glasses? Or glasses and a wig?" Thomasian asked. "Would you know anyone who resembles this general description?"

"Sure, but nobody who's into kidnapping. With lots of curly black hair, he could be Arnie down at the Shell station. Hell, my first thought was he looked just like one of my sergeants from 'Nam."

Her pencil stopped moving across her notebook and her mouth dropped open slightly. Agent Thomasian looked Ed squarely in the eyes. "Your sergeant? Why didn't you say so?"

"Because he never came home. Died in a Viet Cong prison camp."

"What was his name?"

"Hoffman. Bull Hoffman."

"His first name was Bull?"

"Nickname was Bull. That's all we ever called him. I don't think I ever knew his real name."

"What happened?"

Ed hadn't relived this part of his past for some time, and he wasn't eager to relive it now. "Bull's dead."

"Yes," Thomasian said patiently, "but he may have had a brother, perhaps even a father, who looks like him. We can't afford to pass up any leads."

Ed nodded and took a deep breath. "Eight of us

went out on patrol one night in 'sixty-eight. We were in this god-awful terrain, a jungle, but it was all swampy. I don't know exactly what went wrong, but we walked into an ambush. Four guys went down right off the bat, but the rest of us managed to jump into what was left of a bunker, one of theirs."

"Go on."

Susan touched his hand. She knew; she understood this was a painful memory for him. Susan had soothed him through dozens of terrifying nightmares right after they were married. Without her, he probably would have gone off the deep end, he thought, and now they had this new nightmare to share.

"Honey," Susan said, "you don't have to go into details."

Ed shook his head. "It's okay." If it would help the FBI to locate Jonathan, he was willing to dredge up the memories one more time.

Ed continued, "We held them off until nightfall. The sarge went nuts, lobbing grenades at them, shooting into the jungle, wasting our ammo even when they weren't shooting back. He got a bunch of them, too; he was a damned good shot, but we were trapped."

"What did you do?"

"About midnight, the sarge ordered Cozelli, Mendoza, and me to make a run for the rest of our platoon. It was either that or sit there until they came in to get us. It was crazy, but the four of us managed to sneak out of there even though we were completely surrounded."

"Obviously you made it."

"Not far. They captured us and immediately separated us. After they took them away, I never saw Bull or Mendoza again. They threw me into one of their swamp cages. A Cobra division found me before the rats and mosquitoes ate me alive, but they said Bull and Mendoza weren't so lucky. I connected with Cozelli during the medevac to Saigon, right before they shipped me home. Poor Cozelli was in pretty bad shape."

"What were their full names?" she asked. "Mendoza and Cozelli?"

His throat had gone dry. Ed swallowed hard. "Vince Mendoza and Tony—Anthony Cozelli."

Thomasian seemed to be writing down every word he said. As if any of this mattered. "Then it's army record that Hoffman and Mendoza are dead," she said.

"It should be," he answered. "I never saw anything official, but then I didn't stick around for any long good-byes once I was ordered stateside."

"You didn't like Hoffman very much, did you?" she asked.

Ed thought about the answer to that one. Bull was a surly son of a bitch, but you didn't want to see anybody get it at the hands of the V.C. Nobody deserved the kind of punishment those bastards were able to dish out. Not even Bull.

"I guess nobody liked him very much, but there was no bad blood between us, if that's what you mean," Ed answered.

"That's what I mean."

"We were all in the same boat. Nobody could blame our capture on anything except rotten luck."

"Still, it's something I want to check through the computers. You never know."

Susan looked tired. She shifted her position, leaning against him even more heavily. "What do we do now?" she asked Agent Thomasian, but her eyes were on Ed.

"We've more or less put a hold on the local search.

If your son was taken to Virginia by Friday night, he isn't likely to show up back here in Georgia."

"Where are you looking?" Ed asked.

"Well, we're concentrating on getting out the word on the abductor. This composite sketch will be faxed all over the country, and we're working up a psychological profile. I'll have that by this evening. The sketch, along with your son's picture, will be in the hands of every police department and sheriff's office in the country by tonight. Unless he's crawled into a cave, someone will spot Kirby and your boy. Meantime, we have agents from Atlanta to Boston checking out the airport mechanic story. I'll keep you posted on that."

"Maybe someone in one of the airports will identify him," Ed said without too much conviction.

"Perhaps," Thomasian answered, "but it doesn't look too hopeful. The Knoxville airport had never seen him, and what's more, they've never used a free-lance mechanic, as Kirby described himself."

"So where does that leave us?" Ed asked.

"I'm afraid it leaves us with a whole lot of questions and very few answers."

Chapter 16

EARLY Thursday morning the sun finally blinked through the rain clouds. Jonathan shivered from the cold when he awoke in his drafty little room, then he shivered again, remembering how Leon had changed from a crude but well-meaning friend of his dad's to a brutal monster. Jonathan pulled the covers up to his chin and gently touched the bruise on his forehead and the painful split in his lower lip. It throbbed and he wanted to cry, but he didn't want Leon to hear.

It all started Tuesday night when Leon had come home dripping wet and covered with mud. At first Jonathan thought Leon had had too much to drink, because he was suddenly so loud and mean, but then when Jonathan saw the evil burning in Leon's eyes, he suspected the worst. Leon had gone crazy. Jonathan was now determined he would not remain in Leon's house another night. He would run away, as far away from Leon as possible, and, if he could find a phone, he would report Leon to the police.

The police would never let Leon get away with what he had done to Maria, even if he was crazy. Last year he had seen a film at school about child abuse, so Jonathan knew it was against the law to beat up on kids the way Leon had hit them. He hoped the police would lock up Leon for a long, long time.

Jonathan shuddered, remembering how Leon had laughed, drunk with the power he held over the two children, when he pushed them into his room. Leon shoved Jonathan so hard, he'd fallen to his knees. Jonathan began to cry.

"Shut up, dammit. You're nothing but a big baby, just like your yellow-bellied ol' man," Leon had yelled.

"My dad is not yellow-bellied," Jonathan cried.
"You are." Jonathan got up from the floor and took a swing at Leon. He smacked him squarely in the chest, but Leon just laughed. Then Leon's eyes got that funny look again. He stared at Jonathan like a lizard stares without blinking.

"Get out of here, boy. I don't need no aggravation from you." Leon stood there, big and ugly, with his grisly hands clenched into fists.

Jonathan backed toward the bathroom. Maria shrank away from Leon, cowering against the foot of the bed like a small bird under the shadow of a great hawk. Maria's eyes leveled hatred at Leon, but she did not cry.

Jonathan wanted to run for his life, but he didn't want to leave Maria alone with Leon. "Come with me," Jonathan said to Maria. "We'll finish our game."

"Leave her out of this, boy," Leon snapped. "Play your damned game by yourself."

"You can't tell me what to do," Jonathan cried. "You're not my father." He took a step closer to Leon and stamped his foot in defiance.

Leon's hand had flown out so fast, Jonathan didn't even have time to duck. Jonathan's lower lip ripped on the first blow, then Leon smacked him on the head. Now Maria began to cry.

"You wanna fight back, do you, boy?" Leon shouted. A drool of spit slobbered down his chin. "Nobody gives Leon a hard time. You do what you're told or you'll be picking up your teeth, you hear?"

Jonathan fell to the floor and cried, raging inside until he felt sick to his stomach, but Leon just picked him up and threw him against the door. Jonathan had never been hit like that before, and the sheer terror of waiting for the next blow paralyzed his senses. The strength went out of his arms and legs, but somehow he crawled through the doorway into the bathroom. Leon kicked the door shut with a loud thud.

Jonathan crawled over to the toilet, certain he was going to vomit. Then he realized the screaming he heard inside his head was not his own sobs. Maria's cries were muffled by the door a little bit, but there was no mistaking her terror. Her pathetic wail stitched into Jonathan's brain. He finally got up and ran to his bed, but even with the covers over his head, he could still hear Maria crying, if only in his mind.

Then, all day yesterday, Leon had not gone outside, not even to go to the garage, because of the downpour, and Jonathan had watched him grow more and more restless as the hours ticked away. Drinking one beer after another, Leon paced the floor like a caged animal. By nightfall Leon was almost too drunk to walk, but again he yanked Maria from the spot where she had curled up on the couch and dragged her into his bedroom.

Finally, what seemed like hours later, Maria crept out of Leon's room and ran back to her couch in the living room. Jonathan got out of bed in the dark and went to her. He didn't know what to say, so he just sat on the edge of the couch next to her. Maria cried into her pillow, wrenching sobs heaved from deep within her body. After she had cried herself to sleep, Jonathan went back to his bed in the next room.

He guessed he had cried himself to sleep, also. Once asleep, he plunged into a series of swirling, disjointed dreams. They were black and scary dreams, but the vivid scenes instantly dissolved from his memory the moment he woke up.

Jonathan had never lived in fear of any adult, and was, in fact, accustomed to cooperating with all the grown-ups he had known in the past. When he lived with his parents, rebellion had never been a part of his life, but now his instincts told him he had to rebel, not only for his sake, but for Maria's sake as well. Yes, he would run away today.

He ran his tongue over the deep cut on his lip. It stung and felt swollen. He couldn't close his mouth all the way. He wished his mother were here to take care of him.

The rain had finally stopped. That meant Leon would be able to leave the house to go into town today. With Leon gone, he and Maria would finally have an opportunity to run away. All they needed was a head start.

Maria poked her head into Jonathan's room. "We're out of eggs. You want cereal?" Jonathan noticed how her eyes avoided his. Dark bruises sheathed her arms and legs.

"Yeah, sure," Jonathan whispered. "Is he up?"

"Not yet," she answered, then turned and left the room.

Jonathan got dressed and hurried into the kitchen. Coffee was perking; Maria sat at the table with a blank stare on her face as she slowly used her spoon to round up a flotilla of crisp little cereal squares floating in a bowl of milk.

"It stopped raining," Jonathan said.

"I know."

"He'll go to town, won't he?"

Maria shrugged. "I guess. Who cares what he does? He won't take us. He never takes me anywhere anymore."

Jonathan sat down next to her and covered his own bowl of little squares with milk. The cereal had no taste, but maybe that was because his mouth was so sore. "I don't want to go with him," he whispered. "I want to go home, to Georgia. We can run away as soon as Leon leaves the house."

Maria's eyes widened, but then she shook her head. "He'll just catch us and whip the daylights out of both of us."

"Not if we're careful."

"What're you two chumming about so early in the morning?" Leon lumbered into the room, scratching his puffy stomach. The heavy smell of sweat that clung to Leon made Jonathan's nostrils quiver. He wanted to fling curses at Leon and hit him right in the face as hard as he could, but he sat quietly and stared at the burly man with no neck. He had never hated anyone as much as he hated Leon.

Leon shuffled over to the stove and poured himself a cup of coffee. "I guess if you want coffee around this place, you have to get it yourself." He took a sip, then spat the mouthful into the sink. "Tastes like dishwater. You made it too weak; you know I like it strong."

"We're out of coffee," Maria said. "I told you we needed more coffee. We're out of eggs, too."

Leon flashed a hateful glance at Maria and Jonathan. For a moment Jonathan was afraid Leon was going to hit Maria or perhaps both of them again, but he simply dumped the rest of the coffee into the sink. He swallowed some aspirin without any water and then returned to his bedroom.

"What's he going to do?" Jonathan asked quickly.

"I don't know. He doesn't like cereal very much."

"C'mon. Let's wash the dishes. We don't want to act suspicious."

Maria looked at him in disbelief and wrinkled her nose. "You're crazy."

Jonathan dried their two cereal bowls, stacked them on the shelf and put the spoons back in the drawer. He dried Leon's cup while Maria washed the coffeepot.

Soon, Leon reentered the kitchen. "I'm going out to get me a decent breakfast," he said. "Where's your grocery list?"

"Right here." Maria handed him a wrinkled sheet of paper. "You better get milk, too."

"Sure, sure. You see that the two of you stay out of trouble. I won't be long."

"You're going to have breakfast with Judy Mae, aren't you?" Maria asked.

"Nah, we're not getting along so good right now," Leon said. "I think she's found another guy."

Maria's face fell. "She'll be coming back here to visit, won't she? She said she was coming over on Friday."

"How the hell would I know? Maybe she'll run away and marry this new guy."

"But she said she was going to marry you!" Maria's voice trembled.

"Women are like that. They say one thing but they mean another. Goddamn women don't know what they want; they're all alike."

"But . . ." Maria said weakly.

"But what?" Leon growled. "There ain't nothing I can do about it if she wants to run off with another man."

"She said she was going to bring me some . . . things . . . for next month."

"Whenever you want something, write it on the list

just like you do for groceries, and I'll get it when I'm in town."

Maria looked devastated. "I don't even know how to spell it."

"Ask your hotshot brother. He's real good at all kinds of writing, aren't you, boy?" Leon glared at Jonathan before he turned and pushed open the screen door.

Standing by the window, Jonathan held his breath as Leon backed the van over the soggy grass and turned around. The raspy cough of the motor did not sound hopeful. The van might not even make it to town. It sputtered and belched a black puff of smoke, but then disappeared down the road.

When Jonathan could no longer hear the engine, he took a deep breath. "Maria, this is our chance. He'll be gone for a while, and it's not raining. C'mon, we have to get ready."

"I'm scared," she said.

"Well, so am I, but we have to do it; we have to run away."

Maria didn't move. "He'll find us and whip us with the belt. It makes your butt hurt for days and days."

"Maria, I don't believe my house exploded. I think Leon killed my parents and made up lies just to get me in his van. What if your parents weren't in an accident? What if he killed them, too, and your sister?"

Maria looked stunned. "Why would he kill our parents? He was my dad's best friend."

"To get you, to get us, so he could do the stuff he does to us. He's a bad person. I know he killed my parents, and I'll kill him if he hurts us again."

"How are you going to kill him?"

"You'll see, but first we have to get out of here. Pack up all the food you can find in a grocery bag. We'll put everything else in my backpack."

"There isn't much food. We're out of everything."

"Just grab anything we can eat. Crackers, jelly. What about the canned food under the sink?"

"How will we open the cans?"

"Take the can opener." Jonathan opened the drawer and grabbed two spoons, a knife, and the hand can opener. "Here, put these in the bag."

"But Leon will have a fit if we take the can opener," she said.

"Maria!" Jonathan cried in frustration. "Stop worrying about him. He's not going to hurt us anymore."

Maria reluctantly fell to her knees and began to sort through the meager supply of food in the cabinet under the sink. Jonathan hurried into his room and stuffed his jacket, toothbrush, toothpaste, and a comb into his pack. He put on a long-sleeved flannel shirt over his T-shirt, and then grabbed an extra pair of socks, just to be safe. His Cub Scout leader always made them carry extra socks whenever the troop went on a hike.

Maybe he should check Leon's dresser for money? He wouldn't even feel guilty about stealing from Leon. Leon deserved much worse than that. He found fifty cents on top of the dresser. There's got to be more, he thought, dropping the coins in his pocket. One of Leon's jackets, still damp around the waistband from the rain, hung over the closet doorknob. He thrust his hand into the pocket and felt paper. Cash! He had found Leon's money.

Quickly, he pulled out a crinkled handful, but it wasn't paper money. It was his own letter, the one to Brian that Judy Mae was supposed to mail for him. He shoved it into the same pocket with the fifty cents, wondering how Leon had gotten it. Why would Judy Mae give it to him? He bet Leon took it away from her. Maybe Judy Mae didn't even know Leon had taken it.

"Maria," he called, running back into the living room, "put on your jeans, quick." He decided to wait to tell her about finding his letter.

"What's wrong with my dress?"

"Nothing. Fold it up and put it in my pack. You'll be warmer in jeans. We may have to sleep outside, you know."

"Really?" she asked.

"Maybe just one night or two. Depends. Don't forget your money."

Maria dressed in her jeans and a heavy pullover sweater. She carefully folded the faded, threadbare dress and slipped it into Jonathan's backpack along with her windbreaker and toothbrush. After she removed her money from the sofa, she thrust the little blue package toward Jonathan.

"You'd better keep the money in your pocket, so we don't lose it," she said.

Jonathan was pleased she trusted him, but he didn't know exactly how to tell her so. "Okay," was all he said.

Maria reached into another recess in the old couch, under the pillows, and pulled out a flattened plastic bag. Flushing scarlet to the roots of her hair, she pushed the bag into Jonathan's pack next to her dress. "I might need these," she said. "Judy Mae says a woman should always be prepared."

"Right," Jonathan said, wishing he knew what she was talking about. He picked up the bag of food. "There's something else we have to get. Come with me to the garage."

Maria closed the kitchen door quietly, as if Leon, wherever he was, could hear. They followed the muddy path through the graveyard of auto parts to the garage.

"What are you going to take? Leon will know if you mess with his stuff," Maria said.

"He's going to know we ran away, won't he? Remember, we don't care what Leon says anymore."

Maria nodded grimly. Jonathan hurried to the far wall of the garage and stopped under the gun rack. He stepped on a bumper lying on the floor and climbed from it to the workbench. Stretching, he reached for the gun rack and removed Leon's only handgun.

"Where does he keep the bullets?" Jonathan asked.

"Why do you want bullets? Who are you going to shoot?"

"I told you, if he comes after us, I'm going to kill Leon."

Maria put her right hand over her mouth. "You couldn't really shoot Leon, and you know it."

Jonathan began to ransack the tin cans and boxes along the cluttered work space. "I could, too, if I had to, and if Leon catches us, he'll be sorry he killed my parents and kidnapped me because I'll shoot him."

The ammunition had to be here somewhere. He searched through cans holding greasy little engine parts hardly bigger than his finger and swept away dozens of ripped automotive belts. He moved a filthy black rag off the lid of a box that said Dutch Masters Cigars and peered inside. The box contained loose bullets, some long, some short, and two smaller boxes filled with cartridges.

"I'm not sure how to put the bullets inside," Jonathan said.

Maria pointed. "The gun bends in half and you put them in that round part. I saw Leon do it."

Jonathan fumbled with the revolver, trying to release the cylinder.

Maria pointed again. "He did it with his thumb. Right there."

He pushed against a little rounded surface just behind the cylinder, and the front portion of the gun flipped forward. With the cylinder exposed, Jonathan could see openings for five bullets. Most of the loose shells seemed too long for the revolver, so he opened one of the small boxes that said .38 SHORT on the top. Ever so carefully he slipped a shell into one of the five openings. It fit perfectly! He slowly pushed four more into place and tried to close the chamber. The cylinder lurched forward with such a jolt, Jonathan almost dropped the gun.

"Be careful with that thing," Maria warned. "What if it goes off?"

"I'll be careful." He tried again, his hand trembling, but this time the cylinder clicked into place. "Let me put the gun and some extra bullets in the backpack."

Maria quickly shrugged the pack off her shoulder. "Then you carry it. If it's gonna have guns and bullets inside, I'll carry the food." She picked up the brown grocery bag and rolled down the top to create a handle. "We'd better get out of here before he comes back."

Normally the coarse gravel made a crunching sound under their tennis shoes, but today the rain-soaked earth muffled their footsteps. Jonathan was scared, but he knew he had to be brave for Maria's sake. If she suspected how nervous he was, she would run back into the house, destined to remain with Leon forever. He adjusted the backpack, determined he would somehow be strong enough for both of them.

"I don't think we should follow the road," he said. "If Leon comes back, he'll see us for sure."

"Which way do we go?"

"Let's go the same direction as the dirt road, but we'll walk in the woods. If we hear the van, we can duck behind a tree or something."

Maria trekked along behind Jonathan. He kept the gravel-covered dirt lane in view along his left side, but they stayed far enough away that he was certain Leon wouldn't spot them if he returned.

The earth smelled of decay as their shoes squished into the soggy, moss-covered loam, but the rainwashed air felt refreshing and clean. The cleansing action of breathing pure, sweet air was invigorating after being cooped up in the vile little house with Leon. Somewhere in the woods, not too far away, a bird whistled a cheerful little song, the same crisp notes ringing out over and over.

Each step took him farther and farther away from this dreadful place in the woods, and he could barely wait until they reached a phone. The words he wanted to say whirled through his mind. He wanted to tell Brian the whole story about what had happened to him, but he knew he should call the police first. Perhaps, if he could get through to his grandma, she'd tell him what to do. She would also know the truth about his parents.

As much as Jonathan prayed his parents were alive and well, he knew that was too much to hope for. Leon had made up everything about the fire just so he wouldn't figure out Leon had killed them. Maybe Leon even used the same gun he now carried in his backpack. A chill shot up his spine at the thought.

They covered the distance to the black macadam road sooner than he expected. Maria lagged five or so feet behind him, but she wasn't complaining. Jonathan waited for her to catch up.

Jonathan pointed to the right. "I came in from this

direction, from the highway. Which way is the town?"

Maria pointed to the left. "The other way."

"He's probably in town, so let's walk toward the highway."

"Maybe we should try to find Judy Mae?" Maria said. "I think we should tell her we're leaving."

Jonathan shook his head. "Leon might be with her."

"Leon says she found a new boyfriend."

"Let's just walk. We can call her when we find a phone."

They stayed off the blacktop and walked along the shoulder. The air was cool, but they had worked up a sweat, and Jonathan felt good for the first time since Leon had picked him up. If he had counted the days correctly, tomorrow it would be one week since Leon had lured him into the van.

Suddenly Maria let out a yelp and stopped dead in her tracks. In the distance, the familiar yellow van was chugging down the road, moving directly toward them.

Chapter 17

"**D**o you think he saw us?" Maria asked.

Jonathan looked up from the ditch along the side of the road. He had shoved Maria down into the gully, then jumped almost on top of her. They made it into the ditch before the van drove by, but there was no question it was Leon's van. Slowly, the van stuttered up the hill, into the woods and out of sight.

"I don't think so," Jonathan answered. "He would've stopped."

"I thought you said it was safe to go this way!"

Jonathan wondered about that, too. "Well, I thought he was going to town. Didn't you?"

"Now what?" Maria asked.

"We have to keep moving. As long as we're heading away from Leon's place, we'll be okay."

Maria shook her head. "He's gonna come looking for us. He'll whip us both, you'll see."

"Let's go." Jonathan helped Maria to her feet and handed her the bag of food. "We'll walk all day if we have to. We can't stop now."

They followed the winding turns of the lonely road, walking on the narrow dirt shoulder between the paved surface and the drainage ditch which dropped off to their right. They were surrounded on both sides by nothing but trees. Birds chirping somewhere in distant treetops and the occasional chattering of a squirrel were the only sounds besides their own footsteps. A gentle breeze barely stirred the trees; the sky was cloudless. They crossed a bridge, and Jonathan realized it was the same bridge he had seen from the van last Saturday. The water in the little creek pounded against the rocks, the overflow from the recent storm surging into foam. Now it really looked deep.

Jonathan tried to set the pace, but Maria lagged behind if he walked too quickly. At this rate, he thought, it will take us all day just to go one mile.

"Quick, hide," Maria cried. She scrambled down the shallow embankment into the ditch, pulling Jonathan by the arm until he had no choice but to slide after her. "Get down; a car's coming."

Now Jonathan heard it, too. "No, let's flag down the car. They can help us."

"What if it's Leon or one of his friends? Everybody around here knows him; he fixes their cars."

Jonathan hadn't thought about the possibility of anyone siding with Leon, but then again, adults were usually pretty loyal to each other. They might not take the word of two kids if Leon lied and said differently. Crouching low, he crept behind Maria until they reached a spot where a clump of brush grew along the shoulder, partially blocking the ditch from view. They fell facedown into the soggy dirt just seconds before the car rounded the last bend and rumbled by. Jonathan's heart thumped wildly in his chest, but he lifted his head in time to see the rear end of a fairly new white car disappear down the road. Good. It wasn't Leon; that meant he hadn't started searching for them, at least not yet.

They got up and brushed the dirt from their clothes before they resumed walking.

"Look," Jonathan said, "up ahead. There's another road." He pointed to a fork in the road bearing to the left. "Do you know where it goes?"

"No," Maria answered, "I thought you knew the way."

"I do, as soon as we reach the big highway, but maybe we shouldn't go the same way Leon's liable to go when he comes looking for us. Besides, this other road might take us to the highway, where we can hitch a ride."

Maria stopped walking. "What about the bus?"

"First we have to find a bus station, don't we? Do you see any buses out here? Just c'mon."

Maria trudged behind him until they reached the junction of the two little roads. Jonathan looked both ways before they crossed, even though there wasn't so much as the sound of an oncoming car.

The sun was getting warmer, and the blacktop felt hot under his feet. A farm appeared on the left side of the road, a wooded stretch on the right. They passed the farm, and soon another white house and red barn were visible up ahead. One farm looked like the next to Jonathan as the fields and barns melded together with only an occasional stone wall as punctuation.

"Maybe we could find a farmer, ask him to drive us to the highway or the bus station?" Jonathan said.

"I told you, Leon knows all the farmers around here. What if we go to somebody who has seen me at Leon's house? He fixes a lot of cars. He'll just haul us back to Leon. Leon is our legal guardian, you know."

"I don't think he's my legal guardian."

"Well, he's mine; he's got papers, and I'll bet he's got papers for you, too," Maria said.

"Yeah, maybe, but we've got to trust somebody. We'll be walking forever."

"I don't care."

Jonathan hesitated. "Okay, we'll keep walking, but just for a little while. We have to find a phone. I want to call my grandma or Brian."

"Can Brian come get us?" she asked.

"Well, no, but his parents or my grandma could call the police."

"No," Maria said flatly, "no police."

Jonathan looked at her out of the corner of one eye. She was walking faster now, her face set in some sort of grim resolution. "Why not?" he asked.

"No police. I don't want you to call the police."

"Why?"

"I wish we could find Judy Mae," Maria said. "She'd help us."

Jonathan figured Maria wasn't going to tell him the reason she was so terrified of the police, but he saw the fear in her eyes and knew it was real.

"Judy Mae gave Leon my letter, the one I wrote to Brian. I found it in Leon's coat pocket. See." He pulled the letter from his pocket to show her.

Maria stopped walking and examined the letter. "She wouldn't give it to him. He took it from her, or he made her give it to him."

"We can't be sure."

"Well, I'm sure. You can trust Judy Mae. She's the only grown-up I trust." Maria handed the letter back to Jonathan and resumed walking.

Jonathan trusted Judy Mae, sort of, but he didn't want to spend time looking for her. Not now. They had to get much more distance between them and Leon. Getting away from Leon was all he could think of. His hatred for the man boiled inside him with an intensity he could not fully understand, but he knew somehow his instincts were right. Besides,

Judy Mae would probably do whatever Leon wanted her to do, and he was certain Leon would want "his" kids to return, the sooner the better.

They walked and walked. Jonathan was weary and thirsty, but still they walked, until they had covered miles and miles, or so it seemed.

Suddenly the hum of a motor filled the air. A truck was lumbering toward them, churning up a spray of mud and silt as it bumped over ruts and rocks on a narrow dirt road carved between two planted fields. The driver, a tanned, leathery-looking old man, stared straight ahead as he turned onto the blacktop just a few feet ahead of where they walked.

Jonathan decided not to argue with Maria about this, but began to run, waving for the truck to stop. Slowly the truck ground to a halt and Jonathan ran up to the driver's window. Maria lagged behind, standing perfectly still.

"Can you give us a lift, mister, please?" Jonathan asked.

The old man squinted at them. "Where're you heading?" he asked.

Jonathan hesitated, then quickly said, "The highway."

"Which one?"

"I'm not sure of the name."

"Why ain't you two in school?" the man asked.

"We have to go in late today. That's where we're heading."

"You go to that new school over by the bridge?"

Jonathan wondered if the new school over by the bridge was anywhere near a major road, but he didn't want the farmer to get suspicious. He forced a grin. "That's right. Can you take us there?"

"Yeah, but next time you make sure you don't miss the bus. We pay plenty of taxes so those school

143

buses can take you kids back and forth to school, you know?"

"Yessir," Jonathan said, "I know."

"Get in," the man said.

Jonathan waved and smiled reassuringly to Maria. She lingered behind, as if her feet were fused to the road, but finally took a few steps closer. Jonathan made a whirling, hurry-up motion with his hand, and reluctantly she joined him as he raced to the other side of the truck. They got inside and slammed the door.

"Why're you carrying all that stuff?" the man asked when he spotted the backpack and grocery bag wedged between their feet on the floorboard.

"It's just stuff for school," Jonathan answered quickly.

The man pinched his eyebrows together in a frown and grunted. "You two ain't running away or nothing like that, are you?"

"Oh, no, sir. We're just going to school like we do every day."

"What happened to your lip, boy? You in a fight?"

Jonathan brushed his cracked lip with his fingertips. "No, I fell on the playground."

"Where do you live?" the farmer asked. "I ain't seen you two around here before, have I?"

"We're new, just moved into a new house."

"One of those new houses over by the hollow?"

Jonathan couldn't imagine what a hollow was, let alone where it was, but he nodded vigorously, hoping to put an end to the man's stream of questions. Perhaps Maria had been right. It may have been a serious mistake to trust this man; the very truck they were riding in might be one that Leon had repaired. If the man recognized Maria, he would probably turn the truck around and head straight back to Leon's place.

The farmer leaned his head toward the side window and spat onto the road. "Just doesn't make sense for folks to build them big, fancy houses on perfectly good farmland. I say it's a waste. They keep finding new ways to ruin what we've got here."

The man pulled over in front of a driveway that led up a long, gradually sloping hill to a modern school building surrounded by acres and acres of grass. So there was a school close by, Jonathan thought. Leon had lied to Maria about the school. That proved running away was the right thing to do. Leon probably lied about lots of other things, too, especially about the fire and his parents. Jonathan reached across Maria and released the door, nudging her to get out. He jumped out behind her.

"Thanks for the ride, mister. Thanks a lot," Jonathan called. He waited a moment, then waved as the rickety old truck slowly puttered down the road. After the truck had gone several hundred yards, Jonathan began to walk up the long driveway toward the main entrance to the school.

"Wait," Maria said urgently. "Don't go in there."

"Why not? They can help us. We can trust the principal and the teachers in a school. I've got to use the phone."

"Not in that school," she insisted.

"Why not? We have to get through to the police somehow. They'll stop Leon from hurting us ever again."

"No, I'm afraid. The people in those schools know about the papers Leon has; so do the police. They'll make me go back to Leon. Maybe you, too."

"What do the papers say?"

"They say Leon is my legal guardian. He says you can't get much more legal than that. It means he has a right to do with me whatever he wants, and no school or policeman can stop him. The court gave him his rights, and nobody can change it. It's just like a law."

"That's not true. Leon lied to you."

"What if he has a paper like that for you, too?" Maria's eyes filled with tears. "Look, you said we were going to run away to Georgia. You didn't say nothing about going into that school. If you're going to call the police, I'll just run away by myself."

"But the police won't hurt us. They might even drive us to my grandmother's."

"Don't you get it?" she screamed. "They'll make me tell them what Leon did to me. I can't tell anyone about the awful things Leon made me do. Not ever. And you better not tell them either." Tears cascaded down her face. She spun on her heels and ran down the road in the opposite direction the truck had gone.

"Wait, Maria," Jonathan called. "I won't tell, not even the police." She moved much faster than he had seen her move all morning. He chased after her, calling, "I'm coming, Maria, wait for me."

Chapter 18

Inching his way down the rain-soaked lane, Leon navigated the van through the woods. This last downpour had really made a mess, washing a lot of gravel completely off the road surface. Unable to get a grip on the slick mud, his worn tires spun out, spitting chunks of the fine white rock to the rear. One of these days he would have to buy a load of gravel to cover up all the bare spots. There are just too many things to think about when you have a place of your own, he thought, but he knew he mustn't clutter his mind with details like spreading new gravel. He had important problems to solve, and now that he was finally out of the house and away from the kids for a few hours, his mind would be clear and he'd be able to think.

When he reached the macadam road, he paused, debating whether he should go directly to the diner. Something had been gnawing at him ever since Tuesday night, so instead of heading toward Reinholds, he decided to turn right. He picked up speed. Breakfast could wait a few minutes; he had to check the spot where he had buried Judy Mae. Christ, with the way it had poured Tuesday night and all day yesterday, her body could be washed right out into the middle of the road by now. He should have carried her deeper into the woods. Why hadn't he thought of that? He hated to admit, even to himself, that he had been in too much of a hurry to think clearly. Well, he wasn't in a hurry now.

Maybe he could dig a new grave somewhere else? Make it ten, maybe twelve feet deep. Then he could take her out of the shallow grave she was in, and he could do a proper job of laying her to rest. Judy Mae hadn't been a bad sort, just a meddling woman like all the rest of them. Women probably couldn't help being that way, so he wouldn't hold it against her. He'd do it. He'd give Judy Mae a better grave, real deep. Besides, he didn't want to have to worry about her getting washed out of her grave every time it rained.

He slowed down as he approached the wooded area where he had labored in the mud Tuesday night. It seemed so much smaller by daylight. It wasn't even much of a woods, just a scrawny patch of trees on a little hill at the end of a field, a field that was probably planted in corn. The rows were neat, and the slightest hint of green was just beginning to poke through the soil.

Damn, he had buried her too close to that cornfield. Kids would be tromping right in there to steal a few ears when the corn was ready. He had done it plenty of times when he was a kid, and he had even done it often enough as an adult. He didn't want people to come marching by so close to her grave. Why hadn't he noticed this spot was so close to a field?

He had been too nervous to think straight, that's what, but now he was in control of the situation. He would start on the new grave today, closer to home this time, so he could keep an eye on it without driving all the way over to Adamstown.

He passed the exact spot and craned his neck to

see. As far as he could tell without stopping the van, nothing was disturbed. It was okay. He'd dig her up as soon as he had the new grave ready. With that decision made, he turned around and headed back to Reinholds. He wanted to eat his breakfast at Jake's and establish that he knew nothing about Judy Mae's disappearance. By getting that out of the way early on, no one would bother him with a lot of fool questions when people started to miss her. Now that his head was clear, he was starting to think smart again. Damn, he hated it when his mind went fuzzy like it did Tuesday night and he did things all wrong.

He entered Jake's through the first set of double glass doors and pretended to examine the headlines of a newspaper displayed in a rack set up in the vestibule. Everything seemed quiet as usual inside the diner. He opened the inner door and went directly to the counter, taking a stool near the register, where he knew Jake himself would wait on him if one of his waitresses hadn't shown up. No question, one of his waitresses wouldn't be showing up ever again.

"Whaddaya say, Jake. How's it going?"

"I'm running around here like a one-armed paper hanger, that's what." Jake wiped his hand across the stained white apron spanning his more than ample stomach. Just looking at Jake was enough to make a person lose his appetite, but he did bake a fairly decent apple pie. Jake's apple pie was probably the only thing in the diner that wasn't soaked in grease.

"Where's Judy Mae?" Leon asked without looking up from the sticky plastic menu he held too close to his nose.

"Hell, I thought you'd be able to tell me. She didn't

show up for work yesterday or today. Ol' Wanda's bitching up a storm 'cause she has to fill in for her."

Leon noticed Jake's fat wife, Wanda, waiting on the booths along the front window. She looked as if every step would be her last, as if her feet were nothing more than tightly bound clumps of raw nerve.

"Maybe she's sick?" Leon volunteered.

"Hell, she'd better be, or she can find herself a new job. Wanda's called her place a half a dozen times, but there's no answer."

"No answer?" Leon said, trying to look concerned. "Maybe she's in the hospital or something."

Jake raised his bushy eyebrows. "How come you don't know what'sa matter with her? You two are supposed to be pretty thick, aren't you?"

"Used to be. But not anymore," Leon said, his gaze returning to the menu. "Give me number two, sunny side up, and a side order of sausage. Guess I can eat a slab of apple pie with that, too."

Jake leaned over the counter, real close to Leon. "No kidding? Why, just the other day she said you two were finally going to tie the knot."

Leon shrugged his thick shoulders. "Well, I don't know where she ever got that idea. We haven't been seeing too much of each other lately, not since she started hanging out with that new guy."

"What new guy?"

"Oh, some guy she met at the fire-hall dance a couple of months back. I don't go in for dancing much, but old Judy Mae loves to dance, so she'd always go by herself. I knew sooner or later she'd dump me for some tight-assed bastard in dancing shoes."

Jake rubbed his head, dislodging the grease-stained paper hat on his head. "Don't that beat all? And here I thought she was going to marry you."

Leon shook his head pensively. "I thought so, too,

for a while. But I can't compete with one of those slick dancing dudes, if you know what I mean?"

Jake slogged a damp rag back and forth along the edge of the counter. His motion did not intrude upon the built-up layer of grease mired over every surface of the diner. "Goddamn women don't know what they want. Just the other day she was fussing with her hair, asking the other waitress what she should wear when she got married in June. And I thought she was talking about you." Jake shook his head. "You'd think, with her pushing forty and everything, she'd be thrilled to hook up with a hard-working man like yourself." He walked away, still shaking his head, and yelled Leon's order into the pass-through window to the kitchen.

Leon quickly worked his way through a plate of eggs and biscuits smothered with a thick, pasty, brown gravy. Blue veins stood out on the sides of his temples as he chewed oversized hunks of sausage. Sweat formed on his bald head and trickled down his neck close to his ears. He downed his third cup of steaming coffee and devoured a generous slice of pie, then wiped his forehead with the back of his hand. He stood up and handed Jake the money for his bill.

"When you see her, tell Judy Mae I said hello," Leon said, trying to sound casual.

Jake looked at him funny, raising his eyebrows the way he always did when he was confused.

"There's no hard feelings between us or anything," Leon explained. "We just ain't going together anymore, that's all."

Jake rung up No Sale on the register and made change for Leon. "She goddamn better be good and sick is all I can say. Leaving me stuck here short-handed without any notice ain't like her."

Leon smiled to himself when he got back into his

151

van. He would make a quick stop at the grocery store and then hurry home so he could start on the new grave. He might be smart to put Judy Mae on his own property, so he wouldn't have to worry about anyone ever digging her up accidentally. Maybe behind the garage, fifty, no, a hundred yards beyond the outhouse. Yes, he liked the idea of having Judy Mae close. That way he could go look at her grave anytime he wanted to.

When he reached home, he carried the two bags of groceries into the kitchen and set them on the table. "Maria," he called out. "Come put this stuff away."

He glanced into the living room. "Where the hell are those two?" he said out loud. "Maria. Jonathan," he yelled, this time louder.

He checked both bedrooms before he went outside. He walked toward the garage, still calling out their names.

"It's the boy," he mumbled. "I'll bet that goddamn Jonathan talked her into doing something stupid. Son of a bitch, I bet they ran away."

He inspected the privy and made a full circle around the house, checking inside two of the junked cars where he sometimes saw Maria sitting by herself. They were both empty. He went back inside and checked Maria's clothing hanging in his closet next to his own. A couple of pairs of pants she never wore and some blouses and T-shirts hung in their usual places. Everything seemed to be in order. Maybe they hadn't run away, but he'd still have to tan their hides for giving him a scare like that. They were probably in the woods, doing Lord knows what. Whatever, he sure didn't need trouble from them when he had all this digging to do. Goddamn kids, anyway.

The garage door was standing open. He was sure he had closed it. He reached for his shovel, which was right inside the door, but suddenly stopped, his hand still resting on the handle. Something didn't look right. Slowly, deliberately, he studied the interior of his workshop. His workbench was different; things had been moved around. And fan belts were scattered on the floor, and he knew they hadn't been there just the other day. Then he spotted his box of ammo, sitting wide open on the bench. His hand trembled as he checked the contents. The cartridges for his .38 were missing. He shot a glance at the gun rack, then ran closer to make certain. His revolver was gone, too. The kids had taken his gun.

Leon felt fire screaming through the veins in his temples. Suddenly he was having trouble making his eyes focus; he broke out in a sweat. Just like before, just like in 'Nam, he had been betrayed. This changed everything.

Chapter 19

It was late Thursday evening when Kira Thomasian sat at her desk rereading the psychological profile in front of her. She had won a major coup just in securing permission for the Behavioral Science Unit of the FBI to run the bureau's latest weapon in crime detection on such short notice. Her immediate supervisor had argued that the case was too new, she had been on it less than forty-eight hours, and the cases selected for profiling were almost always murders, multiple murders at that. So far there was no indication that Jonathan Grady had been harmed. Still, she had insisted, claiming that her gut reaction to this guy who would boldly take his kidnap victim to a motel meant there was a whole lot more to this case than met the eye. The bottom line was simply that she needed all the help she could get to zero in on Lee Kirby.

Unfortunately, the Behavioral Science Unit didn't have much more than statistics of previous crimes to go on when they fed the information available on the Jonathan Grady case into their computers. In order to compile a vague picture of the man they were seeking, they examined scores of cases involving child molestations, abductions, and murders, focusing on those with a bizarre psychological twist as well as so-called "motiveless" crimes.

The clerk from the motel had done a pretty good job of describing Lee Kirby physically: forty to forty-five, white male, a little over six feet, 200 to 240 pounds, stocky, bald. But Kira was especially intrigued by this psychological approach to catching criminals. The profile agreed Kirby would be a white male, but it also claimed Jonathan's abductor could be homosexual or bisexual. Kirby was most likely a high school dropout, single, living alone, and prone to fits of depression. Without a doubt he did not get along well with his parents, especially his mother, but the most disquieting prediction of all was that Kirby probably knew his victim or someone in the victim's family.

She had seen a similar prediction in her first involvement with a kidnapping. Actually, it hadn't been her case at all, but she had been allowed to tag along, mostly to help with the paperwork, as two veteran agents tracked down a particularly odious creep who snatched young boys from playgrounds and baseball diamonds, then dismembered their bodies in an effort to cover up the fact they had been sexually abused.

With uncanny accuracy the profile had identified the culprit's age, race, and similar information, but all indicators had also led the psychological team to believe the kidnapper knew his victims. It turned out he had been a part-time custodian at the elementary school four of his six victims had attended. Once he got the hang of it, he no longer stuck to the boys from the school but branched out to any little boy who was unlucky enough to cross his path when one of his "moods" struck.

Kira wondered if societies in the past had also bred this kind of sick bastard, or whether it was a phenomenon of modern times. Here she was, not three months after the capture of the Playground Stalker, as the press had named him, facing yet another disappearance in which the victim may have willingly been led away by a familiar face.

"You in some kind of trance?" a voice asked.

Kira looked up into the gaze of her supervisor, Paul Russell. "If a trance would help, I'd be in one," she said.

"What do you have?" he asked.

Kira shuffled through the mountain of paperwork in front of her before she met Paul's steely-blue eyes again. God, he was a hunk. What she wouldn't give for a chance to find out why his wife had dumped him after twelve years of marriage. Either Paul had some personality disorder which sure didn't come through in the office, or the woman was stupid. His smile alone, no matter how infrequently he gave one away, was enough to melt some unnamed part of her anatomy directly south of her solar plexus. Just looking at his clean-shaven face outlined by a full head of dark, wavy hair made it difficult for her to concentrate on the business at hand.

"Not much," she answered. "Kirby's only slip-up so far has been the postcard."

Paul sat down on the one empty corner of her desk, pushing a precariously arranged stack of paperwork off center. "You think maybe Kirby had the kid send the card on purpose, you know, just to torment the parents?" he asked.

"I don't think so. They found little fingerprints, possibly fresh, probably the boy's, on the Gideon Bible in a drawer. Since the motel ran out of their complimentary postcards six months ago, I figure the kid found the cards in the Bible, left there by a former guest."

Paul smiled. "Hey, that's good. I like your style. I

keep forgetting how competent you are for the new kid on the block. You don't need a partner on this one, even if I did have someone to spare."

"Thanks, I think." Kira thought she detected a twinkle in those distant blue eyes, and she suddenly felt that little spot in her gut go weak. Maybe she could get through to this guy if she ever felt like taking on a gargantuan task. Maybe someday when she had time.

"You have any news for me?" She indicated the envelope in his hand.

"Yeah, maybe we got lucky." He dumped the contents of a large manila envelope onto the desk in front of her. "One clear thumbprint on those registration cards proved not to belong to any of the motel employees."

Kira grabbed at the report. "You've got the list of possibles?"

"Not that fast. The computer is doing double-time. If the guy has a print on file anywhere, we have a chance to nail him, assuming this isn't a wild goose chase."

"What are you saying?"

"You've done the usual checks on the boy's parents, haven't you?"

Kira winced inwardly. What kind of world are we living in, she wondered, when the first thing on the procedural list in a kidnapping is to check out the kid's own parents? But too many times, sadly enough, a reported kidnapping was a cover for one or the other parent beating a kid to death.

"Sure, I did some of the usual inquiries," she said, "but we have a third party, remember? The parents didn't have anything to do with hauling the kid off to Virginia. By Friday evening they were fully involved with the Dunwoody police."

"That could be a setup if the parents are working with your third party."

"You honestly believe that?" she asked.

"You don't?"

"No, not at all. I met with the Gradys this morning, and they are really hurting, believe me."

"That's easy enough to fake. You know the stats. Of the thousands of missing children reported last year, only a relative few were snatched by a stranger. Besides the runaways, the rest were taken by a family member."

"C'mon, Paul. There are a lot of numbers out there and they're easy to juggle. Give me credit for knowing a little bit about human nature. The parents are clean. This is legit."

"Would it upset you terribly if we held off on sending out the composite and the kid's photo until tomorrow?"

"I already ordered them out," she said.

He avoided her eyes.

"Wait a minute," she said, "you stopped it, didn't you? Is that why everyone in this place is tiptoeing around me as if I'm the office joke? What do you have on this case that you haven't told me about?"

"Nothing, really," he said.

"Then why not give me a full team, or at least a partner, and let's get to work on finding this kid."

"Okay, I'll get you some help on this as soon as the prints come back from Ident. Maybe someone in my squad will be free by then; if not, I'll check with Stan or Greg to see if any of their people can be pulled over."

Kira suddenly thought she understood what was going on. It shouldn't have taken her this long to figure out why the Grady case was being treated as an untouchable. Along with three of the other supervisory agents in the Atlanta office, Paul was up for promotion to the position of assistant to the special agent in charge of the whole Atlanta operation, and promotions within the agency were usually a dogfight. Paul couldn't afford to pump this up into a full-blown Child Abduction Across State Lines just in case there was a glitch, like a friend or relative playing games with or without the parent's knowledge. If the kid showed up tomorrow with his Uncle Charlie, the agency and Paul would look pretty foolish. The FBI was supposed to be able to tell the real thing from all the child snatching that went on nowadays between rivaling family members.

Paul was playing it safe, letting her run profiles and computer searches to her heart's content, but he was going to be damn certain he had a case before they proceeded with their big guns by letting this go nationwide. The only problem with this thinking was, in the meantime, little Jonathan Grady could be lying dead somewhere in a totally nonpartisan ditch.

"Remember, we're dealing with a boy's life," she said calmly. "The sooner we get the word out, the better our chances of someone spotting Kirby with the kid. He may go underground, if he hasn't already."

Paul drew his eyebrows together into a pained expression, as if he had been slapped. "I know that."

"Then why not move on this?"

"Okay, let's compromise. You ordered the sheets out by nine P.M. Let's just give it until morning, to see if there're any new developments."

Kira let her breath escape through her teeth. Whoever invented the male ego ought to be shot. She said, "Nothing is going to change. We have a psycho, who may be into every perversion in the book." She looked him squarely in the eyes. "You could put my order back into action in two minutes, you know?"

"Wouldn't that make me look indecisive?"

She couldn't believe what she was hearing. Now he sounded almost playful. "Who's going to know outside these walls that you changed your mind?"

"Walls have ears. First thing they should have taught you at the academy."

"Right," she murmured.

"We'll rush the sheets out first thing in the morning, my word."

Her pulse thumped in her neck, but she could see she wasn't going to be able to take this any further. "Okay, nine A.M. Not a minute later."

"You got it. Look, Kira, would it help if I personally teamed with you on this and gave you a hand?"

She thought for a moment. Most of the supervisory agents in the office didn't do as much legwork as the street agents had to do—like she did—but Paul did have a reputation for pitching in whenever he was needed. And even if he was offering out of guilt, his offer was better than nothing.

"Sure," she answered, with an audible sigh, "any help you can give me might get this kid back to his parents in one piece."

Chapter 20

SIDE by side Jonathan and Maria tramped across a muddy field, stepping over the plowed furrows one at a time. The sky glistened with the brilliant blue that follows a heavy rain; the air was cool and bracing as Jonathan sucked in deep breaths through his mouth.

"Look at my jeans," Maria said, "mud clear up to my knees."

Jonathan had mud splattered on his pants, too, and his feet were cold and wet inside his tennis shoes. His inner soles squished with dampness with every step he took.

"I know, but it's safer in these fields, off the roads. Leon can't find us here," he said.

Beginning at the entrance to the school, they had traveled along the narrow country road for some time, but with the first approaching vehicle, Maria had clutched at Jonathan in fear, almost knocking him to the ground.

"Maybe now it would be safe to flag down a car," Jonathan had said. "We're pretty far from Leon's place."

"No," Maria said flatly. "No cars, no police. I don't want to talk to police."

Jonathan saw there were tears in her eyes and she was fighting hard not to cry.

161

"Now that we ran away, I don't ever want to go back there," Maria said. "Leon's got papers. I told you he's got me legally."

"What if it's all a lie?" Jonathan had persisted. He knew Leon was a bad person, but he also knew they had to find someone they could trust to help them in spite of any papers Leon might have.

Maybe Leon really did have papers for Maria; perhaps he even had papers for him, too. But Maria wouldn't give in, and her fear soon transferred to Jonathan. Maybe it wouldn't be as easy to get help as he had hoped. Finally he decided they would have to cut across the fields that stretched out in both directions if they were going to avoid detection. Leon could move quickly in the van, but he would have to stay on the roads. On the other hand, Jonathan and Maria could go almost anywhere on foot, even if it did take them longer.

After noon, Jonathan noticed the sun had begun to dip in the cloudless sky. He pointed. "That direction is west. Let's go that way."

Maria took a deep breath. "Why? I thought you said Georgia is south."

"It is, but if we keep heading west, sooner or later we'll come to a road, and that way we won't be walking in circles."

Maria eyed him skeptically. "Are you sure you know what you're doing?"

"Sure, I'm sure. We learned all about the direction of the sun in Cub Scouts. We just have to follow the sun and we'll be going in a straight line."

"What do we follow at night?" she asked.

"I don't know. I guess we'll have to sleep at night."

Maria shifted the bag of groceries from one hand to the other. "I'm hungry."

Jonathan looked around. "Let's stop and eat over there, by those trees."

They sat down on a large flat rock that was thankfully dry.

"We have a can of tuna fish," Maria said.

"We better save it until we're real hungry."

"I'm real hungry now."

"I mean like for dinner, this evening. What else do we have?"

"Crackers and jelly, two apples, a couple of cans of soup, a box of macaroni, a jar of peanut butter, and a can of baked beans."

"How are we going to cook the macaroni?" he asked.

"I don't know."

"Let's have the crackers and jelly."

Maria carefully spread the runny grape jelly over the little squares. Jonathan ate five, licking the sweet stickiness from his fingers when he finished.

"I wish we had some milk," Maria said.

Jonathan stood up. "We'll buy some later. Why don't we look for water? There're lots of streams and ponds around here," he said, but then he remembered. "We shouldn't drink from ponds; we need to find running water, that'll be safer."

"What's that over there?" Maria pointed.

They walked to the edge of the field, taking care not to trample any of the newly sprouted plants. A tiny stream, swollen with the recent rain, bubbled between two adjoining fields, following the direction of a low stone fence.

"This looks safe," Jonathan said with authority.

Maria fell to her knees and scooped the water to her lips with one hand. Jonathan took a long, slow drink from his cupped fingers and then refilled his hand several more times. The icy water tasted pure and good, soothing his parched throat and cooling his bruised lip.

They continued walking. Jonathan was proud of

the way he remembered what he had learned in Cub Scouts. They kept the sun in front of them as it slowly traveled across the afternoon sky. By now they had crossed over fields and pastures belonging to countless different farms. No one stopped them or even called to them. In fact, they saw no one except an occasional farm worker, and then only from a great distance. Wearily bent over some chore, the farmers paid no attention to two hikers traversing their land.

It seemed as if they had walked a million miles, but still they kept going. Jonathan lifted up his feet and set them down again without thinking, like a machine, as if he, too, were one of the tractors they sometimes saw plowing the horizon of a faraway field.

Then the farms grew smaller and seemed closer together. In the distance, above a clump of trees, Jonathan spotted a sign that looked familiar. He was sure it was a gas station. That meant a road, perhaps the road to Georgia.

When they finally reached the gas station, Maria's face lit up. "I'm going to use their bathroom. I'm tired of going in the woods."

"Be careful, act like you're with one of the customers, and don't talk to anyone. I'll wait here for you."

"Okay, I'll be careful. Don't worry," Maria said before she left the tattered grocery bag with him. "I'll be right back."

He waited in the far corner of the gas station parking lot until she returned, hoping no one would notice how dirty he looked.

"They have a Coke machine," Maria said. "Let's get one." She had washed her face and hands and might have looked almost like the other customers around the gas station if not for the mud smeared on her shoes and the cuffs of her jeans.

"I'll get us one Coke to share. We might need all our money for a bus ticket, remember?"

Maria's face drooped in disappointment, but she didn't argue. She sat down on the bumper of an old car parked next to a row of trees.

Jonathan hurried inside to use the men's room. He washed his face and hands and combed through his hair with his damp fingers. He used the paper towel to brush some of the caked mud off his clothes and tennis shoes, but it was no use. There was just too much dirt. He took a long drink of water from the faucet of the rest room sink.

On the way to the vending machine, he spotted a pay phone. His heart began to pound; this time he wouldn't forget the area code. One of the quarters he had found on Leon's dresser chimed to the inner depths of the phone, and he carefully pressed the three numbers of his grandmother's area code. Then he punched out the rest of her phone number and waited. He hoped he hadn't made any mistakes. His quarter dropped to the little receptacle at the bottom of the phone. He tried again. Nothing.

Jonathan ran over to a man who was pumping gas into a big black car. "Excuse me, mister, your phone's not working," he said politely.

The man tilted his head back to get a better look at Jonathan before he spoke. "It's busted."

"Don't you have another phone? It's real important, an emergency."

"Not for kids we don't. Kids busted the pay phone. They're always busting the pay phone."

"But I didn't do it. I'll be real careful with your phone," Jonathan promised. "You can watch me."

"Do I look like I have time to watch you make telephone calls? Now, get out of here before you catch my boot on the seat of your pants."

The man turned his back to Jonathan and gave

his full attention to the whirling dial on the gasoline pump. Perhaps, Jonathan thought, if he blurted out their story, told the man everything, maybe then the man would listen, but he knew better. This was one of those situations where a kid would be treated as if he were invisible simply because the adult didn't have time to be bothered.

Jonathan gave up and walked over to the Coca-Cola machine. He inserted three quarters and waited for the familiar red can to clunk into the compartment at the bottom. He joined Maria and handed her the Coke. "I guess we should go," he said. "The phone's not working."

She popped open the can and sipped the fizzy bubbles from the cold aluminum. "My dad used to buy us Cokes. We always had Coke when we went out for pizza."

"Yeah, me, too," Jonathan said. "Let's go, bring the can with you."

"The road doesn't go the way the sun is going," Maria observed.

She was right. The road sliced directly across their path, which followed the sun, meaning it was a north-south route. If they turned left, they would be heading south.

Jonathan smiled, feeling happy for the first time in days. They were now hiking in the right direction for Georgia. Traffic was a lot heavier on this road than it had been on any of the roads they had passed today. Perhaps they were getting closer to the interstate, where surely it would be safe to flag down a car. Leon couldn't possibly know all the people just passing through this part of the state. Maybe they would soon come to a city that had a bus station. He walked swiftly, encouraging Maria to hurry whenever she lagged behind. They finished the Coke and, even though Jonathan knew it was wrong to litter, tossed the can along the side of the road.

"It's going to be dark soon," Maria said. "Aren't you getting tired?"

"Let's keep going, just a little bit farther. Look for a good spot to camp for the night."

"What do I look for?"

"Didn't you ever go camping with your family?"

"No," Maria answered, "but once we stayed at a motel in San Diego when we went to Sea World, and we went to Disneyland four times."

"No kidding?" Jonathan said. "We were going to go to Disney World in Florida, and my dad was going to take me to see the Braves play the Pittsburgh Pirates, but now . . ."

"Maybe Leon didn't kill your parents," she said. "Maybe you'll still get to go."

"Yeah, maybe."

Maria tramped beside him in silence. The road grew wider and the cars whizzed by faster. There were no campgrounds as Jonathan had envisioned, only houses and small places of business. They passed several antique shops and real estate offices right in a row, but all of them were closed. Jonathan wondered if he should ask to use the phone at a private home, but somehow that idea seemed scary. They kept walking.

Good-smelling aromas drifted toward them from a big white house with all of its shades drawn tight to the windowsill, signaling strangers should go away. Jonathan realized how hungry he was. Maria must be hungry, too, he thought. He was also dead tired. His knees felt rubbery and his feet burned in his still-damp shoes. In the distance dark clouds were collecting like a thick black collar on the horizon. He hoped the clouds were not a forecast of more rain.

Then, up ahead, Jonathan noticed a giant ice

cream cone atop a small building. The sign said Dairy Queen, but a long red and white banner which read FOR LEASE was pasted over the front window.

Maria followed as Jonathan circled around the small structure. Set in the center of a parking lot, the whole building was probably smaller than his own old bedroom back home.

"I'm gonna try the door," Jonathan said. They rounded the corner and walked to the rear of the building.

A sagging screen door held remnants of dead moths embedded in the rusted mesh. The screen door groaned open easily, but the inner door was locked. Jonathan could see inside through a pane of glass in the center of the door.

"Find a rock or something so I can break the glass," he said.

"What if you set off a burglar alarm?"

"Then we'll run."

The window didn't shatter as easily as he thought it would, and then when it finally gave way, it merely splintered into a thousand weblike veins.

"Smash it harder," Maria said. "Let me try." She pounded with the rock until she created a rift big enough for Jonathan's hand to slip through.

As soon as Jonathan figured how to flip open the dead bolt, the door glided inward. "Leon will never think of looking in here. We can sleep there, by the wall." Jonathan pointed to the only corner that held no counters or rusted appliances.

Her tennis shoes quiet on the stained concrete floor, Maria stepped cautiously into the dust-choked room and then looked to Jonathan for reassurance. He smiled, to encourage her, in spite of what he saw.

Drifts of ancient dirt, thick with mold, covered

just about everything. Dead flies were entombed along the ledge of every window. The old, battered freezers loomed along one wall like sentries warning this was private property. Thou shall not trespass. But the dying sunlight straining through the filth-streaked windows flooded the little room with a stagnant sort of warmth. It would feel good to rest, even here.

"Here's some paper we can use," Jonathan said. A large piece of dusty but sturdy brown paper lay on the floor near a deep sink. Ceremoniously, he knelt, spreading the paper in a double layer on the floor. He tried to ignore the shadows rippling out of the darkness as he ironed out the wrinkles in the paper with his hands.

Maria came closer. "It sure doesn't look very comfortable."

Jonathan tried to smile, but the coldness of the concrete had already seeped upward, chilling his knees. He took off his backpack and Maria set down her bag.

"We should change into dry socks," Jonathan said. "In Scouts we always changed our socks after a hike."

"Okay," she answered, "but it's not going to make my feet any warmer. They're frozen stiff."

They settled close to each other on the hard concrete, and Jonathan carefully opened their only can of tuna fish.

Chapter 21

FRANTICALLY, Leon looked around the garage, trying to make sense of what he imagined must have happened. If the kids had run away *and* taken his revolver . . . what could they be up to? Jesus, he had to get busy on the grave, but first he had to find the kids. He had to find them before they started talking to people, especially before they got the idea of telling some crazy story to the cops.

Jonathan would lie, no doubt, and make up some wild tale about his parents' death. The cops might check it out and blame Leon for kidnapping when all he was trying to do was even the score with Grady. After all, he had a right. Just like he had the right to take Mendoza's kid away from him, he had a right to Grady's kid. Leon's throat tightened. If the cops got wind of this, they'd be all over him. What would that do to his plan? The score would not be settled until he had a chance to grab Cozelli's kid, too. Leon had to take one kid from each of them if he were ever going to get even. That much he had decided years ago when his three good buddies left him to molder in that stinking Viet Cong prison camp just so they could save their own necks. He hadn't forgotten. This was something he'd never forget.

His mind was swimming. He needed aspirin. He

reached up to the gun rack and grabbed his deer rifle. Perhaps they would come home peacefully, without giving him any trouble, but just in case, he put a handful of .30-caliber shells in his jacket pocket before he headed for the van.

Leon fumbled in the glove compartment for his bottle of aspirin and quickly popped four into his mouth. He swallowed them dry as he started the engine. His eyes weren't focusing clearly at first, so he drove slowly. First he would check the surrounding woods closest to his house, and then he would move gradually down the hill. If he did this systematically, he would find them in no time.

The countryside sparkled as it always did after a heavy rain, the air washed free of the impurities created by man. But Leon wasn't interested in the brilliance of the countryside. Right now he had to find Jonathan and Maria. The more he drove, the angrier he became. They were making an ass out of him, that's what. They were no better than their lousy fathers. When he found those two, he'd make them pay. Maybe he'd tie them up. No more Mr. Nice Guy, letting them run around the place, having fun like some spoiled little brats at a summer picnic. He'd teach them. He'd teach them real good.

Finally he had to stop for gas. This craziness was costing him money, too. And the headache was still pounding the shit out of his forehead. He needed more aspirin. He pulled into a gas station he normally didn't patronize on the far side of Reinholds.

"Howdy," the man said. "Fill her up?"

"Yeah," Leon answered, getting out of the van. "Did you see two kids go by here a little while ago? A girl about this tall." He held his hand against his chest. "And a boy just a bit smaller."

"Yours?" the man asked.

"Yeah, doggone them, they're skipping school. Teacher just called me."

"No, I ain't seen them."

Nosy bastard, Leon thought. If he ain't seen them, why'd he have to know if they were mine? People are too goddamn nosy for their own good. He paid the man and sped out of the gas station, his tires squealing against the street.

Now he was even madder, and his eyes still weren't focusing the way they should if he was going to spot those two little sneaks crawling off into some hiding place. He squinted. The sun was too brilliant; the colors of the fields and trees and sky were too bright. Everything hurt his eyes.

Driving much too fast, Leon pressed on. He covered the back road between his place and Reinholds once again. Criss-crossing the network of interconnecting roads he knew like the back of his hand, he went all the way to New Holland before he realized how far he had traveled. Doubling back the way he had come, he pounded his fist against the steering wheel. He had driven for hours, searching in vain, and he didn't know where to look next. They couldn't have gotten this far on foot, he reasoned. They had to be closer to home, probably in the woods hiding within a mile of his place. Maybe they had climbed a tree and laughed at him from some lofty perch as he had driven away to search for them.

Without consciously planning to return home, he soon found himself at the turnoff to his property. Maybe it was just as well. He was tired of driving, and he could look for the kids later. He mustn't forget he had work to do.

Leon found his shovel leaning against the garage and quickly paced into the woods behind the house. Once he passed the privy, he walked faster, searching for the perfect location. Up ahead he saw a small clearing encircled by pine and a couple of hickory trees. God, he thought, that must be the same spot where he had buried a dog once, a long time ago. Maybe it was time old Rover had a little company.

The ground was soft, almost soggy, from the recent rain, and his shovel slipped easily into the earth. He drew a rough outline with the edge of the shovel and began to dig within his marks. He heaped a big pile of dirt on his right, and when the mound became too high, he switched his position so he could stack the shovel loads of soil on the other side of the grave as well. The hole was now three feet deep, no, closer to four. The deeper the hole grew, the faster he dug.

As he burrowed machinelike into the soil, his mind tried to sort through the problems he had to deal with. He wiped the dirt and sweat from his forehead with the back of his wrist and then made a few more violent jabs with the shovel. It wasn't always easy for him to handle more than one problem at a time, and now he had several predicaments to face, none of them really his fault.

First Judy Mae had made him good and mad, poking her nose where it didn't belong. He had seen no choice but to stop her. After all, she was going to mail the letter the kid had written, and then, when she started all that hollering . . . But it was too late to change any of that. Judy Mae was dead, and there was nothing he could do about it except move her to a safer grave.

He dug faster, gouging his shovel into the bottom of the shadowy pit. Now, to make matters worse, he had to worry about where the kids were hiding and what they were doing with his .38. It would serve Jonathan right if he accidentally shot himself. That's the only way a kid like him would ever learn.

Thinking about the kids really made Leon mad. Jonathan was a sharp little kid, but he had brains, too. He knew this running away had to be the boy's idea, but it pissed him off to think Maria had followed Jonathan so easily. It had taken him months to get Maria to do all the things he wanted her to do, and now that she was really getting good at it, Jonathan had to spoil everything.

Dammit, he had been looking forward to grabbing Cozelli's kid soon, but now he wasn't sure what he should do. Perhaps, living with three kids at once might just turn out to be too difficult. They could gang up on him and cause trouble, especially with a little smart-ass genius like Jonathan as their ringleader. He hadn't realized how lucky he had been to have three years with Maria's warm little body in his bed until Jonathan came along. Maria never gave him any trouble because she was scared to death of him, but now all that might be ruined. Damn.

His other option, of course, would be to grab Cozelli's kid and kill the three of them. Perhaps that would be the best solution. Their fathers wouldn't have any trouble making the connection if he left the bodies of the three kids to rot somewhere in a swamp cage. He certainly would make his point that way, but dammit, he would miss Maria, especially now that he didn't even have Judy Mae.

The sweat poured off Leon's head and neck; his shirt was soaked. He pulled it over his head, flung it up out of the grave, then resumed digging. The grave had to be at least five feet deep by now, but little cave-ins along the side walls kept spilling more dirt back into the hole. He was afraid he wouldn't be able to go much deeper.

"She's deep enough," Leon said out loud. He used the shovel to make a few toeholds, then tossed it out over the top of one of the heaps of dirt. Leon slowly struggled to the surface, knocking a considerable amount of soil back into the hole in the process.

He stood back to admire his work. Not bad. Once he filled it in and tamped it down, he would scatter pine needles and leaves over the spot. No one would ever think of digging that deep to find old Judy Mae. She'd be in there forever, that was for sure.

His shirt was covered with dirt, but then so was the rest of him, especially his arms. Tossing the filthy shirt over one shoulder, he planted the shovel into the loose dirt. He had started the trek back toward the house before he even realized how late it had become.

He listened to the house. Everything was dark and quiet. The kids had not returned on their own. When their bellies are empty, he thought, they'll wish they hadn't pulled this little trick.

Leon washed off from the waist up at the outside faucet. The cold water felt good, but he figured he'd better go inside and take a bath anyway, just in case the kids came home. Who was he trying to fool? He was going to have to go searching again. Well, they could just freeze their butts outside in the woods for tonight. He'd look for them again in the morning. Besides, he didn't especially want them spying out the window later on when he unloaded Judy Mae from the van. They were nosy, too, especially Jonathan.

Leon took a hot bath and dressed in clean clothes. He would get all dirty again, but shoveling the dirt back into the hole wouldn't be as bad as digging it out. Maria would just have to wash his dirty stuff tomorrow, as soon as he finished tanning her hide.

He found a can of clam chowder under the sink, then looked in the drawer for the can opener. "Where in the hell does that girl put things? How could she lose the can opener?"

He slammed the drawer shut and used his pocketknife to rip open the can. He heated the soup and ate it right out of the saucepan. He hadn't realized how hungry he was.

Soon it was dark, but he decided to wait a bit longer. No sense asking for trouble. He waited.

By nine-fifteen his eyes were getting heavy. He'd better get to it. Then he remembered he would need the shovel to dig her up. Taking the flashlight from its hook by the door, he headed back into the woods.

The moon glowed from behind ragged blue-black clouds. Shit, he hoped it wasn't going to rain again, at least not until he was finished with Judy Mae. He threw the shovel into the back of the van, tossed the flashlight onto the seat next to him, and headed for the cornfield on the edge of Adamstown.

By the time he rounded the last bend before the cornfield, his weariness from all his digging had faded and he felt wide-awake. He was kind of looking forward to seeing Judy Mae again, and was secretly glad he could look at her one more time without having to hear her talk. Judy Mae always managed to ruin things with her incessant talk.

He was almost there, but something didn't look quite right. Along the road up ahead he saw lights flashing in the darkness. He slowed down. Three cars with pulsating beacons on the roof had encircled the very spot where he had buried Judy Mae. He took his foot off the accelerator. Police cars. He recognized two cars as state police, and the other one must be the local sheriff, parked there, right where he had been parked two nights before. As he drew closer he saw a van with big letters painted on the side, *WGAL*, and at least a dozen men were milling about. One man carried a TV camera on his shoulder, aimed at another man who was talking to one of the cops. Leon hit the brakes.

"Move along," a uniformed state trooper called to him.

"Huh?" Leon said, at first not realizing whom he meant. "What happened?"

The state trooper waved one hand, his index finger pointing to the road ahead. "Just keep moving, sir."

"Can I turn around? I don't think I want to go into Adamstown after all."

The officer glanced over his shoulder. "Back up this way if you want to turn." He pointed to a grassy area along the road.

Leon backed slowly, as if he had suddenly forgotten how to drive. Shifting gears had become an exercise foreign to him. He felt the blood draining from his head; his vision was blurred, but his muscles functioned where his mind failed. He pointed the van back the way he had come and drove very slowly, jerking the accelerator with irregular bursts of gas.

Someone had found Judy Mae! Now what? He had to go home and think. If he could only get rid of his goddamn headache, perhaps he'd be able to figure out what to do next.

Chapter 22

Early Friday morning Kira stood in the shower, the hot water drumming hard upon the top of her head. Quickly she worked shampoo through her dark hair, scratching into her scalp with her fingernails. As soon as the lather built to a creamy white foam, she stepped back into the hot, pulsating jet. She hadn't slept well and was feeling it. Her back was stiff; her feet dragged as if she were pulling leg irons. The shower helped, but not enough.

She stood in front of the mirror blow-drying her hair, but she wasn't seeing her own face reflected back at her. She envisioned the weary, drawn features of Susan and Ed Grady in her mind's eye, as if she, too, were being haunted by the terror they were going through. She felt a chill when she clicked off the warm air from the hair dryer.

Maybe she wasn't cut out for this type of work after all. Perhaps she should consider requesting assignment on something less emotional, like the interstate transfer of stolen vehicles, some boring kind of crime that would not entail terrified parents or little boys who had been kidnapped just a few blocks from home. At first she had been hell-bent on making this into a big production worthy of the tabloids, but now, after yesterday's painful meeting with the Gradys, she was determined to be the one to find their son and return him safely to the warm and comfortable home they had made for him. Even the family dog, a lovable Labrador with big, watery eyes, had appeared devastated when she looked up at Kira from the oval rug centered in front of the fireplace.

With only a cup of black coffee and a piece of dry toast for breakfast, she got an early start for the office. She wanted to be there when the meager data on the Grady case was transmitted to law enforcement officers all over the country. Why, she wasn't sure. She guessed she simply wanted her first real effort at getting some action on this case to run smoothly. With the task completed, she waited, somewhat impatiently, in Paul Russell's office until he showed up for work.

Not much bigger than her own, Paul's office was tucked away in a corner on the second floor. It was sparsely efficient, free of anything that could be called decorative, with not so much as a picture on the wall. Did he choose the look of an army barracks because he was all business, or was he having difficulty relating to things of a feminine nature? She shrugged off that silly notion. A tidy, uncluttered office was certainly no indication Paul had difficulty relating to women. Maybe he needed a woman's eye to advise him in such matters? Either way, how could it possibly be any of her business?

When Paul finally walked in, he looked as if he had a lot on his mind, but then to Kira, Paul always seemed worried or preoccupied. Unfortunately, breaking through other people's shells was not her specialty. She kept reminding herself that Paul had assigned himself to work with her on this case, to help her sort through the mountain of paper shuffling and red tape that was part of the job before an agent ever left the office. He hadn't volunteered to do anything at all about the weird sensations stirring inside her. The task of finding Jonathan Grady was all there was between them, a relationship that couldn't be more businesslike.

"You spend the night here?" Paul asked. He took off his coat and hung it over the back of his chair.

"No, but maybe I should have. I didn't get very much sleep."

"Is that your way of asking for more help?" He sounded gruff, irritated, the way one speaks to an especially tiresome child.

Kira resented his unwavering stare. She just didn't know how to read him, and her physical attraction to the man who was giving her such a hard time on this case was fast becoming an annoyance. She said, "No, I simply couldn't clear my mind. I tossed and turned for most of the night. I know there's some angle to this case we're overlooking."

"There's always an angle we overlook. We can only work with the facts at hand, and on this case, my dear, you've got diddly."

"Sure, I know all that, but I've got a feeling there's something big here I'm not seeing."

Paul fanned through a stack of papers on his desk. He spoke without looking up. "Like what?"

"Like the psychological profile. It figures Kirby would be an acquaintance of the family or someone who at least knew the boy somehow. Just like the Playground Stalker knew most of the boys he grabbed."

"Don't put all your eggs in a psychological profile," he answered.

"That's a mixed metaphor, isn't it?"

"Probably. I'm the last one who would know. I just know it's going to take some hard fact, like Ident coming through on the print, and you might as well stop worrying until you hear from them."

"How would Kirby know the route the boy took every day on his way home from school unless he stalked him and knew his habits? He couldn't have asked for a quieter block. No witnesses we can count on. It's as if Kirby knew the street better than the people who live there."

"Maybe he just got lucky?"

"Maybe, but I don't think so. It's driving me nuts." Kira crossed her long legs and tugged at the hem of her skirt to cover her knees.

"You'll have to learn not to take so much baggage home with you. Too much of this stuff will weigh you down so heavy you might never get up again. You know what I mean?"

"Yeah," Kira answered, "I know, but it's easier said than done. You haven't seen the faces of this kid's parents. It was as if they were aging right before my eyes. I really want this Kirby."

Paul loosened his tie a little. "Your sheets went nationwide this morning?"

"It's all taken care of," she said, hoping the delay hadn't in any way jeopardized the boy.

Just then the fax machine in Paul's office began to hum with the promise of a reproduction.

"This might be what you're looking for." He glanced at the output and handed it over to Kira.

"Thanks." She looked at the first page as the second rolled off the machine.

"What default did you request on this?" he asked.

She looked up from the enlarged photograph of a single left thumbprint with a detailed description of the triangulation patterns the computer had scanned on the whorls, arches, and ridges of the print.

"Ten," she answered, pulling the second sheet

from the fax machine. "Here they are, the ten most likely candidates. No Lee Kirby, however."

"Naturally," he said, smiling as if she should know better. "You got someone at Headquarters lined up to work with us, I presume?"

Now she smiled. "Naturally."

Kira hurried back to her own desk and put a call through to Latent Prints at FBI Headquarters in Washington, D.C. She used to think, before she entered the bureau, that the technology involved with computers scanning hundreds of millions of fingerprints stored in a data bank was foolproof. It was an advanced science, all right, but after the computer did its job, the procedure reverted to some very careful screening by the human eyes of the fingerprint experts in D.C. Thousands of people will have roughly the same classification of loops and ridges in their fingerprints, and by running the patterns through, over and over, the computer will eventually narrow the field to a list of candidates, ranked in order of probability. They didn't dare allow the computer to zero in on simply one person and produce his name in flashing lights. She had in her hand the names of the ten men, out of millions, who were the most likely owners of the print they were trying to trace.

As soon as she reached the print expert who was working on Jonathan's case back at Headquarters, her heart began to race. The thrill of the hunt was in her veins, and she was anxious for a lead, something she could get to work on.

"What do you have on this Rodney James Blackstone?" she asked. Blackstone was number one on her list.

"He's doing time in Leavenworth."

"Any idea if he could've been released recently?"

"No, not yet. We'll try to check that out today."

Kira held back a sigh. Red tape was also a problem in keeping the data bank of fingerprints current. Thousands of deceased were always mixed in with the living because some underpaid clerk just couldn't keep up with the overwhelming volume of corrections and changes that had to be fed into the computer each day.

"How about number two, Leon Hoffman?" she asked.

"He's clean as far as we know. His print came from the military bank."

"Wait a minute. Hoffman?" she cried into the phone.

"Yeah," the voice at the other end said. "No arrests, he's clean."

"Listen, could you do me a great favor?"

She heard what may have been a chuckle. "That's what I'm here for."

"Go back into the military bank and check if this Hoffman guy was in 'Nam. Make sure he wasn't killed in action and get back to me ASAP."

"Will do," he said, "no problem."

"Thanks."

Kira hung up the phone and pulled out her notes from yesterday's conversation with Edward Grady. The name Bull Hoffman, Grady's sergeant, stared at her from the page as she recalled the story of Grady's capture by the Viet Cong. Could there possibly be a connection? One thing was certain: Jonathan Grady hadn't been snatched by a dead man.

Chapter 23

THE jungle is hot, still steamy, even though it is now dark. The three other men huddle together in the bunker, off to his right. He orders them to make a dash for the road, knowing they have a chance to get out of this mess if they stay calm and don't make a sound. One by one they carefully step across the bodies of two of their own men who got it in the ambush, but this time one of the dead is not that stupid hillbilly from Tennessee. Plain as if it were high noon, he sees Judy Mae's smiling face, surrounded by clumps of springy curls, on the body of the dead soldier.

They continue to creep, each step placed cautiously and ever so quietly. They go a hundred yards through inky pools of darkness formed by the overhanging tropical vegetation. The goddamn mosquitoes are eating him alive, but he doesn't slap at them. He inches along, five or six yards behind his men, covering their behinds. Then, out of nowhere, the gooks plummet down from the trees.

Mendoza, Grady, and Cozelli turn and point to their sarge, who is still concealed by the black shadows. "Take him," they say in a chorus of hollow echoes. "We're nothing but grunt; he's got the stripes." The three of them go off arm in arm with the gooks.

Judy Mae stands there in her white uniform, smiling as his hands are tied behind his back and the blindfold, crusted with an ungodly filth, is lashed around his head. He hears Judy Mae talking, chattering away about how she's going to be a good mama to those kids. "We have a responsibility to society to send the kids to school," she says.

Leon bolted upright to a sitting position. He was drenched with sweat. "Holy shit," he said out loud. "Judy Mae got into the dream. She was there!"

He swung his legs over the edge of the bed and sat there, holding his head so it wouldn't explode. He had suffered through the dream so often he knew it by heart, and it was always pretty much the same. They would sneak out of the bunker with the steam rising from the jungle floor like it was some kind of fucking steam bath in a gym. They would go along quietly for quite a ways until those lousy gooks just dropped out of the trees, like it was raining gooks. The ending sometimes varied. Sometimes it would be Mendoza who turned him over to the V.C., sometimes it would be Grady, but mostly the three of them sang out the words together like a goddamn boys' choir.

The dream was always bad enough, reminding him how his men had pointed out that he was behind them, hiding from the ambushers. Those bastards fingered him to save their own necks. His guard in that stinking cesspool of a prison, the one who spoke a little English, told him over and over about his men going home like heroes while he remained imprisoned in the swamp, slowly dissolving into rat meat.

Then, when he was finally rescued, the army lied about what had happened. Said his men had been captured, too, but they had been taken to different prisons. Leon had caught them in that lie. He had asked where they were, said he wanted to see his men, but no, they had already been sent home. Christ, he had been stuck in that hideous cage, rotting for fourteen months, while his good buddies were back in the States, probably going to church suppers, their chests plastered with fucking Medals of Honor.

Leon shivered. Any recollection of his endless term in that prison still gnawed at his gut, and the dream always riled him, but now Judy Mae was part of it, too. How had she gotten into his dream? She didn't even know the whole story of his capture and imprisonment. She didn't belong there. His head pounded. His head always pounded after the dream, but today it was worse, like a vise grip squeezing across his forehead until the pain roared through him.

Closing his eyes to keep out the light, he pulled on his pants. Then he remembered the kids had run away. He had been so absorbed in this new addition to his dream, he had forgotten he had to look for them again this morning. They could do him harm if they shot off their mouths to the wrong person; especially Jonathan. The kid was no different from his old man, and old Grady didn't have any trouble fingering him when he wanted to save his own skin, that was for sure.

Leon put on a shirt and his shoes and socks and grabbed his aspirin bottle. It was empty. He opened the new bottle he had bought at the general store and gobbled six of the yellow pills. Leon liked the way they went down easier because of the smooth coating on the outside. He'd try to remember what the label looked like so he could buy another bottle of these.

He fumbled with the burner on the kerosene stove, thinking that Maria had served a purpose.

She wasn't such a bad little girl; it had to be Jonathan's idea for them to run away. Maria had seemed happy enough before Jonathan arrived, even if she hadn't talked a whole lot. Now everything had changed. He was almost sorry he was going to have to get rid of both of them as soon as he found them.

At first he had thought he could whip them and tie them up, but now he was certain that wouldn't work. Jonathan was too rambunctious, too smart for his own good. He would have to silence Jonathan once and for all, and now because of Jonathan, he would also have to quiet his little Maria.

He thought of the dozens of enemy soldiers he had managed to snuff during the war. Lousy gooks had it coming, all of them. He remembered one he bashed to death with the butt of his rifle. That son of a bitch tried to slice him even as his head was being pounded into meat. Seeing the brains of a gook splatter into quivering slime had given him a great deal of pleasure at the time. Killing Jonathan would also give him a certain sense of real satisfaction.

One good thing, Leon chuckled to himself, getting rid of Jonathan and Maria wouldn't pose any extra work for him. Why, he had the perfect setup; he could use the grave he had dug for Judy Mae. It was plenty big enough to hold two kids.

Finally Leon got the coffee perking. It smelled good. Maybe he'd scramble up a few eggs; he looked inside the refrigerator, but then suddenly slammed the door shut. He heard a car coming up the road.

The first thing he spotted was the outline of the driver's hat. One of those Smokey the Bear hats the Pennsylvania State Troopers wore. A chill prickled the back of his neck, then outrage fired through him. What were the state police doing here? He bet they had found Jonathan and Maria wandering around, crying like babies because they had spent the night in the woods. Well, he hadn't told them to run away; it wasn't his fault if they were cold and hungry.

But no, Leon thought, what if it wasn't because of the kids? What if that goddamn Jake had spilled his guts? What if Jake had told the cops how Judy Mae had bragged about getting married and how much in love she and he had been? Jake had no right, not after he had explained so carefully that the two of them had broken up for good. Judy Mae was seeing another guy, wasn't she? He had to get the cops busy looking for him. Leon could almost visualize what a sweet-talking smoothie like the one he had made up for Judy Mae would look like. Tall, good-looking, and blond. No, dark would be better. Dark and slick with those extra little lifts on his shoes because he wasn't real tall, that's what he would tell them. But maybe he shouldn't know too much about the guy who had stolen his girlfriend away from him. He didn't want to appear too concerned about losing Judy Mae, or they'd just say he had been a jealous lover. He had to think carefully before he said anything.

Leon wiped the palms of his hands down the front of his pants. Maybe he should pretend he wasn't home, but by now they had probably seen the kitchen light. Maybe they could even smell the coffee. He hadn't done anything to warrant a visit from the law, and they had no business driving up his private road like they owned the place. His mind jumped. He had to get control of himself. He had to stay calm.

Leon squinted through the window. The state police emblem on the side of the car swung toward him as the cop on the passenger's side threw open his door. When they had both gotten out of the car, they just stood there for a moment taking in the scene.

Leon noticed the one who had been driving un-snapped the little belt that crossed over the grip of his service revolver and lightly rested his hand upon the gun as they approached the door.

The cop who had been the passenger, a tall, fair-skinned pretty boy, knocked on the screen door and waited.

Leon swabbed his hand across his lips, turned off the coffee and walked to the door. He opened the inner door and talked through the screen.

"Yeah?"

"Good morning," the cop said. "Are you Leon Hoff-man?"

"Yeah, why? Did I forget to register the van again?"

The cop smiled. "No sir. May we come in?"

Reluctantly, Leon stepped aside, but he did not make any move to open the screen door. The one cop held the screen door for the other as they stomped their heavy boots into the room. The cops were both big men, and now with the three of them standing in the tiny kitchen, the room seemed filled beyond capacity, far too crowded for Leon to inhale a simple breath of air.

Leon cleared his throat. "How about some coffee? It's fresh."

"No, thanks." Pretty Boy did all the talking while the other one strutted like a goddamn G-man over to the doorway leading to the living room and looked around. He didn't even ask, just decided to stick his nose where it didn't belong, all the while resting his hand on the butt of his gun.

"We've been called in to assist the local sheriff with a homicide," the cop said. "We've been told you knew the deceased, Judy Mae Detweiler."

Leon knew what they'd be looking for. He had to be cool, act surprised. He had seen enough shows on TV to know how to act, and besides, they didn't have a thing on him. "Judy Mae deceased? You mean she's—"

"Dead," the cop finished for him.

"My God, what happened?"

"Like I said, it was a homicide. She was strangled."

Leon reached for one of the kitchen chairs and sat down. "I don't believe it," he said. "Why, she was over here, visiting, in this very room, about a week ago."

"What was the date?"

"Oh, I don't know. Last Saturday, I believe. That was the last time I saw her."

"Saturday the eighth was the last time you saw her?"

Leon lowered his head. He could feel the eyes of Pretty Boy and the other cop singeing into his flesh, but he didn't let them know they were getting to him. He stared at the floor when he said, "Yeah, we haven't been seeing too much of each other ever since she started going out with that other guy."

"What was his name?"

Leon looked up. "Oh, that I don't know. She said she met a guy at a dance, at the fire hall."

The other state cop stepped closer to the kitchen table, almost elbow to elbow with Pretty Boy. The two of them exchanged knowing glances. "How long had you been going with the decedent?" Pretty Boy asked.

His mind fastened on the word, decedent. God, he wished the cop wouldn't call her that. Leon cleared his throat again. "We weren't exactly going together. We've been friends for a year or so. I met her at the diner where she works."

"And there was no talk of marriage between you?"

Leon could feel a growing wetness in his armpits.

He knew his face was covered with sweat, too. "You know women. She talked about marriage; I listened. I'm not the marrying kind myself. I just wanted to be friends, you know, have a beer and a few laughs every now and then."

"How'd you feel about her dating this other man?"

"I was kind of glad, even if he was a dago. Got Judy Mae off my back a little bit. She was the clingy type, if you know what I mean."

"You said he was a dago. You met the man? You knew him to be an Italian?"

"No," Leon answered quickly. "I never laid eyes on him. That's what she told me. That's all I know."

"Where were you Tuesday, the eleventh?"

"Let's see." Leon pretended he was thinking. Then he noticed the box of cereal on the table right where Maria had left it yesterday. Would the cops figure out it was the kind of cereal kids usually eat? He had to be ready if they asked questions about the kids. A bead of sweat rolled into his eye.

"Tuesday, the eleventh," Pretty Boy repeated.

"Oh, yeah, Tuesday I worked the whole day on Chuck Weaver's Pontiac. Didn't finish until late, so I was really beat. What a job that was."

The cop was writing away in a notebook. "This Weaver live around here?"

"Sure, just outside of Reamstown, he'll tell you." Leon felt his gut sinking deeper and deeper into the pit of his bowels. This guy asked his questions too fast, one right after the other. How was anybody supposed to think that fast?

"What about Tuesday night?"

The light in the kitchen was suddenly too bright. Leon felt the hot yellow glare searing into his eyes. "That was the night it was raining, wasn't it?" he asked.

"The storm began Tuesday evening."

"That's right, I was home all night, right here, trying to fix my TV. Damn thing's on the fritz again."

Pretty Boy took a step closer to Leon. "You didn't see Ms. Detweiler on Tuesday?"

"Nah, I ain't seen her since Saturday."

"What about Wednesday? Did you see her Wednesday?"

This sonofabitch didn't give up easily, Leon thought. His shirt was sticking to his back, and his head was pounding like a goddamn jackhammer, but he was doing all right. They didn't have a thing on him.

"I didn't see anybody on Wednesday. It rained too hard to go anywhere."

"And nobody came to see you?"

"No, nobody."

"Mr. Hoffman, do you live here alone?"

Leon wiped his sleeve over his forehead. "Yeah, why?"

"You don't have a daughter, or a young girl who lives here with you?"

"Oh, I used to have a girl I took care of for a friend. She went to live with her aunt."

The cop closed his notebook. "I see."

Leon picked up on the tone of the cop's voice. He didn't believe his story. Leon was sure of it.

"Well, thank you for your cooperation," Pretty Boy said. "We may return with more questions as soon as we learn more about the decedent's activities over the last few days. You have a phone here?"

"No, no phone."

"Okay, thank you."

Leon felt his face fill with hot color as the cops pushed open the screen door and walked outside. He watched through the window as Pretty Boy opened up his little notebook again and copied the license number from the van. He had no right to do that, Leon thought, fuming at the nerve of these guys. Cops were all unreasonable bastards. Before he got into the patrol car, Pretty Boy looked back toward the house, his eyes narrow slits, probing as if he could see right through the walls. Pretty Boy slipped on his sunglasses, then got into the car. The other cop started up the engine and drove away.

Leon had to get the hell out of Pennsylvania, and he had to do it fast. Maybe he should go all the way and head for the border? If he pushed real hard, he could make it to Canada before dark. His mind was swimming again. There were so many details he had to figure into his plans, and he didn't like feeling so confused.

He rushed into the bedroom and grabbed a couple of shirts, underwear, his other pants, and some odds and ends from the top of his dresser. Stuffing everything into an old duffel bag, he remembered extra socks. His money. He kept all the money he had in a shoe box on the top shelf in his closet. Always seemed safer than a bank. It wasn't very much, but he'd find work somewhere. Tools, he'd need tools if he was going to work in Canada.

He tossed his bag of clothing into the van, then backed the van right up to the garage door. The rear of the van open, he began to throw in his best tools. Don't want to load her down with too much junk, he thought.

Finally he took the box containing the rest of the .30-caliber shells for his deer rifle. The rifle was already on the floor in the back of the van. Staring at the confused mess of tools and junk, he finally remembered one more thing. He went back into the house and pulled the two blankets from his bed. He might need these to wrap up the bodies of the two children he was hoping to find before he headed for the border. He wanted to be neat about the whole thing, just the way he had been neat with Judy Mae.

Chapter 24

Kira reread the report from latent prints that had just cranked through the machine. Rodney James Blackstone was doing hard time, ten to twenty, and there was no possibility of parole for a long, long time. Scratch candidate number one.

The name Leon Hoffman stared at her from the page. Early that morning she had started the wheels in motion to get the military records she wanted. Little by little, information had begun to trickle in. No report of his death anywhere in the military data bank made her wonder why Ed Grady was so certain his sergeant never came home. She was planning another run out to Dunwoody to see the Gradys later today. She made a note to ask him about that.

Suddenly, like a distant recollection, her senses detected the aroma of Old Spice after-shave lotion in the room. What a great scent, one she remembered fondly from her very first date. Back when she was still in junior high school, she had gone to a movie with a tall, long-haired boy who used to sit behind her in history class. She soon found out she had very little in common with this particular young man, but she had maintained a soft spot in her memory for the clean, straightforward male scent that had intoxicated her on her first one-to-one date with a boy. She still believed no leather or musk or wild animal scents were needed by men who were honest with women. It was pretty ridiculous, but the sentiment persisted in her mind. She looked up to see Paul Russell standing in the doorway.

"I can almost hear the gears spinning in your head," he said.

"It's this Hoffman thing. He's got to be our man."

Paul sat down. "I just got a call from somebody in General Sanford's office with the information about Mr. Grady's capture in 'Nam."

Kira slapped her hand against the desk. "Dammit, I put that call in. Why didn't they contact me directly?"

"I'm your supervisor, remember?" Paul said gently. "And we are partners on this case, aren't we?"

"That has nothing to do with it, and you know it. Doesn't anybody in the Pentagon believe a female agent can handle an investigation? What are they afraid of, that I might mess up my manicure?"

Paul chuckled, but not unkindly.

Kira went on. "Does every woman in the agency have to go through this crap if she needs information from the military, or is it just because I'm new?"

"I think if they got a call from a new agent who was a male, Sanford would channel it through me also. He doesn't trust anybody new; he probably doesn't even trust me."

Kira felt her face redden. "You think I'm overreacting, don't you?"

"I think you are the most dedicated new agent to hit the Atlanta office in the last ten years."

"And who preceded me ten years ago?" she asked.

"Me."

She studied the fine lines radiating from the corners of his eyes. Finally she said, "You love your work, don't you?"

"I love it so much, my wife dumped me for another man who wasn't so wrapped up in his job. Now, that's the sort of dedication J. Edgar would have been proud of."

"I'm sorry. I didn't mean it that way."

Paul nodded. "I know. But then, you understand, because you feel the same way about your work as I do, or at least I think you do."

Kira felt her face flush, the heat traveling all the way up to her scalp. Was she so weak she could fall in love with a man she hardly knew? Just because he had finally moved in to give her a hand on this case didn't exactly make him a knight in shining armor. After all, only an hour or two ago he had been growling at her. His confession about the collapse of his marriage meant nothing, although it was nice to have him confide in her like that. Any kind of dialogue that sounded like two people trying to get to know each other was better than the usual screaming and yelling that passed as conversation between agents who were trying to work together. Dammit, that solar plexus thing was happening again.

Kira smiled at him. "Thanks for being patient with me. I guess I expect too much too soon from the big shots."

"Always remember the big shots aren't real people. Don't let them bother you," Paul said. "Now about the phone call."

Kira pulled her legal pad closer and picked up a pencil. "I'm all ears."

Paul opened his mouth as if to contradict that comment, but apparently thought better of it. He said, "Grady was ambushed just like he said. There were eight of them, four got hit. The other four who were later captured by the V.C. were separated. They took Grady and Cozelli to a little swamp hole that the Marines liberated about four months later, although they had no contact with each other while they were in there."

"Part of the demoralization?" Kira asked.

"Probably. Hoffman and Mendoza went to a worse place up the river. Somehow Mendoza and another guy from a different outfit escaped after, I think, six months. Hoffman did the most time, fourteen months of pure hell, from what the army hospital reported."

"Was he injured, physically, I mean?"

"When they finally found him, he had a broken collarbone, broken fingers, infections everywhere, stuff like that, but they said he had the crazies really bad."

"No wonder," Kira answered. "After fourteen months of torture."

"Anyway, he was eventually brought home and admitted to Wadsworth Veteran's Hospital in Los Angeles."

"So he didn't die in Vietnam?"

"Nope, and he didn't die in the hospital either."

Kira stopped writing and looked up. "When was he released?"

"He wasn't. One day he just walked out the door. He never returned to any V.A. hospital for further treatment, as far as they know."

"But wouldn't he have that post-traumatic stress disorder? And if he just walked away—"

"The hospital records are on their way, as soon as somebody at Wadsworth has time to dig up the files for us, but yes, it seems he would have suffered all

198

kinds of psychological distress, to put it mildly. The guy at the Pentagon said if he's still alive, and has not had intensive therapy, he must be a walking time bomb."

"Or a kidnapper?" Kira asked.

Paul nodded grimly. "I made a few other checks for you."

"What do you mean?"

"Since I got tied up in that staff meeting this morning, I started feeling guilty about you practically winging it on your first big case."

"If you had known it was a 'big' case, would I have it at all?"

"No, but now that you do, don't you want to know what I've got?"

"Go ahead." Kira looked at the light fixture hanging from the ceiling, wondering how long it would take until she was considered a "real" agent who didn't have to be treated as if she were going to trip over her own feet.

"This is going to cost you."

"How much?" she asked.

"Dinner."

Kira raised one eyebrow. "Your place or mine?" Now Paul flushed. Good, she thought. It serves him right.

"Yours," he said through a smile. "Now, are you ready for this?"

"What do you have?"

"I ran a check on Anthony Cozelli. Married, one kid, lives in Harrisburg, Pennsylvania."

"That's it?" she asked.

"Vincent Mendoza, the other guy, also married, lives in Los Angeles. Two kids."

"So?"

"His older girl was kidnapped almost three years ago when she was ten years old."

Kira stiffened, her eyes wide. "Same age as Jonathan. Did they find her?"

Paul shook his head. "No. It was like she dropped off the face of the earth. Not a trace."

"If Hoffman has some axe to grind with his former soldiers, he might be grabbing their children in some kind of weird revenge plot."

"That's the way it reads to me, too."

"Okay, Mr. Supervisor, I owe you dinner, but now I need your permission to put out an APB on Hoffman."

"Permission granted."

"And if this is a serial kidnapper, I think we're going to need more help. Get somebody to dig up the files in Los Angeles on the Mendoza girl."

"You got it."

Kira paused for a moment, then said, "Paul, one other thing."

"What?"

"From your experience, what are the Mendoza girl's chances? There's never been a ransom note or any contact?"

"No contacts, and since she's been missing three years now, she's probably long dead."

"Hoffman may still have her. It's been done before."

Paul shook his head. "You're thinking of that case in California, years ago. Steven something."

"Right. That creep kept the boy for seven years, pretended he was his son, then he grabbed another boy."

"At random, remember? If Hoffman has some sort of vendetta, he isn't playing house with the kids."

Kira cleared her throat over a lump that had suddenly appeared. "But the Mendoza girl might still be alive. There's a chance, a slim chance."

"Sorry," Paul said, "but I don't believe there's any chance she's still alive. And, now that Hoffman has had the Grady boy a week, I'd say he's probably dead by now, too."

Chapter 25

ED Grady absently raked his fingers through his hair with one hand; the other hand rested on the top of the refrigerator door. He stared into the almost empty refrigerator. He hadn't expected Susan to do any grocery shopping under the circumstances, but he also wished he could find something sweet and gooey. He searched, hoping for a surprise, a piece of streusel coffee cake like Susan always used to bake, or even a can of beer to deaden his senses. Anything to help him forget today was a milestone: one week since Jonathan had been kidnapped. Would they forevermore see life in terms of such morbid anniversaries? Two weeks since Jonathan was kidnapped, one month, six months, a year, ten years? His heart felt as if it was being squeezed from within.

He pulled a covered bowl across the shelf toward him, then shoved it back again. Leftovers from one of the many dinners Claudia had lovingly prepared for them. It was her way of helping, and Ed was grateful, but he also knew a casserole did not make up for the loss of his boy. He slammed the door shut. Dammit, where was Jonathan? Who had taken his son?

Ed felt the cold tile of the kitchen floor through the

thin soles of his bedroom slippers. He had pulled on a pair of pants and a T-shirt this morning, as he had every morning this week. Today he had not even bothered with shoes. Perhaps Monday morning he would go into the office, even if just for an hour, to see what was happening. Somehow, he had to go on living.

Susan padded into the kitchen, the slapping of her bedroom slippers against the floor the only sign that life still flowed through her tiny frame. If it were not for the slippers, she would be as silent as a ghost, the specter of a childless mother, searching in vain for her lost progeny.

"You want some breakfast?" she asked, her thoughts plainly elsewhere.

Ed tried to clear a raspy static from his throat before he answered. "Not really. Well, maybe a little. How about you?"

Susan shook her head helplessly. "I'll just put on some coffee."

"I could scramble some eggs for us. We have to eat something," he said.

"I know. Maybe later. Claude will bring us something soon."

"Susan, darling, Claudia can't feed us indefinitely. We have to pull ourselves together for Jonathan's sake."

Susan spun around to face him. "What do you want from me? You expect me to spend the day baking bread and putting up preserves?"

Ed swallowed hard. "No, of course not. I just meant we've come to depend too much on Claudia's good nature, that's all."

"And who does Jonathan have to depend on?"

The sound of their son's name triggered the tears Ed had seen so often during the last week. More tears than any woman should ever have to shed during a lifetime, and his lovely Susan had shed them in only seven endless days. He took her in his arms.

"Why am I fighting with you?" she said through her tears. "Oh, Ed, I must be losing my mind."

"It's okay. We're both wound pretty tight."

Susan dabbed a tissue at her eyes. "I'd fix breakfast, but Claudia said she'd be over early today, to bring us one of her egg soufflés. She's late."

Ed gently patted her shoulder. "She's got her own household to run. Maybe something came up."

The doorbell rang. Susan forced a weak smile. "There she is now."

Together, Ed's arm still around Susan, they went to the door. More and more frequently they walked through the house this way, supporting each other in an unspoken need. Ed had to touch Susan frequently, to feel her physical presence, just to be certain his entire world hadn't come crashing down around him. Even though she had never expressed it out loud, Susan was apparently feeling the same craving for a guarantee that her husband would not suddenly disappear as her son had.

He knew he had to get some sort of professional counseling for Susan. Even their family doctor had said so when he prescribed a sedative to help her sleep. He immediately felt guilty for thinking Susan was the only one who needed help. He was going to need just as much counseling as Susan, and they both might need marriage counseling. Little barbed comments, the need to snap at one another, had taken the place of their total despair.

At the front door Ed squinted into the morning sun and saw Claudia was not alone.

"I'll just put this in the oven to keep warm. You remember Detective Fernandez, don't you?" Claudia nodded toward the detective and then spirited her foil-covered oblong pan off to the kitchen. The warm, pungent aroma of cheddar cheese and bacon lingered in the air.

"Yes, of course. Please come in and sit down." Ed walked with Susan toward the long, sectional sofa. Fernandez glanced around the room as if to appraise the situation, then took an adjacent chair.

Fernandez looked uncomfortable settling into the deep cushion on the back of the chair. He tried to straighten his perpetually rounded shoulders, then gave up on the effort and hunched forward in their direction, awkwardly propping his elbows on his knees.

"Any news from the FBI?" he asked.

"Not really," Ed answered.

"Something just came to our attention. We're not certain if it's a connection, but we don't want to overlook anything in a case like this. It might be the first break we've had since the postcard."

Susan's entire face lit up as though she had just received a shot of adrenaline. "What is it?" she asked urgently.

"Maybe nothing, but then again, it may be a link to your boy."

Susan appeared ready to burst through her skin. Ed took her hand and gently flattened it between his own hands to calm the tension he felt rising between them. They were desperate to latch on to any clue, any link to Jonathan, no matter how frail it might be. Like a ball being bounced from hand to hand, they had to keep the volley going. Even the press had lost interest in Jonathan. He had gone from hot topic to old news in just one week.

Fernandez cleared his throat. "We got a call from the state police in Pennsylvania. They're investigating a murder in a little town not too far from Reading."

"Murder! Oh, my God," Susan cried.

"I'm sorry, I should have explained it was a woman, not a boy."

Susan let out a breath combined with a sigh of relief. Ed's heart had crawled up into his throat, thudding against his Adam's apple.

Fernandez referred to his notepad and went on quickly. "A woman named Detweiler was found dead, buried in a shallow grave a couple of miles from where she lived. A farmer out walking with his dog discovered the body. The police searched the woman's apartment last night. They didn't find much except for a torn envelope."

"How does this relate to Jonathan?" Ed asked, his heart rate slowing to its normal pace.

"The envelope was addressed to Brian Nowlin, but it doesn't match up with Jonathan's writing on the postcard."

"You have the envelope?" Susan asked, lurching toward the edge of the sofa.

"Just a copy." He held out a sheet of white paper with a facsimile of the envelope centered in the middle.

Fernandez was right. It didn't look anything like Jonathan's precise little lettering.

Claudia came into the room and sat on the other side of Susan. "Sue, we don't know a soul in Pennsylvania, and, of course, we can't imagine anyone who might have Brian's address except—"

"Jonathan," Ed finished for her. "What does this mean?" he said to Fernandez.

"The police up there wanted us to check out Brian, thought he might be a relative of the dead woman or something, but when the request for information came across my desk, I thought of Brian's connection with your son."

"So you think Jonathan's kidnapper has something to do with the death of this woman?"

Fernandez nodded. "It's certainly possible, so as soon as Mrs. Nowlin said they didn't know anyone in Pennsylvania who might write to her son, we walked over here to tell you."

Claudia squeezed Susan's hand. "This may help the FBI to find him, Sue."

Fernandez went on, "We should pass this on to the Atlanta Field Office, so they can contact the police in Pennsylvania. Give me the name of the agent in charge of the case, and I'll get right on it."

"Agent Thomasian, Kira Thomasian," Ed answered. "You can call her from here." He pointed to the portable phone on the coffee table.

"Did they look everywhere in that woman's apartment?" Susan asked. "Jonathan could be tied up somewhere."

"That I don't know," he said, "but don't worry, I'll tell the FBI to cover the place thoroughly."

Ed put his arm around Susan and leaned back into the pillows of the sofa while Fernandez made the call. Susan snuggled against him, but he could feel her stiffen, tensing with each number Fernandez punched on the touch-tone dial.

It took forever for the call to go through to Agent Thomasian's office, but when she finally answered, Fernandez carefully repeated the particulars of this recent discovery. Ed listened, hoping and praying this mad killer didn't have Jonathan. Why would a killer want Jonathan in the first place? Nothing about this whole nightmare made any sense.

"Maybe we should fly to Pennsylvania?" Ed mumbled more or less to himself, but Susan whispered a yes.

For the longest time Fernandez nodded to the receiver, listening in silence. Finally he held the phone out to Ed and spoke: "Thomasian wants to talk to you."

Ed crossed two fingers on his other hand while he placed the receiver, still warm from Fernandez, against his ear. "Yes?"

"Mr. Grady," she began slowly, "I think we're finally getting somewhere."

"What is it? Why didn't you call us?"

"This is something we just got minutes ago. I've been trying to get an identification on the fingerprint they found at the motel, and it just came through." She paused. Ed heard her clear her throat. "It matches up with somebody from your past, somebody you thought was killed in 'Nam. I think your old sergeant, Leon Hoffman, has Jonathan."

Ed felt the veins in his temple slowly clog with lead. "But Hoffman was killed, everybody said he was."

"That's all you're going on, what everybody said?"

He tried to remember. So many were killed, so many names were bandied about, but he had never tried to follow up on the dead. It would have been far too painful when he first got out, what with all his night sweats and headaches. He was so glad when all of that finally stopped, he could think only of getting on with his life and putting the war far behind him.

"I guess I never saw anything official, I just assumed—" His voice broke off.

"Well, to the best of our knowledge, he's very much alive, and now with this possible connection to a homicide, we may be able to zero in on him."

"What about Jonathan?" Ed asked weakly. "Any sign of him being in Pennsylvania where this woman was . . . found?"

"That'll be our next step. I'll check into it and get back to you."

"Thanks." Ed hung up the phone.

"What is it?" Susan asked. "What did she say?"

"My old sarge. Bull. She thinks he kidnapped Jonathan."

Susan put her hand over her mouth and whispered, "But how? You said he was dead."

Ed's mind quickly jumped to his capture in the swamp. He had been too terrified to scream. He even remembered with shame that he had pissed his pants at some point after the Viet Cong guerrillas had grabbed him. But Bull had screamed and sworn enough for the four of them, wild, incoherent stuff, the rantings of a man crazy with fear of what the Viet Cong were capable of doing to him. Ed could still picture the crazed look in Bull's eyes, eerily reflected in the moonlight, just before they put the blindfold on him.

Ed cringed, remembering how he had yelled out for the sarge to shut up moments before the rifle butt went crashing down on Bull's head. He had tried to warn Bull, but it was too late. The gooks didn't want to hear all that yelling, so they shut Bull up before they dragged him away. Within seconds they dragged him away, too, in the opposite direction along with Tony Cozelli. He never even saw which way they took Vince Mendoza.

Bull had every right to be deranged with fear, Ed recalled. He was pretty insane at first, too. He had heard about the torture and the beatings, and it was all true. He still carried a scar on his throat from where one of his guards had crushed out a cigarette. And the rats. The thought of the slow, insidious way the rats gnawed on a cage or even a man's leg still made his stomach churn. But he had been lucky—he had lived through his four months of hell. Plenty of guys had died in those stinking cages. Too many. Stories passed from prisoner to prisoner, and he had heard about the mindless torture allegedly inflicted on Bull, like the grenades the V.C. exploded just close enough to scare the hell out of a prisoner but not close enough to kill. And then he had heard that both Bull and Vince had died. Ed rubbed his hand over his forehead, vaguely aware his fingers were trembling. Vince had been a damn nice guy, and he recalled thinking at the time that even crazy old Bull didn't deserve what he' must have gone through.

How could Bull still be alive? From the rumors he had heard, it didn't seem possible. But if Bull had survived and was somehow responsible for Jonathan's abduction, if it were true . . . Slowly, the long-submerged memories began drifting back into his mind.

Ed got up and walked to the bathroom. He didn't want Susan to sense how desperate he was feeling. It was all coming back to him. Just remembering the maniacal flashes in Bull's heartless black eyes every time he killed one of the enemy was enough to make his blood run cold. That crazy sonofabitch actually *enjoyed* killing. His poor little boy. If Bull had him, Jonathan didn't stand a chance.

Chapter 26

JONATHAN wondered what time it was. It was early Friday morning, he knew that, but it was still dark outside. He tried to wiggle his toes, but it was hard to tell if he even had toes. He had never been so cold. Pulling his knees up almost to his chin, he burrowed his hands deep into his armpits, but it didn't help very much. The numbness just wouldn't go away.

After the sun had set Thursday evening, the former Dairy Queen had been enclosed by a dreary, overcast night. Later on, dark, jagged clouds shrouded the moon, and dampness seeped up through the concrete, making their bed on the dirty floor as cold as it was hard. At one point he had snuggled closer to Maria, seeking warmth, but she had stiffened. He moved away again, and although he remained close, their bodies did not touch. The gloom of the cold darkness whispered about him, and he cried to himself. For a long time he had trembled, teeth chattering, until exhaustion finally took over, bringing him sleep.

After the first glow of daylight began to creep into their hideout, Jonathan stretched out his legs. He ached everywhere. Pain shot up his back as he pulled himself to a sitting position. Desperately wanting to cry to release some of the pain, he instead bit the insides of his cheeks. He had to hold back his tears so Maria wouldn't hear.

Just then Maria rolled toward him and groaned. She buried her face in her thin cotton dress which she had tried to fashion into a pillow.

"I'm so cold," she whimpered.

"Me, too," Jonathan answered. His throat felt scratchy, just like it always did before he got a sore throat or the flu. Please God, he prayed, please don't let me get sick.

"What do we do now?" Maria said, opening one eye to the gray morning.

"We can eat something, then we'll go look for a phone. I want to call my grandma."

Maria's teeth chattered. "Shouldn't we try to call Judy Mae?"

"We'll call her later. First I have to talk to my grandma."

"Then let's go. I'm freezing."

Jonathan stood up. His head felt light. "It'll be better if we eat breakfast here. No one can see inside."

"Okay," Maria said, but she didn't get up. She coiled herself into a tight ball on the hard floor.

"Listen, I'm going to go outside and look around." He took off his jacket and handed it to her. "Here, take this, I'm not cold."

He tossed his lightweight jacket over her before he headed for the door. The gray clouds were knitted together with no trace of the sun. The sky seemed low, like a heavy blanket he could reach up and touch. He hugged his arms around his chest and hurried to the rear edge of the Dairy Queen lot. A row of saplings separated it from a farm. He could see a run-down barn in the distance but no signs of people. In the shelter of the trees he relieved himself, and then decided his throat was scratchy because he was thirsty.

He had no idea where they could find water. Little streams crisscrossing the many fields they had navigated yesterday had provided more than enough water, but no streams approached the uneven, cracked blacktop of their Dairy Queen retreat.

Something shiny on the ground caught his eye and he walked through the trees into the adjacent field. An old hubcap filled with water lay in the ditch between two newly planted rows. He stooped next to it and examined the murky water. Everything from his Cub Scout training told him the water was unsafe to drink, but it had to be rainwater, didn't it? The hubcap was rusted around the edges, but it looked shiny where the treasured cup or two of water lay waiting.

He scooped up a bit in his hand and held it under his nose. He didn't smell anything bad, so he greedily slurped it into his parched throat. The water was sweet-tasting, slippery smooth as it went down. Ever so carefully, he picked up the hubcap and carried it back to Maria.

The screen door stood wide open, the broken spring hanging as a reminder that Jonathan hadn't closed it properly, and it could no longer close itself. He butted the inner door with his rear end so he wouldn't have to release his grip on the precious water and eased the hubcap inside.

Maria had somehow managed to go back to sleep, huddled under the folds of Jonathan's jacket. Ever so carefully Jonathan placed the water on the floor near where she slept and then inched across the wrinkled brown paper, settling next to her.

He remembered all the times he had crawled into his mom and dad's bed, usually early on Saturday or Sunday mornings. It was always warm and so cozy. The sheets on their big king-size bed emitted the sweet aromas of his mom's lotions and perfumes and his dad's smell, which wasn't perfume or even after-shave. It was just the way his dad always smelled. Remembering those days of warmth and love brought tears to his eyes again.

He sniffed back the tears, but he knew he couldn't sleep, not now. He was wide-awake and eager to get moving so they could find a phone. He thought about waking Maria, but decided to let her sleep just a little while longer. Her eyes seemed sunken and hollow even as she slept, and today might be another long day for both of them.

After a bit Maria stirred and rubbed her eyes.

"Oh, good, you're awake." Jonathan said.

Maria stretched, looked around the dismal room, then finally focused on Jonathan.

"I have to go to the bathroom," she said.

"Go outside, in the back, by those trees. No one can see you."

Maria got up and grunted. "It's easier for a boy. Everything is always easier for a boy."

Jonathan wished she knew how hard the last week had been for him. His sudden move to Leon's shack following the news about his parents' death had been bad enough, but no one could have ever prepared him for the anguish of seeing Maria being molested or the terror of being abused himself. Then came the realization that there was no fire, no explosion, just Leon and whatever hideous means of murder he had vested on his unsuspecting parents. Jonathan was feeling more and more homesick for a familiar face when he remembered that today he finally might be able to make contact with his grandma and Brian, or maybe both.

Maria stomped back into the room and closed the door. "I hate this place," she said matter-of-factly.

"I found some water," Jonathan said.

"It looks dirty."

"Maybe a little, but I drank some and it didn't hurt me."

"Poisoned water doesn't kill you right away. You'll probably drop dead in an hour or two, and then I'll be all alone."

"It's not poisoned," Jonathan said. "It's rainwater with a little dust or something in it. That's all."

Still, Maria refused to drink the water. She took a sip after she brushed her teeth and swished it around her mouth, but quickly spit into the dingy stainless steel sink where a family of spiders had taken up residence.

"I hate spiders. Let's get out of here," she announced.

"Don't you want more to eat?" Jonathan asked. "You only had two peanut butter crackers."

"They make me too thirsty."

"Here, eat your apple." He handed her one of their two apples and took a bite of his own. It tasted cold and grainy, but he forced himself to eat every bit. He thought of poor Snow White and the wicked queen who gave her a poisoned apple. They didn't have to worry about wicked queens or poisoned apples, but he knew Leon was a far greater threat, and Leon was very real.

As soon as they had eaten all but the seeds of their apples, Jonathan quickly repacked the crackers and peanut butter into Maria's bag. He spilled the last few drops of water into the sink and tried to wedge the hubcap into his backpack.

"What do you want with that thing?" Maria asked.

"I don't know. It might come in handy, like for carrying water."

Maria eyed him suspiciously. "I thought you said

we'd get a ride today, that we wouldn't have to sleep like this again without water or a bathroom."

"I know, but I kind of like this old hubcap."

"Oh," she said, apparently satisfied with that explanation.

Jonathan put his jacket back on and zipped it up to the neck. They stepped outside and walked around to the front of the building. Now the sky appeared even gloomier, a wintry day misplaced into spring. It felt as if any second it would rain, a cold, hard-driving rain. Maybe it was cold enough to snow. Jonathan saw his breath fog the air in front of him.

Cars rushed by in both directions as they approached the narrow two-lane road. Jonathan said, "Why don't we try to hitchhike? Leon's not around. He won't know any of the people just driving by. It'll be all right."

Maria looked much too tired to argue. "Okay, I guess we're pretty far from his place," she said.

Jonathan held up his thumb the way he thought you were supposed to. "Hey, what's that across the street?" he said suddenly.

Maria looked. "A diner. I think it's closed."

"No, right inside the door. There's a telephone!"

Chapter 27

Leon slammed the rear doors of the van and rushed back into the house. He took a quick look around the place, but there wasn't time to worry about anything else. The cops would return. When, he didn't know, but he was certain they wouldn't quit bothering him until they had figured out a way to pin Judy Mae's death on him. Well, he just wouldn't be here when they came back. Outside again, he got into the van and checked the fuel gauge. After all that driving yesterday, he needed to stop for gas. He figured he'd spend the morning searching for the kids, then, whether he found them or not, he'd have to head for Canada.

The wind had shifted and he could feel a penetrating chill in the air; another storm was brewing. On the horizon leaden-gray clouds boiled angrily, closing in, another sure sign of rain.

If he only knew where to start, if he had some idea where Jonathan and Maria might be hiding. He drove much more slowly today, hugging the shoulder and looking from side to side along the road, studying everything that moved for a trace of the missing kids. He had to find them quickly, but he knew yesterday's mad speeding back and forth over the narrow roads had not produced results. How would Jonathan be thinking? What kind of crazy scheme had he talked Maria into?

Suddenly he hit the brakes and stopped dead right in the middle of the road to Plowville. Of course, why hadn't he thought of it sooner? Jonathan was on his way to Ohio, to find his grandmother! They were heading west!

Leon reeled the van in a tight circle, his tires singing against the crumbly macadam along the shoulder. Back on course, he pressed the gas pedal to the floor. There was no sense looking here, he thought, as he sped toward a junction where he could connect with the road leading west.

He neared Route 222 and slowed once again. Not only was the traffic heavier, but there were people walking here and there along the road. Most were simply strolling from a car into a restaurant or roadside shop, but he couldn't afford not to check every pedestrian he saw. Jonathan and Maria could be pretending they were part of one of these little outings. He had to be certain he didn't miss them if they had gotten it into their heads to fool old Leon by hiding in a crowd.

With each passing minute, Leon grew more and more nervous. What if the cops had already picked up the kids? They would start asking Jonathan and Maria questions, just as they had done with him, and the kids might say something about being all alone during the storm on Tuesday night. Leon knew the cops would wheedle it out of them. They would say that he had came home late, dripping wet, his shoes covered with mud. They might also start talking about how they came to live here in Pennsylvania with him in the first place.

Another possible scenario blazed through Leon's mind. Jonathan might get through to his grandmother on the phone. She would call the police; they would notify the FBI. A whole swarm of cops and detectives would descend on him. He was doing the right thing to run away to Canada. They'd never give him another moment's peace if he stayed.

Dammit, he never should have left Jonathan and Maria home alone. He should have tied them up in the garage. But one thing was certain, the kids had to be around here somewhere. How far could they have gone on foot?

A few raindrops began to splatter against the windshield, just enough to interfere with his vision, but not enough to require windshield wipers. He'd find them soon, he hoped, before the rain became too heavy, and he'd drag them into the van, by their necks if he had to. Once he drove them back to his place, it wouldn't take very long to fill in the grave. Before the cops even thought about returning, he'd be far away, safely on the road to Canada.

Leon bit his lower lip. But what if he didn't find them? Well, he'd keep looking until noon, but then he'd have to give up and head north. Maybe he could make it all the way to Canada before the cops even figured out he had hit the road. They wouldn't know which way he was heading. Hell, they probably wouldn't even start looking for him for a day or two. He'd have a pretty good head start by then.

His palms were sweaty against the steering wheel. He stretched his fingers and moved his hands to fresh places on the wheel. Then, up ahead, he saw several children huddled in a group on the right side of the road, but there were also people milling about outside a gas station on his left. The van sputtered and slowed as his foot slacked off the gas pedal. The cars whizzed by, interrupting his line of vision. He spotted a child in a red jacket. Didn't Maria have a red jacket? No, now he remembered. Hers was blue. It was simply too hard to examine both sides of the road at once. Blaring its horn, a pickup truck raced by the slow-moving van, passing it on the left.

"Fuck you, asshole," Leon shouted toward the rear end of the truck as it sped away. He pulled over to the side of the road and stopped. His sweaty hands trembled with rage. His mouth twitched.

There were simply too many places to investigate in this populated area. He hated places with swarms of people, and the roaring din of the traffic was getting to him. He slapped his hands over his ears and tried to see across the road. But the blur of passing cars and trucks had washed into shades of green and brown, like the blur of branches and vines climbing the trunks of great trees in a jungle, a hot, steamy jungle.

His eyes wouldn't focus and his head began to pound again. The faces of the children across the road bled together. All he could make out were skinny legs, just like Maria's. Leon felt sweat running down his neck. God, he remembered how he used to sweat when he was in the cage. Grady and Mendoza, or at least their kids, were still making him suffer after all these years.

Leon cushioned his head against his arm on the steering wheel and rested for a few moments. After the hammering in his forehead relaxed a little, he looked up. He could see the children more clearly now, and they were all too young, maybe six or seven. A woman, maybe their teacher, held the hands of two of them. Jonathan and Maria were not a part of the group.

He slowly pulled out into traffic and proceeded down the highway. The next time he saw a gathering of people along the side of the road, he slowed, edging over until he found a place where he could come to a complete stop. That worked better, and once he was satisfied Jonathan and Maria were not there, he moved on. He followed this same procedure two more times, the second time pulling into the vacant lot of an old Dairy Queen.

He squinted through the raindrops, trying to get a better look at a couple of kids hanging around the diner across the street. He didn't think the diner was open this early, but someone was holding the outer door so they could enter the vestibule.

These two looked older, taller, more like Jonathan and Maria's size. Funny, ever since he had started his search, every kid he saw looked like Jonathan or Maria from a distance.

Chapter 28

With bristly, cold raindrops peppering their faces, Jonathan and Maria waited several minutes for a safe opening in the steady stream of cars. Finally they dashed across the two lanes of macadam. The diner was closed but there definitely was a phone inside a little vestibule that also housed a cigarette machine.

"Why don't we just wait right here until they open?" Jonathan asked. "Then we can call my grandma."

Licking a large raindrop from her lip, Maria nodded.

"You'll like my grandma," he said, grinning. "She's nice and she'll let you stay in Columbus with me if you want."

Maria pointed to a car pulling into the diner's parking lot. "Look, here comes a car."

The car parked close to the building and a woman and a man got out. They ignored Jonathan and Maria and went around to the rear of the diner and let themselves in. A few minutes later the woman unlocked the front door.

"You two are early. We don't serve breakfast until ten this time of year," she said.

Jonathan thought she looked fuzzy and warm, a

lot like Judy Mae. "We don't want to eat; we just need to use the phone. It's real important."

The woman looked them over.

"I have to call my grandma. I won't damage the phone, I promise."

The corners of the woman's mouth crinkled into a smile. "Well, I guess you can do that."

The woman held the vestibule door open for them and then disappeared back inside the darkened diner. A faint light was visible through a door that probably led to the kitchen. Jonathan heard pots and pans begin to clank and rattle from somewhere within.

Maria stood close behind him, near the cigarette machine, while Jonathan fished in Maria's hoard of money for change. His fingers were so cold it was hard to pick up the coins.

"Hurry up," Maria said. "Call her."

He was careful not to make any mistakes. He slipped two dimes into the slot and pressed the 0. The dimes immediately shot back into the change return.

"Operator," a woman's voice said.

"I want to call Columbus, Ohio, please. Six-one-four." Jonathan paused and took a breath, hoping he remembered the area code and number correctly. "Seven-six-seven . . . four-three-one-nine."

"Is this a collect call?"

Jonathan wasn't certain he understood what that meant, but he quickly said, "Yes."

"Your name?"

"Jonathan Grady."

"One moment, please," the operator said.

Jonathan heard a melodious beeping, then the ringing of the phone. It rang three times. He wondered if his grandma really was ill, as Leon had said. Maybe she was in a hospital; maybe she was dying.

She had to be there, she just had to. On the fourth ring he heard a faint voice.

"Hello."

"Grandma!" Jonathan cried into the phone.

"One moment," the operator interrupted. "I have a collect call from Jonathan Grady. Will you accept charges?"

"Oh, my, yes," his grandmother said. "Yes, of course. Jonathan?"

"Go ahead," the operator said.

"Grandma!" Jonathan cried again, tears streaming down his face. "It's me."

"Jonathan, baby, where are you? We've been so worried."

"I'm in Pennsylvania. I'm not sure where. We're on a highway and there's—"

Suddenly, brusquely, big, beefy fingers clamped down over Jonathan's mouth, knocking the phone from his hand. A familiar odor, stale and heavy with beer and sweat, clutched at his throat just before his mind went blank.

Chapter 29

Leon heard a terrified voice screaming through the dangling telephone receiver, "Jonathan, Jonathan," over and over again. That was close. The kid almost told the old lady everything. His hand covered half of the boy's face. His other hand clutched Maria's throat.

Savagely, he pulled Jonathan away from the pay phone and hissed into the boy's ear, "We're gonna go quietly, so no one inside this place hears us. You make a sound, I'll strangle Maria."

Leon grabbed Jonathan by the arm and slid his other hand around until he had a firm grip on the back of Maria's neck. His fingers dug into Jonathan's skinny little arm, and he knew, even though the kid was wearing a jacket, he was inflicting enough pain to make Jonathan follow quietly.

"Okay, walk."

Maria's eyes were frozen with terror, but she didn't scream. She didn't move. Leon tightened his grip on her neck and gave her a shove, propelling the two of them through the vestibule door and down the three steps to the parking lot.

"We're gonna cross the road real careful like and get into the van. You've had me crazy worrying about you," he said.

The boy's legs went rigid, so Leon grabbed Jonathan by the neck, too, squeezing until the kid stumbled forward. At the same time, he relaxed his hold on Maria. He wasn't worried about Maria making a run for it. She was afraid of her own shadow and would follow quietly. Jonathan was different, of course, and Leon kept his grip firmly, painfully, tightened around the boy's scrawny neck. They had to wait a few moments for a break in traffic, then he half dragged, half shoved Jonathan and Maria across the road and into the waiting van. Leon made certain Jonathan sat in the middle on the wide front seat so he wouldn't have a chance to pull anything. Maria sat trembling, next to the door.

"Where are you taking us?" Jonathan finally demanded, tears streaking his dirty face.

"Home. Where else?" Leon answered, trying to keep his anger in check. Losing his temper here would only make Jonathan bolt and try to run away. There were too many cars around. He had to take both of them home, into the privacy of his own place, before he dared show them how angry he really was.

"I talked to my grandma!" Jonathan cried. "She's not sick at all. You lied to me."

"I got there just in time. You tell that poor old woman a lot of fool things, you'll worry her into having a heart attack. I told you she's not well."

"I don't believe you," Jonathan persisted. "You lied!"

Leon gripped the wheel tighter and spun out of the Dairy Queen lot, making a left-hand turn to go back the way he had just come. The raindrops, which had continued to splat large and heavy against the windshield, now grazed his line of vision in a steadier rhythm. He flicked on the windshield wipers. Watching them slog into action, he remembered he needed new wiper blades. How had he for-gotten to replace the wiper blades again?

It was going to be one hell of a storm, and he had to take care of the kids and get on the road to Can-ada before traffic was snarled to a crawl. Maybe it would be better if he took them along. He could dump them somewhere along the road, buy himself a little more time.

Maria was whimpering to herself in the corner, Jonathan was sobbing and sniffing. Perhaps their whining and crying would upset him too much. He usually made his foolish mistakes when something upset him. Taking them along wasn't worth the risk. He would stick to his original plan and return to the house. Nothing could be more convenient than the grave he had dug for Judy Mae, all ready and wait-ing for him to use.

Leon wanted some small part of his plan to work out. He wouldn't be able to line up the three kids in a row and shoot them the way he wanted. He wouldn't be able to leave them to rot in a swamp, or at least a creek or riverbed. That part was too bad. There just wasn't time to make Cozelli's kid pay his old man's debt, but Jonathan and Maria were going to even the score for him with Grady and Mendoza. That thought brought a slight smile to his lips.

"It was bad for you to run away. You know that, don't you?" Leon said calmly.

"I want to call my grandma again," Jonathan sputtered.

Leon reached out and slapped Jonathan across the face. "Just shut up. You're not calling nobody." He stepped on the gas, casting great silvery plumes of water all over a woman who had just gotten out of a car parked along the shoulder. He didn't look back. Why should he? He had plenty of problems of his own.

The kid blubbered, wiping his face with his sleeve, but he piped up again through all the tears. "I want to call my grandma."

"You're not doing nothing, except going home with me, so quit your bellyaching," Leon roared.

This kid was going to drive him crazy. Wasn't it just like Grady to have a kid who was a smart-mouthed pain in the ass? Maybe he couldn't silence Grady, but it was going to give him a great deal of pleasure to shut up his kid, permanently.

"What the hell did you do with my .38, boy? I told you not to go messing with my stuff, didn't I?" Leon turned, getting a glimpse of Jonathan's owlish eyes, peering right back at him without the slightest waver. This kid had a way of looking through a person, he thought.

"We tried it, in the woods behind the garage," Jonathan said. "I think I left it there, on the ground."

"Shit, didn't your old man teach you nothing? You don't play with guns, and you don't leave them on the ground where they might get wet." Leon pulled out of the line of traffic and passed a slow-moving delivery truck. "I should have known fuckin' Grady wouldn't teach his kid nothing. He didn't even deserve to have a kid," he said half to himself.

Leon shook his head, concentrating on navigating the van through the pelting rain. Traffic crawled; visibility was terrible. Why did everyone have to creep along just because of a little rain? He wanted to pull out and pass all these chickenshit drivers, but you never knew when a cop might be looking for someone who was going too fast. Those cops loved it when they could write up a speeding ticket, but they weren't going to nab him. Not today. It was only another four or five miles, then this whole ordeal would be over.

Chapter 30

$\mathbf{T}_{HE}$ rain swirled against the windshield of the van. Jonathan watched the windshield wipers slosh back and forth, squeaking on the upstroke, groaning on the downward slide. He knew they couldn't trust Leon, but he wasn't sure what to do about it. For now, he planned to watch him very carefully.

"When he stops, let's make a run for it, okay?" Jonathan whispered to Maria.

Maria squirmed in her seat but didn't answer. She watched Leon out of the corner of one eye, probably trying to determine if he was listening to what Jonathan was saying. Jonathan knew Leon was concentrating on driving through the storm, but he also knew it would not be a good idea to make him mad. He had heard the hatred in Leon's voice when Leon grabbed the phone away from him. He knew Leon had meant it when he said he would strangle Maria.

Soon Jonathan recognized the dreary woodland approach to Leon's private road. The gravel lane had turned into valleys of mud and deep puddles. Leon charged over the swamplike road, his face fixed in a contorted grin. Why was he in such a hurry? Jonathan wondered. What was he going to do to them?

Leon spun the van into his regular parking place for a second, then threw the gearshift into reverse.

He backed up a few feet, then proceeded down the narrow path between the mountains of derelict cars toward the garage. This didn't make sense, not the way it was pouring. They were parking far from the house for a reason. Jonathan guessed Leon was going to take them into the garage for a whipping.

The van shuddered to a stop.

"Stay close to me," Jonathan hissed to Maria. Eyes watchful and filled with fear, Maria nodded.

Maria gathered up her grocery bag with its few remaining supplies and slid off the seat. She raced into the open garage to escape the downpour. Jonathan slipped his arms into the straps of his backpack and hurried after her, but in spite of the short run, they were drenched by the time they were inside.

Jonathan shook his arms and stamped his feet and looked up into the long, steel barrel of Leon's rifle.

"Little change of plans," Leon said. "We're going to take a short walk in the rain. Head out behind the privy."

Jonathan's heart thumped wildly, pounding all the way up into his ears. Maria walked out into the rain, but Jonathan simply stood there, his feet welded to the floor. There could be only one reason Leon wanted them to go into the woods. He was going to shoot them, and Jonathan could see no way for them to escape.

"Walk," Leon said, prodding the rifle into Jonathan's back. "I ain't got all day."

Jonathan slowly began to walk behind Maria, not even feeling his feet connect with the soggy mud. Maria took a few more steps, then looked back, her eyes pleading with Jonathan to tell her what to do. His face must have told her he had no ideas, not even a faint one, for she turned again and continued to trudge forward through the driving rain.

They approached a tiny clearing heaped high with several piles of earth. Maria stepped to the side, avoiding the first mound, just as Jonathan saw a deep hole gaping between the little hills of dirt.

"Hold it," Leon said, "this is as far as you're going."

Jonathan and Maria stood at the edge of the hole. One of the banks of dirt closest to the rim had started to erode from the rain, sending little rivulets of mud cascading over the side. The bottom was filled with water. Jonathan couldn't tell how much water, but it looked deep.

Leon stood right behind them for a moment, then suddenly grabbed Jonathan. Leon pushed one fist against his backpack, shoving Jonathan dangerously close to the slippery edge.

"This here is your new home," Leon said.

Leon's grip on the backpack had Jonathan trapped. He twisted, turning to look at the madman who wanted to push him into this pit of mud and water. Leon's face was so red Jonathan expected to see brains explode right through his ears. His usually dull eyes were on fire, bulging under his rain-soaked brows, but Leon didn't take those eyes off him for a second. Jonathan flailed his arms, struggling to extricate himself from the shoulder straps of the pack. The ground beneath his feet gave way and he began to sink into the hole.

"No!" Jonathan yelled. He freed one arm from the pack, but as he did, Leon pushed him, hard. Jonathan half slid, half fell headlong into the black pit.

Hearing only the piercing shriek of Maria's scream, Jonathan quickly righted himself, relieved to see the water was not even an inch deep. From his knees he looked up at Leon's towering, long legs, which stretched all the way up to his fiery-red face. Next to the giant Leon, Maria stared down at him, screaming and crying in total disbelief.

"What are you going to do to us?" Jonathan cried.

"I'm planting you in a swamp hole. Just the way your old man left me in 'Nam. He left me in some hole in a swamp, but I'm alive and you're dead." Leon tossed Jonathan's backpack into the hole after him. It landed with a splat, spraying Jonathan with mud. Leon laughed loudly, the rain continuing to beat against his head.

Jonathan stood up and tried to climb the side of the pit. The earth gave way under his hands and crumbled back into the hole on top of him.

Leon laughed harder. "Go ahead, make it easier for me. Maria, you'd better go help him. You like him better than you like me, anyway."

Maria stared at Leon but did not move. Jonathan stopped trying to climb for a moment and looked up. The rain ticked against his eyelids, making it hard for him to see. He could feel the darkness of the mud surrounding him, and now he finally understood Leon was planning to bury them alive.

"I said, go help him, dammit. Get in there, girl," Leon said. He reached over and struck Maria's shoulder lightly. His tap was all it took to send her tumbling down into the cavity. She landed on her knees next to Jonathan.

"That's better. Now you two can do whatever you want. You can write letters together, you can run away, you can even call your grandmothers, because you're going to be together for a long, long time."

Leon threw the first shovelful of soggy dirt into the hole. It landed on Maria's foot. She cried out in terror and reached for Jonathan, but the next load of dirt came crashing down on her back.

Jonathan grabbed for his backpack as the dirt came flying at them by the shovelful. His mind screamed silently and his heart thudded even faster, louder. He didn't know it was possible for a heart to pound so furiously, and he feared it would just stop beating. Surely he would die long before the dirt covered them up. With each new blast of dirt from the shovel, Jonathan scraped the mud from his arms or legs as if it were burning coals.

Leon snickered. "That's pretty good. You afraid you're gonna get dirty, boy?" Leon was beside himself with laughter. He slapped his knee and then tossed another load of mud at Jonathan. "I always said you were smart, kid."

Jonathan clutched his backpack to his chest and pulled at the zipper. Clods of dirt were skyrocketing all around them. They were sinking deeper into the mud as the rain quickly transformed the earth Leon was shoveling into a slimy ooze. The zipper was now covered with little clumps of mud, but Jonathan continued to struggle until he got it open.

He yanked a shirt and the old hubcap out of the way and stuck his hand deep into the pack, probing until he touched the cold, hard steel of Leon's revolver. The dirt was flying into his eyes, but he now had his finger on the trigger.

"Get over against that wall," Jonathan said to Maria, jerking his head in the direction he meant. "Stay behind me."

Maria crawled into the corner of the pit close to the muddy wall, and Jonathan backed up against her. He held his backpack upside down, his arm extended upward. His pencils and pens and his school notebook tumbled out into the mud, but the gun was firmly in his grip inside the pack.

"Hey, Leon," Jonathan yelled. Now his heart had

moved up into his throat, making it difficult for him to speak. He yelled louder, "Leon, look at this."

The dirt stopped flying for a moment, and Leon's great hulking shoulders leaned over the edge of the grave. Rain dripped from the top of his bald head.

Jonathan held his arm as straight as he could, pointed the backpack at Leon, and squeezed the trigger. The loud retort startled Jonathan and he flew backward, pinning Maria against the dirt wall behind them. Maria screamed and covered her ears. Jonathan's own ears were ringing, but he aimed, the gun still inside the backpack, and pulled the trigger one more time.

Jonathan was stunned by the force radiating up his arm. His whole body trembled, but he looked up in time to see the crazed look on Leon's face just before he fell to the ground.

The hot gun pressed against Jonathan's fingers. The pit was filled with the odor of the exploded gunpowder. He examined the jagged hole ripped through the bottom of his backpack. It had worked. He had stopped the torrents of dirt from burying them alive.

Quickly, Jonathan picked up the old hubcap and began to gouge toeholds into the soggy mud wall in front of him. Some of the holes immediately eroded and collapsed, but several held.

Maria still cried uncontrollably; her nose ran, but somehow she understood what Jonathan was trying to do. They dug their feet into the weakened mud wall and clambered one on top of the other, trying to get out of the grave.

Finally, by using Jonathan's shoulder, Maria reached the crest. She pulled herself up over the side and then lay down on her stomach with her arms extended to Jonathan. He struggled, falling back into the mud several times, before he was able to scale the impossible slime.

Jonathan caught his breath and stood up. They were both completely covered with mud. Maria even had little blobs of dirt on her eyelashes. Then he saw Leon.

A bright red spot on the front of his jacket faded into a circle of pink as the rain washed away the blood.

Maria stared, then took one step closer to Leon. Her mouth hung open for a moment before she found the words to speak.

"Holy Mother of God," she whispered. "You killed Leon."

Chapter 31

KIRA couldn't believe how fast things were happening. Police work, even within the venerable FBI, was usually a plodding, painstaking process, but ever since her talk with the expert from latent prints this morning, information on the Grady case just kept falling into her lap.

First, Fernandez's tip about the murder in Pennsylvania. Within minutes she was on the wire to the state police up there, and sure enough the dead woman was a known girlfriend of none other than Leon Hoffman. If his fingerprints all over her apartment weren't enough, they had the envelope addressed to Jonathan Grady's best friend, tying Hoffman to the kidnapping with a double noose.

Then, not more than fifteen minutes after she had talked to the Pennsylvania police, she had another call from the Gradys, this one a bit more frantic, about the boy reaching his grandmother by phone from somewhere in Pennsylvania. The grandmother kept the line open by running next door to use her neighbor's phone to call the FBI and the phone company. Smart lady, Kira thought.

Another agent, assigned by Paul, monitored an open line to the phone company, reporting back to Kira. The pay phone Jonathan Grady had used turned out to be about twenty miles from where they had found Hoffman's girlfriend in a shallow grave. The gap was closing, and there was no question in her mind Hoffman was their man. She was concerned, however, about how the boy's call had been cut off so abruptly. Jonathan had probably slipped out of Hoffman's sight long enough to make the call, but then he must have caught the boy in the act. Damn, she thought, this could be bad news for the boy, but at least Hoffman hadn't killed him. At least not yet.

Now for the hard part. She had to get permission, a waiver actually, to stay on the case. Once they had evidence that a missing was known to be in another state, normally the FBI from that state would follow through. It saved a lot of wear and tear on agents, not to mention air fare. She had, in fact, just transferred the case file to Pennsylvania. Technically she was finished, but her gut told her it wasn't always that easy.

She hurried into Paul's office with the news about the pay phone Jonathan had used to contact his grandmother. Paul's eyes lit up when she finished her story, and he leaned back in his chair, lacing his fingers behind his head.

"Great," he said, "so we're done with it, and since you are fast becoming a kidnapping expert, there's a case I want you to look into over on the west side of Atlanta. Parents just reported getting a ransom note postmarked South Carolina."

"Wait a minute," Kira said. "I want to stay with the Grady case until I see Hoffman's ass in jail."

Paul grinned. "And I'd like to see his balls nailed to the wall of his cell, but it's out of our hands. Send all that you have on the case to Greenberg in Philadelphia. They'll take over from here."

"Greenberg already has everything. He delegated

the case to the resident agent in Harrisburg. A guy named Vern Wentzel pulled duty on it."

Paul leaned forward in anticipation.

Kira drew in a deep breath. "Listen, I know it's out of our jurisdiction, but I also know you can send me up there if you want to. If for no other reason, I can back up the local agents until they're fully familiarized with the case."

"Crissakes, Kira, they can get into this in ten minutes. The guy is leaving a trail wider than Sherman's march to the sea."

"I know that, too, but I want to be in on the collar. I want to bring the boy home to his parents."

Paul shook his head. "You gonna bake him cookies, too?"

Kira was afraid she was going to cry. Damn Paul for making her beg. She knew he could okay a trip to Pennsylvania for her to follow up on this. It had been done before.

"Paul, if you won't assign me, then I'd like to request vacation time starting right now."

He looked at her blankly. "You want to go up there now?"

"Yes, I want to be on the next plane."

Paul shook his head again and stroked the side of his temple with his fingertips. "Women," he mumbled.

"Yes, I'm a woman. I may also be a pain in the ass, but you owe me."

"Whoa! Why do I owe you?"

"You held me back on this investigation at the beginning, now give me a break. It's my first case." Her voice cracked. "I want to be there."

"You make it sound like you're tracking the crown jewels. This is small potatoes. They'll have this guy in cuffs before dark."

"Then I'll be back home, with the boy, tomorrow."

Paul picked up the phone and began to punch out numbers for a call. "Bring your car around to the front and wait for me. I'll be right out."

"Who are you calling?"

"I'm making arrangements for us to fly to Pennsylvania."

Kira's mouth dropped open. "For us? You're going with me?"

"Yes, I'm going with you," he barked. "I'm your partner on this, aren't I?"

Kira broke into a grin. "I want to call the Gradys, let them know where I'll be just in case they hear anything."

"And where will you be?"

"The Dutch Country Motor Inn on 222, just off the Pennsylvania Turnpike."

"For crying out loud, don't they have regular places like Holiday Inns up there?"

"Greenberg said this place will be closer to the command center. They're setting up at a local sheriff's office, a place called Cocalico."

"Looks like you were planning to be there with or without my consent."

Kira felt her face redden. "I'm sorry, Paul. It's hard to explain how I feel about this."

"I know," he said, getting up from his chair. "So get moving; we don't have all day."

Chapter 32

E<small>D</small> stared at the ringing phone, almost afraid to pick it up. He had been unnerved by his mother-in-law's telephone call from Jonathan, confused because his son had called his grandmother rather than his parents, and now he wanted to keep the line open. Surely Jonathan had tried to call home and failed because the line was busy. That had to be it.

"If it's one of those goddamn reporters again, hang up," he said to Susan as she reached for the phone.

"Shh," she said, holding her hand over the mouthpiece. "It's Kira Thomasian."

Ed sat down. Every time the phone rang, the stiffness in his neck tensed into a tight knot at the base of his skull. He tried to work it out, massaging the back of his neck with his fingertips.

This morning's new developments were clicking into place, and the FBI was finally making sense of what had happened to Jonathan. But Ed felt particularly helpless at the moment. All he wanted was a couple of minutes alone in the same room with Bull Hoffman, but on the other hand, every time he even thought about Bull and what he may have done to Jonathan, all he could do was tremble.

Susan hung up the phone and turned to him.

"She's on her way to Pennsylvania. The FBI from Harrisburg is taking over because they're certain Jonathan is still in that area, but Miss Thomasian is going to assist them. She says if she goes in person, it will cut down on the briefing time for the Harrisburg man and they'll be able to get right to work."

Ed began to pace. He didn't belong here, twiddling his thumbs in Atlanta, if his son was being tortured by that crazy son of a bitch in Pennsylvania. Yet he couldn't go to Jonathan if it meant leaving Susan here alone. She needed him, now more than ever. He stopped walking and stood in front of the wide picture window in the living room. Slowly he scanned the sloping, green expanse of his own front lawn until his gaze settled on the low-hanging branch of the old magnolia tree where he had suspended a swing for Jonathan. He closed his eyes and took a deep breath.

"Ed?" He heard Susan behind him.

He turned and put his arms around her. "It won't be long. They'll find Jonathan now that they know where to look. Don't worry."

She pulled away from him and studied his face. "The waiting is really getting to you, isn't it?"

"Sure, it's enough to drive you nuts, knowing Jonathan called your mother just a few hours ago, and here we sit, waiting for God knows what."

"Miss Thomasian gave me the address and phone number of the motel where she and the other agent would be staying."

"What other agent?"

"I'm pretty sure she said Mr. Russell. Paul Russell."

"Where will they be?"

"Near where Jonathan made the call to Mother." Susan hesitated a moment then continued. "Ed, maybe we should be there, when they find him."

He cringed inwardly. God, how he wanted to be there, but what if what they found wasn't their bright-eyed son, but a mangled corpse? He couldn't put Susan through that. He wasn't even certain he could handle it himself.

"Wouldn't the FBI have something to say about us getting in their way?" he said.

"Pennsylvania's a pretty big place, and Agent Thomasian didn't warn us to stay away."

"Susan, I want to be there for Jonathan, you know I do. I'd also like to get my hands on Bull, but . . ."

"But you're afraid we may walk into something that we're least expecting. That's it, isn't it?"

Ed sat down and pulled her into the large chair with him. "I've been itching to get out of the house and do something all week, and now I just don't want you to see what Bull might have done to Jonathan. That bastard is crazy. They don't get any crazier."

"Stop thinking like that," Susan said sharply. "If Jonathan was smart enough to get away to make a phone call, he's smart enough to get away again. What if our baby ran away from Bull and is alone out there all by himself? He needs his parents."

"You're prepared for what we might find?" he asked.

Susan stood up. "You get on the phone and make reservations for us to fly to Harrisburg. I think that might be faster than flying into Philadelphia."

"Sue, I could go alone. You could have Claudia stay here with you."

She shook her head. "I'll pack for both of us. Get the first flight out of Atlanta, then call Claudia and ask her if she could stay here while we're gone. Just in case Jonathan tries to call home."

Ed hurried into the kitchen and grabbed the phone book. He felt his heart rate accelerate as he flipped through the pages looking for airlines. Just when he was about to come apart at the seams, Susan had finally regained her strength and pulled the two of them back on the right track. God, she was one helluva woman. Now, if they could only return from this trip a happy family of three . . .

The phone rang. He snatched it from the hook before the first ring was over. "Hello."

"Is this Ed? Ed Grady?"

Ed's blood ran cold. He thought he recognized the voice as one from a long, long time ago. "Yes, who's this?"

"You probably won't remember me, but we served in 'Nam together. This is Vince Mendoza."

"Vince? You got out of there?" Ed stammered.

"Yeah, it's been a long time. You okay, buddy?"

"Sure, I'm fine. I thought you . . . didn't make it home," Ed said, his voice cracking.

"Listen, Ed, some FBI agent called me, said your son was kidnapped. I can't tell you how sorry I was to hear that."

Ed's mind raced, trying to put the pieces together. "I guess they were checking on my story, to see if I was telling the truth about our old sergeant, Bull. They think Bull kidnapped our son."

"No, I don't think they doubted your story," Vince said. "They just wanted to verify a report they had about my daughter, Maria."

"What happened to your daughter?"

Ed heard Vince suck in a deep breath. "She was kidnapped, too, almost three years ago."

Chapter 33

JONATHAN squeezed his arms around his chest, trembling from the cold. He gaped at the massive body stretched out on the ground in front of them. His ears still rang from the two gunshots he had fired at Leon, but the numbness in his brain was starting to fade. What he had done when he pulled that trigger was slowly beginning to register.

"What do we do now?" Maria cried, rain dripping off the tip of her nose.

Jonathan shivered. His teeth chattered. "I don't know."

A sudden gust of wet wind lashed the trees above their heads into a frenzy, pouring even more rain down upon them. The mud on Maria's face washed down toward her throat. Her wet hair was slicked against her head with two muddy fish-hook curls falling into her eyes. Her nose was running, but she didn't seem to be aware of it. Jonathan suddenly realized he was crying.

"Shouldn't we do something?" Maria asked.

"Yeah," Jonathan said, sniffing back his tears, "I guess so. Let's get out of here."

They tramped through the muddy forest back toward Leon's house. Jonathan couldn't find the words to speak, but deep inside he was screaming.

He had killed Leon and surely would be punished, even though Leon deserved it. Maybe the judge would take that into consideration when he was sentenced; maybe he would just have to go to a youth camp for juveniles. Once, he had read a story about a boy who had been sent to a youth camp for stealing cars. But killing Leon was much worse than stealing cars.

The house looked older and even dingier in the bruised daylight. With the dark clouds pushing down upon the tall trees, the day seemed to be changing into night even though Jonathan was sure it was still afternoon. But then he couldn't be certain about the time, or anything else for that matter. His life was coming apart, and all he wanted was to lie down someplace warm and dry and cry himself to sleep.

Maria opened the door cautiously, drawing out the agonizing squeak of the screen door. Jonathan followed her inside. She flicked on the kitchen light. Everything looked the same.

Jonathan strained to hear even the slightest sound. Nothing. They walked into the kitchen, the old floorboards creaking beneath their feet, and stopped in the middle of the room. The house was still. Even the faded yellow electric clock on the wall seemed to be silent, but the red second hand continued to sweep around in a mindless circle. It said twelve o'clock—noon. Jonathan wondered if it could possibly be midnight.

They began to peel off their sopping-wet jackets and sweaters. The house was cold and damp, and Jonathan could hear Maria's teeth chattering in the quiet.

"You should take a hot bath," Jonathan said, "and change your clothes."

Maria stood there trembling. "I'm so scared."

"It's over, remember? Leon's dead."

Her eyes were swimming in tears. "What's going to happen to us?"

"I don't know."

"What should we do?"

"First, we should change our clothes, I guess. You go first."

"I'm afraid to go in there by myself," she said.

"Stop it, Maria," Jonathan said sharply. The truth was she was beginning to frighten him, too.

Maria took a few hesitant steps into the living room. "All right, I'll take a bath, and I'll wash my hair. It's full of mud," she said weakly.

"Okay," Jonathan answered. While Maria bathed, he stripped down to his underwear and wrapped himself in a blanket. Still shivering from the cold, he sat on the edge of the bed in the little room that had been his. He clutched the blanket tightly, doubling it around him, but he couldn't get warm.

He was also completely exhausted. His arms weighed heavy, and he was haunted by the sensation that had rippled throughout his body when he'd fired the gun. The powerful force of the weapon still echoed through his veins. But as tired as he was, he didn't want to lie down in Leon's house. After he had a chance to wash off the mud and change his clothes, he wanted to leave this place forever.

The hot bath soothed some of the tension in Jonathan's aching arms and legs. He dressed in clean, dry clothes, the ones he had left behind when they ran away, and dumped all his muddy things into a heap on the floor. He found a dry jacket in Leon's closet. Naturally it was far too big, but it would do until he got to his grandmother's house or the police station or wherever he would end up. He wasn't quite so anxious to get on the road again. He guessed it might make sense to wait here at least until it stopped raining.

He found Maria at the kitchen table drinking a glass of milk.

"Leon finally remembered to buy milk. You want some?" she asked.

"I guess so." Jonathan sat down across from her.

Maria poured another glass of milk and placed it in front of him. The weight of the glass made his hand tremble. He didn't feel strong enough to lift it to his lips.

"What should we do?" she asked.

"Maybe we should wait until the rain stops. Then I have to find a phone and call the police."

Her eyes peered at him from within dark circles. "Are you gonna tell them you killed Leon?"

"I have to."

"Why? Can't we just run away? We could go to Georgia and look for your dog. There's nobody to stop us now, so we could hitchhike."

Jonathan thought about that. He'd like nothing better than to go back to Georgia and find Ginger, but maybe it would be smarter to confess his crime and get it over with. They'd go easy on him because he was just a kid, and he would explain how Leon had asked for it. He'd tell the police Leon had hit them and how he was going to bury them alive. Maria would back up his story, and once the police knew everything, maybe they would feel sorry for two kids who had to ward off attacks from a beast like Leon.

"No, I'll go to the first house we can find and ask to use the phone. My grandma will tell me what to do."

"Do you think I should call Judy Mae after you call your grandma?" Maria asked.

Jonathan shook his head. "She's not going to be happy that I killed Leon."

"Do you think you'll go to jail?"

"Not a real jail. They have special jails for kids."

Maria looked confused. "Even if it's for kids, you'll be locked up, won't you?"

Jonathan nodded and took a sip of his milk. The wind moaned through the cracks around the kitchen window, and Jonathan suddenly pictured himself sitting on a narrow cot in a drafty little cell, locked away from his grandma and Maria. It seemed all the bad things that had ever happened to him had happened in just this past week, and all because of Leon.

"What will I do while you're in there?" Maria asked.

Jonathan swallowed the last of his milk over the knot that had surged up in his throat. "I'm sure you can stay with my grandmother. You'll like her."

"I've never been to Ohio."

"It's okay. It's a lot like Pennsylvania."

"I hate it here. California was better."

"That's because of Leon, because he was here and he was awful."

"Okay, I guess Ohio will be better than here, if your grandmother will let me."

"She will. She's nice."

Maria suddenly sat up straight. Her eyes wide with fear. "What was that?"

Jonathan had heard it, too. A strange, strangled sort of noise just outside the kitchen. They sat, staring at the closed door.

"Did you lock the door?" Jonathan whispered.

"The lock doesn't work. Leon never locked it."

They waited, listening. A slow, groaning creak told Jonathan someone was pulling open the screen door. A neighbor or someone driving by had probably heard the gunshots and called the police. His heart thumped, knowing it had to be the police, coming to take him away.

A dull thud against the inner door echoed throughout the kitchen before the door actually swung inward. Jonathan couldn't believe what he saw. Cumbersome and unsteady, Leon stood there, his dripping-wet clothes streaked with blood. He didn't speak. He just leaned against the door frame and glared at Jonathan and Maria.

Chapter 34

Slowly, Jonathan got up from his chair and stood next to Maria. He hadn't killed Leon, but there was no question Jonathan had hurt him real bad. The front of Leon's shirt was streaked with red, and even from this distance Jonathan could smell the odor of Leon's blood mingled with the claylike mud covering his clothes. Leon clutched the rifle in his left hand, the barrel leveled directly at them.

Leon stood riveted in the doorway, still staring at them. Tiny, beady spots of bright yellow reflected from the kitchen light into the depths of his gray, zombielike eyes. Jonathan wanted to run, but his feet would not move. Besides, they were trapped. There was no way he and Maria could get around Leon to reach the door.

Leon still had not spoken. He just stood there, squeezing his right hand against his left shoulder. Blood continued to trickle through his fingers no matter how tightly he pressed the wound. Finally, he staggered to the kitchen table and sat down heavily. He propped the rifle across the span of his knees, but his finger never left the trigger.

"I need a medic," Leon snapped. "Mendoza? Grady, I've been hit. Don't just stand there. Get the fuckin' medic."

Jonathan heard Maria begin to whimper. He reached out and squeezed her hand, but he was ready to cry himself. He shivered, feeling cold chills pulsate up his spine.

Leon rocked back and forth, still clutching his shoulder. "Goddamn gooks is everywhere," he mumbled. "The sneaky little bastards just drop out of the trees."

"Mendoza?" Leon squinted at Maria as if his eyes were not focusing. He shook his head and squinted harder. "What the hell you waiting for? I told you I got hit."

"Why's he calling me by my last name?" Maria whispered, tears running down her face. "What's the matter with him?"

"I don't know, but we gotta get away from here," Jonathan whispered back, his eyes still on the rifle. "I think he's gone crazy."

"Mendoza," Leon howled, this time even louder. He picked up the rifle and pointed it at Maria. His breathing was heavy, his dull, glazed-over eyes seemed alien, disconnected from the rest of him. It was as if Leon wasn't really seeing Maria even though he was looking right at her.

Leon wiped the back of his hand across his mouth. "Mendoza, go get the medic, that's an order. You even think about running away and leaving me here, I'll blow Grady's fuckin' brains right through the fuckin' wall."

Maria's face went blank and her hands began to tremble. She looked like she was going to faint. Jonathan's own gut twisted with stabs of pain.

"I think he wants us to bandage his shoulder," Jonathan whispered to Maria, "but we should try to make a run for the door."

"He'll shoot us if we run."

Jonathan thought for a moment. "Maybe while

we're bandaging his shoulder, we can get the gun away from him?"

Maria sniffed. "All we got is Band-Aids."

"We can use a towel or washcloth or something to mop up the blood."

Jonathan tried to recall his first-aid training from Cub Scouts, but the sight and smell of Leon was making him sick to his stomach. Pressure to the wound was all he could remember, but he wasn't positive that rule applied to a gunshot wound. He was certain they had never discussed anything about gunshot wounds in his Cub Scout classes, but he also knew if they didn't do what Leon wanted, they wouldn't live long enough to have a chance to get away from him.

Maria moved sideways, crablike, until she reached the doorway to the next room. Then she ran through the living room and on into the bedroom. All the while she was gone, Leon aimed the rifle at Jonathan's head. Jonathan took quick, shallow breaths, afraid to breathe normally, for fear Leon's finger would squeeze that trigger. He stood perfectly still, not even blinking his eyes.

Maria hurried back into the kitchen with an armload of towels and washcloths and one bed sheet. "This is everything from the linen drawer," she said. "The sheet's too big, but we can cut it up."

She dumped the linens on the kitchen table. Leon's head had rolled to one side and his eyes were half closed, but the rifle still followed Jonathan.

Noiselessly, Jonathan took one step away from Leon and whispered to Maria. "As soon as we give him first aid, make a run for the door. We can flag down a car and try to get help."

"I'm scared," Maria answered. "Maybe we should just do what he says."

252

"Maria, he was going to bury us in that hole. Maybe he'll make us go back there."

"Not me," she cried. "I'll never go back into those woods again."

Leon opened his eyes and jerked his head upright. "What's that you said? Mendoza, get over here and do something about this goddamn hole in my arm, and get me a slug of whiskey." Now he pointed the rifle at Maria.

Maria took a stiff, gray square of terry cloth that had probably once served as a washcloth and put it against the soggy front of Leon's shirt. "You have to take off your shirt," she said.

He struggled to pull his good arm out of his jacket and shirt, and Maria tugged on the other side, freeing the wounded shoulder. A deep black hole surrounded by darkened flesh gaped at them.

Maria shrank back, her face pinched into an expression of both loathing and terror. Her nostrils tightened and her face drained of color. She folded a towel and tried not to look at the tortured, ripped flesh in front of her.

"He's got a bottle of whiskey under the sink," Maria said to Jonathan. She dabbed at the wound with the towel, her eyes all but closed.

Jonathan fell to his knees in front of the sink and searched for the whiskey bottle. His mind was spinning. He was just as scared as Maria, but he didn't want to help Leon. They had to get away. Maybe Leon would fall asleep after he had some whiskey to drink. If they could stop the bleeding, perhaps they could talk him into taking a nap.

Jonathan looked over his shoulder at Leon. Maria was still swabbing away the blood. Leon's finger rested on the trigger of the rifle, sometimes twitching when Maria pressed too hard. Even though Jonathan was certain Leon was in a lot of pain, he was also certain Leon was capable of pulling that trigger. He knew it was wrong, but he wished he had killed Leon. Going to jail would be easier than this.

Maria leaned against Leon's shoulder, holding the swab with two fingers.

"You have to push so fuckin' hard?" he growled, his chest heaving. "Where the hell's my whiskey?"

Jonathan pulled out a bottle labeled Jack Daniel's. He remembered a scene from an old cowboy movie he had watched on TV where the doctor poured whiskey right on a bullet wound. It must have worked, for the cowboy was alive and well at the end of the film. Carefully, he filled one of the Flintstone jelly glasses with the whiskey, wincing from the smell. Jonathan carried the glass and the bottle back to the table.

Leon downed the liquor in two huge gulps, and as soon as he had finished, Jonathan turned the bottle upside down, dumping the remaining Jack Daniel's over Leon's bare shoulder.

"Holy fucking Christ," Leon roared, knocking the bottle right out of Jonathan's hand. It crashed to the floor, exploding into a million shards of splintery glass.

Jonathan and Maria jumped back from the bellowing hulk as he loomed to his feet in front of them. Leon kicked over a kitchen chair and waved the rifle in their faces, his own face flaring to a brilliant red.

"Maria!" Leon shouted, his eye twitching. "What are you doing here?"

Maria blanched, stammering as if Leon's outburst had physically knocked the wind out of her. "We hadda climb out of there. We didn't want to die in that big hole."

Leon looked confused. Eyes squeezed together, Leon studied Maria's trembling shoulders and watched as she twisted her fingers together in a ner-

vous little dance. Then, as if he had suddenly become aware of Jonathan's presence in the room,
Leon turned and stared at him.

A film of sweat covered Leon's face, and big, blue
veins popped out on his thick throat. "Now I remember what happened. It was you."

Jonathan froze, expecting a bullet to hit him at
any moment. He closed his eyes and waited, but no
bullet came.

Leon said, "I ought to finish you right now, you
sneaky little bastard."

Trembling, Jonathan slowly opened his eyes.

Leon's eyes looked black and hateful as he stared
at Jonathan. "I'm not gonna let you off that easy,
boy. It'll be better if we go get Cozelli's kid and do it
the way I planned. My first plan was the best all
along, that's what, and I'm gonna off the three of
you just like I always said I would."

Jonathan shrank away from Leon, not understanding the plan he raved about. Leon's rifle wa-
vered, pointing toward Jonathan's feet as he
pressed a small towel, folded into a thick wad,
against his shoulder. The bleeding had finally
stopped.

Maria cut a long strip from the bottom of the sheet
and wound it around and around under Leon's arm
and across his chest until the entire shoulder was
covered.

"Get me a shirt and a jacket," he ordered Maria.

Maria ran into the bedroom and returned with a
red-and-black-checkered shirt and a worn denim
jacket. She helped him ease his wounded arm into
the sleeve of the shirt.

"Hey, my old huntin' shirt. Sonofabitch, that's
good," Leon said. "I'm going huntin' for two prize
bucks and a doe. I'm gonna nail all three of them at
once, that's what. That's pretty good."

Leon pushed his right arm through the sleeve of the old jacket, but simply draped the other side over his left shoulder. He held the rifle in such a way that the jacket covered most of the weapon, all but the butt, which poked out under the jacket, and the tip of the barrel, which always seemed to be pointing right at Jonathan.

"Get in the van," he said. "We have to take a little trip to Harrisburg."

"No," Maria cried. "I don't want to go."

"Nobody's asking what you want. Just get in the van. I got a score to settle, and no matter what happens to me now, I'm gonna take care of this first."

Chapter 35

THE throbbing pain in Leon's shoulder clawed all the way down to his fingertips. He needed his pills for the shoulder but now also for the headache. At first he hadn't even noticed the headache, but it was there. The goddamn headache was always there.

He pushed the kids through the door into the almost blinding daylight. The rain had finally stopped, and the sun was trying to burn through the remaining clouds, but all it produced was an annoying frosty glare that stung his eyes.

"Get in the back," Leon ordered.

Taking the kids along to Harrisburg wasn't part of his original plan, but he didn't have time to do it any other way. Besides, he had a new plan: Jonathan and Maria could help him get Cozelli's kid. He couldn't wait around for the boy to come strolling down the street where he could grab him as he had done before. He'd use Jonathan and Maria, or maybe just Maria, to lure the Cozelli kid into the van. Once he had all three, the rest would be easy.

Maria looked at him with her eyes ready to flood over with another bucket of tears, but he shoved her into the nearly full back portion of the van. His tools were heaped against the rear doors, so they wouldn't be able to get out that way, but there was always the sliding door on the side to worry about. He would have to tie them up.

"Hand me that rope, kid," Leon demanded, looking squarely at Jonathan.

The boy picked up a length of clothesline coiled at his feet and held it out to Leon. Leon saw the hatred festering in the boy's eyes, but he also remembered it was the boy who had planted this slug in him. At first he thought it was one of those louse-infested bastards from a V.C. patrol, but then he remembered. He was pretty sure he remembered it was Jonathan who had done it. A little slug in the shoulder was not going to kill him, however, and now he had the upper hand. Jonathan, Maria, and Cozelli's brat would all be dead in just a little while. He'd be able to head for Canada knowing he had done the whole job. Just the way he had always planned it.

Leon's plan was so much better than simply killing the three fathers. He could have picked them off easy if he had wanted to, but that would have been too fast and too neat for those three lying traitors. Each with a dead kid to remember, Mendoza, Grady, and Cozelli would suffer inwardly for the rest of their lives. And he would finally have his revenge.

Pain ricocheted down Leon's left arm when he bound the rope around the two kids. He forced them to lie flat upon the scattered blankets and rumpled clothing strewn over the floor of the van, and then he lashed their hands and feet, using double loops. He yanked the rope as hard as he could with one hand, all the while a cold sweat dripping from his forehead into his eyes. Kicking with one foot, Leon wedged his duffel bag between Jonathan and the side door. The two of them, lying side by side with the rope zigzagged across their arms and legs, looked like two trussed turkeys. He decided to pull one of the blankets loose, and threw it over them.

Perfect. If anyone should look into the van, they would see two kids, cozy and warm, resting on the floor under a blanket.

"Something's poking in my back," Jonathan said. "Can't we sit up?"

"Shut up or the barrel of this rifle will be poking in you. I don't want to hear another sound out of either one of you, you understand?"

Leon knew from the terror in their eyes they would be quiet. Damn Jonathan was probably up to something, or else he wouldn't have asked to sit up, but he was smarter than the kid was. No matter how smart Grady's goddamn kid was, he was smarter because he would be the one who was alive when all this was over.

He started the van and drove down the muddied, gravel lane. He hunched over the wheel and drew up his bulky shoulders almost to his ears. That seemed to relieve the pain a little. His pills; he had almost forgotten.

He pulled over just before reaching the macadam road and groped into his glove compartment. It was hard to open the bottle, everything was harder to do with this nagging pain jabbing his shoulder, but he kept telling himself not to rush. The kids were right where he wanted them. In a matter of minutes he would be on the road, so he didn't have to worry about another visit from the state cops. Harrisburg wasn't far. He was determined to finish what he had started, even if it was the last thing he ever did.

Leon drove slowly. There was no sense in calling attention to himself. He knew the turnpike would be the fastest way to Harrisburg, but he also remembered that Pretty Boy cop had written down his license number. If they had any ideas of tracking him down, the turnpike would be too risky. It would be easy for the cops to radio ahead to all the exit booths to set up a roadblock. No sir, they couldn't fool him into taking a road that was so closely monitored. He would stick to the county roads, like he had done before, and then follow 322 straight into Harrisburg no matter how much longer it took.

He adjusted his rearview mirror so he could see the floor in the back of the van. The two little mounds under the blanket lay perfectly still. He could barely make out the faces on the heads sticking out from under the blanket, but he could see Jonathan and Maria were being good. Too bad they hadn't thought about being good before, but then it really didn't matter. He kind of liked the idea of just getting rid of all three kids at once. Now that he thought about it, it would have been far too much trouble to try to keep three kids at his place, especially without Judy Mae.

Traffic was much heavier than usual as he approached the little town of Brickerville. Then he noticed the orange warning signs: CONSTRUCTION AHEAD. He inched along, following behind a silver tanker truck polished all shiny, like a mirror. He could see from the way the oncoming traffic was backed up that the area under construction must stretch out for miles. There was no way to pass, and there was no way to turn around. He crept along at barely fifteen miles per hour for miles and miles.

Daylight faded quickly. With the cloud cover from the storm still lingering, twilight was moving in early, gathering like a scum over the gray fields along the road. It was growing cooler and windier, and Leon suddenly wished he had changed into dry pants and shoes when he was back at the house. He flicked on the heater, figuring what little warmth it provided would have to do.

The drive continued to go slowly, with two more pockets of construction before he reached the outskirts of Harrisburg. By the time he pulled over and located Cozelli's address in the glove compartment, it was almost dark. He'd never be able to lure the kid outside at night. Shit, things just weren't working out according to plan. The pain thumped in his shoulder; his head was splitting. Then he spotted a little park along the road.

He drove into the empty parking lot and stopped close to a clump of bushes. A swing set and a circular slide sat off to the right, but it was too dark and too cold for any children to be out enjoying the playground. Leon turned off the engine and got out of the van. He walked around to the sliding door on the other side and yanked it open. The little eyes peering at him widened in fear.

Leon chuckled. "It's about time you two learned how to behave. Now we're going to spend a nice quiet night sleeping in the van."

Jonathan opened his mouth to speak, but Leon climbed into the van, pushing the two of them farther from the door with his feet. He closed the door behind him and positioned the duffel bag behind his back. Every movement was agony. He drew his knees up toward his chest and rested the deer rifle against one leg. Finally he slumped back against the door and let out a deep breath. The thudding in his head was giving him double vision. He squinted, positioning the rifle so it was pointed at Jonathan's head. Both kids looked terrified. He liked the way they looked, like they were going to shit their pants. He grinned in the near darkness.

"Now ain't this cozy? You two just go right to sleep and you'll be alive to see the morning. Try anything, anything at all, and I'll blow your heads clean off your shoulders."

Chapter 36

JONATHAN trembled under the dirty woolen blanket. The scratchy little fibers made his nose itch, and he had to pee. He was much too afraid to ask Leon to untie him so he could go to the bathroom, so he prayed he could hold it in until morning. Wetting his pants would only turn this day into a worse nightmare.

The sun had faded, leaving the back of the van in foggy darkness. Jonathan didn't know where they were. From the floor of the van he hadn't been able to see anything but the sky and the rooftops of buildings. Earlier, he had seen a sign for the State Capital Motel, but he didn't know what city was the capital of Pennsylvania. He wasn't even certain they were still in Pennsylvania.

Leon had parked the van in a dark place, the shadowy outline of some tall trees looming above them. The only light came in through the rear window, distant and not very bright. Jonathan's wrists ached where the rope cut into his flesh; his back was stiff from the hard steel floor of the van. The odor of the whiskey he had poured over Leon's shoulder lingered on his clothing, making the stale air in the small compartment even more disagreeable. Jonathan's mind was far away, disconnected.

Maybe this was all a bad dream. If he had thought it would do any good, he would have cried.

The keen, steady whine of the wind pressed against the windows of the van, whistling a lonesome croon. Jonathan thought he heard strange, eerie sounds rustling somewhere outside. He was sure it was not a human sound. Maybe it was just a toad or a cricket, but it was probably something much worse.

He remembered the monsters he used to visualize at home whenever the stairs creaked at night. His dad always said it was nothing more than the house settling, but Jonathan never believed such a scary sound could be explained away so simply. But now he knew deep down inside nothing out there could be worse than the terror that was right here in the van. Leon and the long steel barrel of his deer rifle were his only real concerns on this cold, starless night.

Jonathan tried to fall asleep, but sleep didn't come. It was the same lonely feeling he had experienced every night during the long week since he had arrived at Leon's house. He tried thinking about the happy days back in Georgia with his parents. He remembered playing catch with his dad in their backyard. Sometimes they used to go to the park, but usually they just tossed the ball back and forth while his mom prepared dinner. He liked to stand there, trying to pitch his best curve to his dad, while the good smells of fried chicken or spaghetti sauce drifted out through the back door. Jonathan wasn't real good with his baseball mitt, and he sometimes still dropped the ball, but his dad never criticized him. His pitching arm had improved, though, and he could throw the ball even farther than Brian could. Brian probably missed playing catch with him, too.

Jonathan's hot tears finally let go, gushing down his cheeks. He turned his head toward Maria so Leon wouldn't see him crying. She, too, was whimpering into the blanket, ever so faintly. Leon groaned, shifted his weight, then groaned again, settling into a different position.

Suddenly, the single beam of light that had filtered into the van from a distant porch or street lamp flickered off, leaving them in total blackness. He didn't remember it ever being this dark in Georgia. He squeezed his eyes shut as tightly as he could.

The morning sun shone through the filthy, rain-streaked windows of the van. The wind whipped through the trees, finally chasing away the last of the storm clouds.

Jonathan's wrists had gone beyond pain, and now he felt the same burning sensations through his socks where the rope spanned his ankles. His neck ached as he lifted his head to see where Leon was. The bald head was slumped forward, almost touching his chest, but one stubby finger still curled around the trigger of the rifle. Jonathan didn't make a sound. Maria slept next to him, her face smudged with the vestige of what must have been a steady flow of tears during the long night.

Finally Leon began to stir. Jonathan saw him swallow a whole handful of little yellow pills before he poked the rifle into the blanket near Jonathan's feet.

"Wake up, you two. We got things to do."

Jonathan turned his head toward Leon. "What do we have to do?" His voice was now almost as scratchy as Leon's, and his throat felt cottony and dry.

"Take the ropes off," Maria begged. "My arms hurt."

"Yeah, sure, but first let me figure out something." Leon got out of the van and looked around. He leaned back inside, pointing the rifle at them.

"There's some kind of privy here, so I'm going to untie you. We'll all go over to the toilet, together. Just walk naturally, and make it quick, and no noise, you hear?" Leon motioned with the rifle for them to sit up.

When the ropes came off, Jonathan felt lightning shoot into his hands and little needles stab the soles of his feet. As they walked a few yards to the rest rooms, he could see they were in a park. It wasn't much more than a baseball diamond and a play area for little kids, but it was a pleasant enough neighborhood park. He thought of running to one of the houses he could see in the distance, but his feet hurt so badly, he could hardly walk, let alone run. Then there was also the certainty that even if he could get away, Leon would kill Maria just to get even.

· Leon pointed to the door of the ladies' rest room and motioned to Maria. "Wait right outside when you're done. You take off, I'll shoot Jonathan." He then followed Jonathan into the men's room. "I'll be watching the whole time, so no funny business."

They returned to the van, and Leon ordered Jonathan and Maria into the front seat, Jonathan in the middle. Leon got in the other side and propped his rifle against his left leg.

"I'm hungry," Maria said.

Leon slicked his tongue over his dry lips. "You're a real pain in the ass sometimes, you know that?"

Maria began to cry, but Leon ignored her as he started up the engine. "First I'm gonna get some gas, then if I see a place, I'll get us something. You say one word, one word at the gas station, I'll kill you both."

Little beads of sweat had formed on Leon's upper lip. He needed a shave, and the bristly hairs looked as if each had a tiny globe of moisture attached. The glazed look had returned to his eyes again, too, and Jonathan knew Leon was in pain. Perhaps if the pain got worse, he and Maria might be able to get away, but in the meantime he sat quietly, waiting whatever came next.

Leon pulled into a gas station and told the man to fill it up. The man hardly glanced at Jonathan and Maria, but even if he had, Jonathan didn't know how to make eye movements that would convince anyone of the danger they faced.

Leon pulled a twenty-dollar bill from his pocket and handed it to the man. "You know where Winston Road is?" Leon asked him.

The man pointed. "Go down to that first light and turn left. Keep going and you'll see it on the right, about two miles or so."

"Any place where I can get a cup of coffee around here?"

Now the man looked at them a little closer. "Not too much open yet, but you'll pass a McDonald's on the way to Winston Road."

"Thanks." Leon wiped the sweat from his face with the back of his hand and started up the engine. He drove directly to the drive-through window at McDonald's and spoke into the microphone when a voice asked if he could take their order.

"Give me an Egg McMuffin and three cups of coffee, lots of cream and sugar."

Leon paid for his order and drove about two blocks away before he pulled over and parked.

"You each get a cup of coffee now. If you do what you're supposed to do and don't make any mistakes,

I'll take you back there for some breakfast." He handed each of them a large cup of coffee, two little containers of cream, and four packets of sugar.

"I don't even like coffee," Maria said.

"Suit yourself," Leon said as he bit into his sandwich. He sipped the hot coffee and munched the food, chewing with his mouth open.

The aroma of the hot egg and Canadian bacon sandwich was almost enough to drive Jonathan crazy. Except for the glass of milk he and Maria had drunk at Leon's house, they hadn't eaten anything since yesterday's meager breakfast at the Dairy Queen. That seemed centuries ago. Jonathan poured all the cream and sugar into his cup and slowly sipped the overly sweet mixture. He had never liked coffee either, but it warmed his sore, parched throat and didn't taste as bad as he thought it would.

Reluctantly at first, Maria sipped her own coffee. She made little faces after the first few sips, but she eventually drained the cup.

As soon as Leon finished eating and drinking, he tossed his bag of trash out the window and drove down the street. He slowed to study the signs at every intersection until he finally spotted a street marker for Winston Road. He swung around the corner and advanced slowly, scrutinizing the modest little houses along both sides of the street. He checked an address he had scribbled on a scrap of paper.

Finally he pointed. "There she is. That's Cozelli's place."

Jonathan looked at a small yellow house with a neatly manicured front lawn. A scraggly little pine tree was centered in the small patch of brownish-green grass, and a few trimmed shrubs bordered the short driveway leading to the garage. Leon drove past the house and then abruptly made a U-turn. He stopped two houses away, on the other side of the street, and shut off the engine.

"Now we wait," Leon said.

"Where are we?" Jonathan asked.

"That doesn't matter, kid. What matters is what Maria is going to do here."

"Me?" she asked, surprise registering on her face. "What do I have to do?"

Leon smiled. "We're going to sit here awhile, until we're sure they're up, and then you're going to go over to that yellow house and ask the Cozelli kid to come out to play. His name is Billy. When you get him outside, ask him if he wants to see the brand-new puppies you got in the van."

"What brand-new puppies?" Maria asked.

"There aren't any puppies, you know that, but he'll follow you to have a peek, and then the four of us will go back to McDonald's for a real breakfast."

"What if he knows I'm lying?"

"That's your job, to sound convincing as hell so he comes over here with you."

"What if he doesn't want to see puppies?" Jonathan asked.

"Shut up, boy. Nobody asked you. Every kid wants to see puppies."

"But what if he doesn't?" Maria persisted.

"Then you say whatever you can think of to get him over to this van. If you do anything to scare him away, I swear I'll blast Jonathan clear into the next county, then I'll come to get you."

Chapter 37

KIRA and Paul booked an early flight out of Atlanta, but a delay at the airport kept the plane idling on the tarmac for close to an hour before takeoff. When they finally landed in Philadelphia, a driving rainstorm was drenching the city. The airport TV monitors announcing departures and arrivals flashed like little square Christmas trees, and the usually courteous airport personnel looked frazzled and tired. No one seemed to care that Kira and Paul had missed their connecting flight to Harrisburg.

"When is the next flight?" Kira asked as politely as she was able to through clenched teeth.

"We've had some delays because of the storm. The last commuter to Harrisburg leaves at 10:45 P.M.," the airline clerk answered without even looking up from his computer keyboard. "Be at Gate Eleven on the lower level at ten-fifteen for boarding."

Kira turned to Paul. "Now what? We're going to waste two hours waiting for the flight. Couldn't we drive it in less time than that?"

Paul shrugged. "Sure, but not on a night like this. Traffic will be tied up, and we'd be lucky to find a rental car and get out of the parking lot by ten. I say we wait."

Kira let out a deep breath. "Shit. Doesn't the fact

that we're FBI agents mean anything? There must be another way to get to Harrisburg."

"None that I know of," Paul answered calmly. "How about coffee and a sandwich? I'm hungry."

Anxiety over the delays had wired Kira almost to the point of totally losing her composure, but the tension suddenly flowed out of her. She realized she was seeing a side of Paul she really liked. His even, steady keel in a frustrating situation was just the sort of thing she needed to develop herself. They were opposite personalities in many ways, but she was certain their differences could mesh together nicely. The two of them could be a great team, and she wasn't thinking about a working team. Getting to know Paul on a personal level was something she was looking forward to, and she only wished their first meal together could be in a quiet, out-of-the-way candlelit restaurant, under different circumstances.

She smiled in spite of the less than ideal situation. "Okay, let's find a coffee shop."

For most of the two-hour wait they sat under dusty yellow lights in a crowded snack shop that reeked of stale oil from the deep fryer. They talked over coffee and giant Reuben sandwiches, layered with hot sauerkraut and plenty of mustard.

The spicy food seemed to turn to a concrete lump the moment it hit Kira's stomach. Any other time she would have relished the opportunity to hear about Paul's reasons for joining the bureau and the stories about his first few years on the job, just to get to know him better. But tonight her thoughts were with the little boy, some sixty miles to the west, who had been kidnapped by Leon Hoffman.

"This thing is probably going to give me nightmares," Paul said, finishing his sandwich, "but it was worth it."

Kira nodded as she took her last sip of coffee. "We may have a worse nightmare waiting for us when we find Hoffman," she said.

"If we find Hoffman. It's a big state."

"We should have taken another airline."

Paul grinned. "What we should have done is let the Harrisburg office take this case right out of our hands. We could be having a nice Italian dinner and a good bottle of wine at Alfredo's in Atlanta."

"Touché," she said, "but now that we're here . . ."

Paul stood up. "Now that we're here, let's go nail Hoffman's ass. C'mon, it's time to find Gate Eleven."

After another delay in takeoff, the commuter flight landed in Harrisburg at 11:35 P.M. They hurried inside the terminal, and Kira put through a call to Special Agent Vern Wentzel at the Harrisburg FBI Resident Agency. The night switchboard operator placed her on hold for what seemed like a lifetime, but finally came back on the line with instructions for them to wait outside the main baggage claim.

"Vern Wentzel is sending a uniform from the local sheriff to pick us up," Kira said.

"The old red-carpet treatment."

"Do you think this means Wentzel's out there at this time of night working on the investigation?" Kira asked.

Paul chuckled. "Either that or he's pissed as hell because we don't trust his R.A. to handle the case."

Paul was right, of course. She was prepared for at least some resistance from the resident agent. After all, it was unusual for agents from a field office as far away as Atlanta to cut into his turf, but on the other hand, Wentzel was supposed to give them every courtesy and assistance in a matter as urgent as this. Jonathan Grady was in imminent danger, and finding Hoffman before he harmed the boy was their only priority. Wentzel could lick his wounded ego when all this was over.

Within a few minutes a sheriff's patrol car pulled over and a young officer not more than twenty-five got out. He quickly threw their two carry-on bags into the trunk of the car and opened the rear doors for them.

"I'm John Lenhart. I got orders to take you to meet Agent Wentzel," he said.

"Where are we headed?" Paul asked as the officer drove out of the airport parking lot.

"Cocalico sheriff's station, sir. That's the jurisdiction where the murder took place."

"So, Wentzel's working late?" Kira asked.

"Oh, no, ma'am. When he got your call about missing your flight, he went over to the motel to get some sleep. I was at the office anyway because I pulled the late shift, so I said I'd be happy to pick you up."

"We appreciate your help," she said.

"No problem, ma'am."

"You work with the FBI before?" Paul asked.

"Not me personally. We don't get too much of your kind of crime. Cocalico's a small town."

"Must be nice," Kira said.

"Oh, we get our share of fights to bust up at the local taverns, and plenty of traffic violations, but this is only our second murder this year. I've never been in on a kidnapping across state lines."

The officer accessed the Pennsylvania Turnpike at Harrisburg and drove the forty-plus miles east to Cocalico. As soon as they exited the turnpike, Kira saw why there was no big crime spree in the area. Sprawling fields and widely scattered houses dotted the countryside on the outskirts of the town, and Cocalico itself was hardly more than a few houses and small places of business. They passed a school and several churches, and even though it was late, Kira thought it was odd she didn't see even one other car on the road.

"I guess folks around here go to bed early," she said. "I don't see anybody."

"Well, tonight they're having a special dance at the fire hall. A live band's playing, a group from Reading," John Lenhart said proudly.

This live band must be something special, Kira thought. Funny, if you don't have a whole lot of grand expectations out of life, you can be satisfied with very little. She'd have to remember that.

The cold wind whisked through the trees along the side of the road. The warmth of a couple of beers and a live band might be just the thing on a night like this, Kira thought. She cinched her coat closer around her body.

"At least the weather's cleared up," Lenhart said. "We had one heck of a rainstorm today. Even flooded in a few places."

When Kira got out of the car at the sheriff's station, the cold air penetrated her coat. The ground was still damp, and wide puddles of rainwater indicated it had indeed been one heck of a storm. The walkway to the entrance was dark, lit only by one exterior floodlight. Night had taken possession of the little town, and it was a blurry, unfriendly kind of darkness. She hurried inside, following closely behind the officer and Paul.

Vern Wentzel, who looked as if he hadn't had a good night's sleep in a week, was inside waiting for them. He stood up when they entered and offered his hand to Paul. Kira thought he resembled the Archie Bunker character from the old TV show, even the same white shirt without a tie, and she prayed his resemblance to the character who was so stubborn and bigoted was not a portent of things to come. Wentzel said hello to her, realizing she expected a handshake, too, only after she extended her hand to him. Some things really take time, she thought.

"Well, what do you have so far?" Kira asked.

Wentzel looked puzzled and flashed a questioning glance at Paul.

"Agent Thomasian is the special agent in charge of the Grady kidnapping," Paul said matter-of-factly. He didn't go on to explain he had come along to make certain she didn't mess up, or even just to see what in the hell she was going to do now that they were here. For a change Kira could have kissed him.

"Oh," Wentzel mumbled. "I guess I should have remembered that. It says Agent Thomasian right here at the bottom of the report."

"Call me Kira, please." She had a feeling it was going to be a long night.

"Please sit down." Wentzel lined up two chairs in precise order next to the desk before he positioned himself in a large swivel chair. "First of all, you have a message from Mr. and Mrs. Grady."

"Yes, I told them I'd be here. I'll call them in the morning."

"Oh, they didn't call from Atlanta. They're right here at the motor inn. Checked into Room Seventeen earlier this evening. They'd like to know if you can meet with them in the morning."

Kira sighed. "I should have known. Okay, I'll get back to them. Now what do you have?"

Quickly, Wentzel shuffled through the paperwork in front of him. "Let's see. You want to start with the murder of the Detweiler woman?"

"Okay, shoot," she said.

"We had the local coroner do a preliminary postmortem this morning, but we have to wait on some of the lab work. So far we know edema of the larynx and fractures of the surrounding cartilage point to death by strangulation."

Archie Bunker continued reading. "Let's see . . . nasal passages were clear, no needle marks, pupils were equal. Oh, yes, the doc said her uterus was not enlarged, but it did appear she had sex shortly before she died. They sent the vaginal scrapings to the lab."

Paul shifted his weight in his chair. "You're not going to read that whole coroner's protocol, are you? It must be ten pages long. Let's concentrate on the stuff that points to Hoffman."

"You think the murder was committed in the woman's apartment?" Kira asked.

Wentzel nodded. "Probably, but we have no witnesses. The lab people from Harrisburg went to work after we talked to you. They're busy analyzing fiber and hair samples. The prints Ident sent up from D.C. match the ones we found all over her place, except for the doorknob."

"What about the doorknob?" Kira asked.

"Wiped clean, not a print."

Paul shook his head. "Why would the killer wipe off only the doorknob and leave prints elsewhere? That sounds pretty stupid."

"Okay," Kira interrupted. "We've got Hoffman as the woman's boyfriend, and his prints are everywhere in her apartment, except for the doorknob. We have the Grady kid calling his grandmother from a short distance away. There's also the envelope addressed to the boy's friend. Did you check out Hoffman's place of residence?"

Wentzel nodded again. "Two state policemen went to his house first thing this morning. They didn't get anything, but Hoffman seemed to be sweating bullets. Then, after the bureau put the information about the Grady kidnapping through to Harrisburg,

I ordered the state troopers back at about sixteen hundred. By then Hoffman and his vehicle were gone."

"Figures," Paul said. "What'd they find?"

"They found the Grady boy's backpack in a deep hole in the woods behind the house. A recently fired .38 was inside the pack, and get this, it looked like the gun had been fired from inside the thing. Had two bullet holes and powder burns on the inside, but no blood. That stuff went to the lab. They did find fresh bloodstains and broken glass on the kitchen floor."

Kira jumped to her feet, almost knocking over the chair. "Why in hell didn't you tell us that before?" she shouted.

"You said to tell you about the murdered woman first," Wentzel answered, looking wounded.

"Bullet holes in the kid's backpack! Blood on the kitchen floor! That could be the boy's blood."

"We don't know that yet," he answered.

Kira thought she was going to explode. She released her grip on the edge of the desk and glared at Wentzel. Paul slid her chair forward, against the back of her knees, and reluctantly she sat down. She lowered her voice. "Did you go over the house personally? In light of the kidnapping?"

She saw the redness creeping up Wentzel's neck into his thinning hair. "Not yet," he said.

"How about his vehicle? He drove a van when he abducted the boy."

"Yeah, we got that. The troopers got the license number when they were there the first time. It's a Dodge van, registered to Hoffman."

"Okay," she said. "Let's drive over to Hoffman's place, now."

"It's almost one in the morning. Wouldn't you rather wait until daylight? I've reserved some very nice accommodations for the two of you at the Dutch Country Motor Inn. That's where the Gradys are."

Kira clenched her hands into fists until her fingernails stabbed into her palms. "The motor inn can wait a little while, thank you," she answered as she got up and walked toward the door.

Paul was on his feet. "Might as well get moving on this," he said, more or less to Wentzel.

Wentzel followed, slipping his arms into a heavy jacket as he walked.

"You need me for anything else?" Lenhart asked Agent Wentzel.

"No, son, I'll drive them. You go on, get some sleep."

The officer smiled and pulled Kira and Paul's carry-on bags from the trunk of the patrol car. He hurried off, driving just a bit too fast down the deserted road. Perhaps, Kira thought, he still had time to catch the last few numbers by the live band at the local fire hall.

Chapter 38

THEY drove up the long, rutted lane and approached Hoffman's residence in darkness. Kira stared at the bleak visage of the tiny house illuminated in the glow of Wentzel's headlights. It looked like something out of an old horror flick, every bit as dismal as the Bates Motel. Paul and Kira got out of the car and stood waiting while Wentzel pounded on the door. He paused, knocked again, then entered the unlocked house. He disappeared into the black obscurity and turned on a few lights, including one on the exterior, right next to the door. Even when it was lit up, the house was surrounded by a monotonous gloom.

"Nobody inside. There's also a workshop, over there." Wentzel pointed toward the trees beyond the house. "Seems Hoffman is a self-employed auto mechanic."

"Did the state troopers check out the workshop?" Paul asked.

"Not in light of the kidnapping. They just wanted to check it out in reference to the murdered woman," Wentzel said. "Want to take a quick look in there first?"

"Why not? You can learn a lot about a man from the place where he works," Paul said. "Do you have a flashlight?"

"Sure do." Wentzel quickly rummaged through the trunk until he located two flashlights, then led the way through what appeared to be Hoffman's personal junkyard to the garage.

He pulled a chain, flicking on a single naked light bulb hanging from a long cord in the center of the drafty little building. Kira studied the mounds of gaskets and belts and discarded auto parts, most of which she couldn't even identify. She stubbed her toe on a corroded car battery sitting more or less right in the center of the floor. She had never seen such a mess. She remembered Paul's surprisingly efficient office back in Atlanta. Perhaps you could learn a lot about a man from the place where he worked.

"Look, Paul, on the far wall." Kira had spotted a row of rifles and a shotgun. "Hoffman's arsenal."

Paul walked closer and shined a flashlight on the gun rack. "Looks like a rifle is missing. There might be a place for a handgun up there, too."

"Maybe the one we found?" Wentzel offered.

Paul and Wentzel moved some of the greasy rags and smaller auto parts like hubcaps, searching the workbench. Kira examined a disarray of fenders and a badly dented bumper leaning against one wall so she could avoid handling the smelly, black sludge congealed like a scum over everything in Leon Hoffman's world.

"I don't see anything in here that might help us," Paul said finally. "Why don't we go into the house?"

By now Kira's fingers ached from the cold, and she welcomed the move into the house. She held the screen door while Wentzel opened the inner door; she and Paul followed him inside.

"Strong odor of booze in here," Kira said, looking around the dingy, gray kitchen.

Wentzel pointed to the shattered glass on the

floor. "That's the broken liquor bottle I told you about. Bloodstain's right next to it. Lab boys took samples."

"Okay, let's start looking," she said. "Something has to turn up, anything that might give us a hint as to where he took the boy."

Paul stepped over the broken glass and moved into the living room, turning on lights wherever he found them. "Charming place. There's a couple of bedrooms in here and a bath."

"I'll start in the kitchen," Wentzel said. "You two can work in there."

Kira and Paul began in the living room, going over every piece of furniture inch by inch, but they found little more than a dismembered TV set. Paul looked under every drawer and shelf, even the windowsills, for taped-on items, but found nothing. Kira tugged at the battered couch, pulling it away from the wall. "Hey, look at this," she called to Paul.

"What do you have?" he asked.

"A box of sanitary napkins jammed behind the couch. I thought he lived alone."

"The girlfriend, remember? The one he strangled."

"No woman would keep her pads behind the couch in the living room. She'd leave the box in the bathroom."

"Well, let's go look in the bathroom," Paul said.

Kira followed him, but stopped in the first bedroom. She kicked at a pile of muddy clothing heaped on the floor. "These must belong to the boy."

Paul picked up the pants; particles of crusted mud fell from the filthy corduroys on the floor. "They're kid-size, all right, and still damp."

Kira knelt next to an old army duffel bag tossed in the corner near the bed. She felt the muscles in her throat grow tight. These were Jonathan Grady's clothes. She even found a school workbook, fifth-grade math, and neatly penciled in the upper right-hand corner of the cover was the boy's name. Where had that sick bastard taken Jonathan? There had to be something else. She kept searching, removing all the bedding from the little bed and emptying all the dresser drawers. Meanwhile, she could hear Paul had shifted his search from the bathroom into the other bedroom. He called out to her, reporting he had found loads of stuff in Hoffman's closet.

She had grown weary and was moving much slower. Her limbs felt heavy, as if she were trying to walk through the shallow end of a swimming pool, but she continued to search the room where Hoffman had kept Jonathan. The constant reminders, Jonathan's school books and his folded T-shirts, kept her going. She just wished she knew what she was looking for.

Finally she gave up on the little bedroom and went into Hoffman's room. She sat on the edge of the bed and studied the small mountain of boxes Paul had hauled out of the closet.

"A regular treasure trove," he said, looking up at her from the floor where he knelt. "Hey, you look like it's way past your bedtime."

"Hours and hours, but I'm all right."

"Why don't you lie down while I sift through this junk?"

"On Hoffman's bed? I'd rather have a root canal."

Paul laughed. "He had some of the boy's clothing in here, too. See, on the right side of the closet."

"He's been missing only a week. Why so much clothing?" she asked. She got up and walked closer to the closet. Suddenly she reached out and ripped a shirt right off the hanger. "This is a girl's blouse. This isn't Jonathan's."

She pulled open the dresser drawers and began to tear through the contents. She stopped dead when she came to a folded stack of girls' underpants. "Get Wentzel. What does his report say about the occupants of this house?"

Wentzel followed Paul back into the bedroom. "The girl's stuff would have belonged to Hoffman's adopted daughter," he said. "At least he claimed he had adopted her."

"What adopted daughter? You didn't mention a daughter," Kira said, suddenly wide-awake. "Where is she?"

"I don't know. The state police didn't see any signs of the girl first time out. They asked about her, but Hoffman said she had gone to live with a relative."

"What's the name of this girl?"

"Marissa, Maria, something like that. All we have on her is the hearsay of some of the people Judy Mae Detweiler worked with. It was in the police report. They claimed Hoffman had adopted a girl, the daughter of an old friend who had been killed, but he kept her pretty much at home. Didn't even send her to school."

"Nobody ever bothered to report that fact to the school authorities?"

Wentzel shook his head. "Doesn't look that way."

Paul moved the chair he had used to reach the upper shelf in the closet, scraping the legs noisily on the wooden floor. "How old did they say the girl was?" he asked.

"Somewhere around twelve or thirteen."

Paul looked at Kira. "Are you thinking what I'm thinking?"

"The Mendoza girl. I'll bet he abducted her and kept her alive for the past three years, passing her off as his adopted daughter."

"I've heard screwier things."

Kira sat down again. "Well, that explains the sanitary napkins. Okay, if this is what we've got, two kids may be in danger, especially since Jonathan tried to make that phone call this morning."

"Except Hoffman surely knows the kid didn't reveal anything but the name of the state he was in," Paul said. "Hoffman doesn't know the FBI is on his tail."

Wentzel forced a cough to get their attention. "But Hoffman knows the state police are on his tail for the Detweiler murder, or at least he probably took off for that reason. Who's this Mendoza girl?"

"The daughter of someone who was in Hoffman's unit over in Vietnam, same as the Grady boy's father," Kira said. She looked at Paul after she spoke the words, then suddenly felt the color drain from her face. "Oh, my God. The other guy, what was his name? Didn't you say he lived in Harrisburg?"

"What other guy?" Wentzel asked.

"The other guy in Hoffman's patrol," Paul answered for her. "His name is Anthony Cozelli, and the army had an address for him somewhere in Harrisburg."

"Are you willing to go with me on a hunch?" Kira asked.

Paul grinned. "Hell, we've come this far, why not?"

"Paul, I'm serious. I'm sure Hoffman took off for Cozelli's place. If the Mendoza girl and Jonathan Grady are still alive, I'll bet he's got them with him."

"I'd say it's worth looking into," Paul answered. "What do you think, Vern?"

Vern Wentzel nodded; he still looked a little confused.

Kira felt her hands trembling. Hoffman was playing out a twisted scenario, but perhaps they finally had a place to focus their search. "Mr. Wentzel," she said, "could you wake up someone at your office and see if they can pinpoint Anthony Cozelli's address? We have to talk to Mr. Cozelli, wherever he is, and warn him not to let his kid out of his sight until we get somebody there. What time do you have?"

Wentzel looked at his watch. "It's after four. C'mon, we can make some calls from the motel. We're too far from Harrisburg to use the car radio, and I haven't seen a phone anywhere in this place."

"Good. If we get the ball rolling, maybe we can locate Cozelli before Hoffman does. Cozelli's house has got to be Hoffman's next destination."

Wentzel sidestepped a pile of junk on the bedroom floor and headed for the door. "You're going to have to brief me on these other kids you're talking about," he said. "I didn't read anything about them in your report."

"It wasn't there," Kira answered flatly. "I'll fill you in as we drive, but for now I think old Hoffman is in this for the shock effect, and I'm afraid we're now talking about three children in extreme danger."

Chapter 39

KIRA hurried into the backseat of Wentzel's car, and in moments they were speeding down the dirt road, spewing loose gravel away from the rear tires. The storm clouds lingered, hiding any trace of the moon or stars. The thick blackness of the night in this desolate countryside was unnerving. Except for the two straight beacons emanating from the car, there was no light, no signs of life anywhere.

She closed her eyes and leaned her head against the back of the seat, just for a second. The events of the day swam through her mind. The bloodstained floor and the bullet-riddled backpack still posed unanswered questions. She may have made this mad dash to Pennsylvania just a few hours too late to save any of the kids who might be in Hoffman's clutches.

Please, God, she prayed, let Jonathan and the girl be alive when we find them. Was it possible Hoffman had imprisoned Maria Mendoza for three years without harming her? As hard as she tried, Kira still couldn't figure out his motive for abducting the children of his former soldiers in the first place. Hoffman had to be psychotic, and if he was, what would he do if he got his hands on the Cozelli child? She shuddered, envisioning a gruesome execution-style murder of three children.

She was grateful Paul sat in the front seat exchanging small talk with Wentzel. Men can always find a common ground in sports, she thought. How they could worry about the 76ers and the Atlanta Hawks at a time like this was beyond her, but at least their interest in each other's opinions gave her an opportunity to withdraw from the conversation.

Paul seemed to sense she needed a moment or two to recover from the intensity of the last twenty-four hours. Was this bit of sensitivity another pleasant discovery, a side of Paul she had never seen before? She was beginning to feel very close to him, in spite of the logic that told her it was foolish to become romantically involved with her supervisor.

Her head suddenly jerked forward when the car came to a stop at the Dutch Country Motor Inn. She had slept, if only for a few minutes, and her weakness embarrassed her. If Paul was aware she had dozed off, he said nothing when he jumped out of the car and opened the rear door for her.

The desk clerk was wide-awake, smiling as if he enjoyed working the graveyard shift in this lonely spot near the junction of Route 222 and the Pennsylvania Turnpike. The clerk recognized Wentzel and puffed himself up, as if just knowing about an FBI activity somehow linked him with an important investigation.

"You have rooms for the two agents I told you about?" Wentzel asked. "Mr. Russell and Miss Thomasian."

"I certainly do," he answered. He pulled two keys from a board on the wall and placed them on the counter in front of Kira and Paul, but he spoke to Wentzel. "I put them close to your room, in case you have to get together to discuss your investigation."

"Good thinking," Paul answered. "Keep this all under wraps, will you?"

"Oh, yes, sir," the clerk said solemnly. "Just let me know if there's anything you need. Anything at all."

"Hoffman's ass in a sling would be nice," Paul whispered to Kira as they walked away from the desk.

"I'm going to get on the phone," Wentzel said. "I'll get that address."

"If Cozelli is still in the area, get a stakeout on his house, and don't forget to warn him not to let his kid out of his sight until we get there," Kira said.

"Right," Wentzel answered. "I'm going to shave and change my shirt. I'll meet you back here in the lobby in a few minutes."

"Okay," Kira said, "but ring my room if you get through to Cozelli before then."

Wentzel hurried off down the corridor. Kira looked at Paul. "You must be tired," she said.

He hesitated, then said, "Kira, you know Hoffman may have grabbed Cozelli's kid already. He's had all day to make his move. We may be closing in on him after the fact."

"Let's try to think positively," she said as she let herself into her room.

Kira washed her face and reapplied her makeup. She didn't use much, but she felt undressed without it. When she slipped her makeup case back into her shoulder bag, she checked to see if her service weapon was loaded. It was. The bureau had recently changed over from a .38 revolver to a semiautomatic .45, and she hoped she had spent enough time on the firing range with the new handgun. Wasn't that always the way? Just when she had become a crack shot with the .38, she had to get used to the feel of a new weapon.

She thought about unloading and dry-firing the .45 a few times, but that would be a waste of precious time. She also thought about strapping on the shoulder holster packed in her flight bag, but rejected that idea as well. When the time came, she wanted her weapon right in her hand. She combed through her hair and went out to the lobby to wait for the men.

"Ms. Thomasian." She heard her name being called, just slightly above a whisper. She turned to face Ed and Susan Grady. They didn't have to say the words. Their eyes were pleading, begging her to tell them whatever she had learned.

"What are you doing up so late, or are you up early?" Kira asked.

Ed said, "I asked the desk clerk to call us when you came in. We couldn't sleep anyway."

There was no doubt they hadn't slept. Pouches of weariness sagged under their eyes. Susan Grady's face looked pasty, like a woman who had suffered a long illness.

Kira pointed to a sofa facing two chairs. "Let's sit."

"Did you find Jonathan?" Susan asked.

"Not yet, but we will. We have a lead."

Moments later Wentzel, short of breath, hurried into the lobby.

"This is Agent Wentzel of the Harrisburg FBI," Kira said.

They shook hands, and Wentzel sat down before he spoke. "Cozelli must have moved recently. He had the phone disconnected, and the closing bill went to a P.O. box. They're working on an address through the electric company and other agencies, but they take time."

Ed Grady stiffened noticeably. "Wait a minute. Are you talking about the Cozelli who was in 'Nam with me?"

"I was just about to tell you what we have so far," Kira said. Briefly, she explained the possibility of

Jonathan's kidnapping being connected to the disappearance of the Mendoza girl, and how they feared the Cozellis' child might be next. Susan held her head and began to cry.

Ed jumped to his feet. "I don't believe it. This is crazy."

Kira grabbed his arm and pulled him back down to the sofa. "Of course it's crazy. We're not dealing with a rational person."

"I had a phone call just before we went to the airport," Ed replied. "It was Vince Mendoza, the girl's father. He told me the FBI called him because of Jonathan's kidnapping, and he wanted to let me know how sorry he was. He thinks his little girl is dead. It's been three years since she disappeared."

"I know," Kira said. "She may be alive. Hoffman had clothing for a young girl at his house."

"But Bull might go nuts if he realizes you're after him. There's no telling what he might do to the girl and Jonathan."

Kira nodded. There were no words she could think of to relieve his terror. She was scared to death herself. Turning to Wentzel, she said, "We've got to speed up this process, especially if we can't reach Cozelli by phone."

Paul walked into the lobby and motioned to Wentzel. "Listen, maybe we should drive on in to Harrisburg. Did you get through to Cozelli?"

"No phone. We should have his address any moment. If he has a P.O. box, he's probably still in town."

Susan looked up from her hands. "What if he doesn't even live in Harrisburg anymore?"

"Then we do something else," Paul said. "Cozelli sure as hell isn't in this motel."

"I agree," Kira said. "Let's get out of here."

Ed Grady stood up again. "I want to go along. I have a rental car, we could follow you."

Kira wanted nothing more than to make their pain go away, but she had to remember what they might come up against when they finally cornered Hoffman. "I wish I could say yes," she said gently, "but it might be dangerous. There could be gunfire, who knows what sort of violence."

"And our son will be right in the middle of it," Susan Grady cried, tears streaming down her face.

Before the tears had a chance to well up in her own eyes, Kira stood up. "If you really want to help, you'll stay right here, out of our way. I'll call you if I learn anything at all." She hurried to the car ahead of Paul and Wentzel.

Outside, a golden sun was beginning to rise over the rounded hills to the east. The early morning turnpike traffic into Harrisburg was light, and by the time they reached the R.A.'s office, Cozelli's address was waiting for them.

"Thank God his electric was hooked up yesterday. They had him in the computer. Winston Road," Kira said, holding the information out for Wentzel to read.

Wentzel looked at the address. "Shit, that's all the way on the other side of town. We're lucky it's Saturday; traffic might not be too bad."

"How about the stakeout and a helicopter?" Paul asked as they dashed back into the car.

"They're on their way."

Chapter 40

LEON kept his eyes on the front door of the yellow house. Goddamn that Cozelli. He had it pretty good, living here in style like he was some kind of big shot. Cozelli's place wasn't as fancy as Grady's fucking palace down south, but it was a hell of a lot better than his own little shack. It wasn't fair, after all the time he had spent in that lousy swamp, that the men who turned their backs on him should be living like kings. They didn't know what it was like to suffer, but now maybe he would change all that. When each of his three good buddies had a kid to bury, they'd think twice before they ever crossed old Leon again.

"I'm hungry," Maria said loudly.

"You don't get no breakfast until you do what we've been practicing," Leon answered.

"But I'm hungry now."

"Don't do it, Maria," Jonathan whispered to her. "Don't listen to him."

Leon reached out and slapped Jonathan, missing his face and instead cuffing his ear. A stab of pain ripped through his bad shoulder because of the sudden movement. A cold sweat broke out on his forehead. He held back another swipe at Jonathan and shouted, "You stay out of this, boy. What we're doing here's got nothing to do with you."

Jonathan shrank back against the seat, making himself very small. Maria was trembling; but that was good, Leon thought. She was too scared not to listen to what he was telling her to do. The whole time they had sat in the van, waiting in front of Cozelli's house, he had rehearsed Maria until she knew exactly what she was supposed to say to the Cozelli kid. She looked harmless, even slightly pathetic, and he could see no reason why the boy wouldn't want to play with her. She was older than him, of course, but if she had a whole litter of puppies to show off, the kid wouldn't actually have to want to play with Maria; he'd be interested in seeing those puppies.

"Okay, let's pretend the kid opens the door. What do you say?" Leon asked Maria.

Maria sat up straight. "I say, Hi, Billy, my name's Maria. I just moved in down the street. You want to come out and play with me?"

"Yeah, then he says hi. Then what?" Leon urged.

"Then I tell him about the puppies."

"Say it. Say the words." Leon was feeling the pain again. He fumbled for the bottle in his jacket pocket and spilled six yellow tablets into his hand. One pill jumped out of his hand and landed on the floor near the gas pedal. Dammit, he was almost out. He gobbled what was left. He'd have to stop at a drugstore as soon as he was finished here.

Maria repeated her tale about the new puppies and wouldn't Billy like to take a peek? Their little eyes were almost open, and they were just as cute as they could be. Maria would point to the van and say her dad had them in the backseat because they were on their way to the vet to have the puppies checked. Billy could hold one if he wanted to.

"Then what?" Leon asked.

"Then Billy and I walk over here and we get in the van and we all go to breakfast," Maria answered.

"How do you know this kid Billy?" Jonathan asked.

Leon glared at him. "Don't ask a lot of fool questions, boy, unless you want another smack on the head. I'm not in the mood." He turned his attention back to Maria. "Now what do you say if his mom or dad come to the door first?"

Maria thought for a moment. "I say I'm the new girl from down the street, and can Billy come out to play and see our brand-new puppies?"

"Okay, I guess you've got it. Just remember, you say anything else, you and Jonathan are dead. Him first, then you. You understand?"

Maria chewed on the insides of her cheeks, but she didn't cry. "Yes," she said.

Leon checked his watch. The little numbers on the dial had become too blurred for him to read. He blinked. He still couldn't focus, but he was sure it was after seven, maybe it was almost eight. It didn't matter. Billy was sure to be awake. Kids always got up early on Saturdays to watch the damn cartoons on TV, at least Maria always had. "Okay," he said. "Go ahead, just remember everything I told you."

Maria opened the door and slid off the seat of the van. She crossed the street and slowly approached the Cozelli house. She stopped walking for a moment and glanced over her shoulder.

Dammit, she's not supposed to look at me like that, it makes her look too suspicious, Leon thought. I told her not to act suspicious. He quickly rolled down the window and waved for her to keep going.

His fingers clutched the stock of the rifle spanning his knees, and he realized he was soaking wet from his own sweat. Sweat was running down his neck into the bandage Maria had wrapped around his shoulder. A little bead of moisture clung to the tip of his nose. He let go of the rifle and wiped his face with the back of his good hand and then rubbed his palm down the leg of his pants. He didn't even try to blot the palm of his left hand. The left arm was now so stiff he could hardly move it. He was going to need a doctor as soon as he reached Canada, that was for sure.

Maria stood in front of Cozelli's door and knocked. She looked back over her shoulder again. Leon shook his head. Jonathan would have understood what to do without making so many mistakes, but he hadn't dared send him to get Cozelli's kid. Jonathan was too full of tricks and surprises, and Leon knew he was better off having him right here where he could watch him. He glanced to his right. Jonathan had inched away from him after Maria had gotten out of the van, and now the boy somehow looked different, sort of shifty-eyed, like one of the Viet Cong bastards who had guarded him all those months. Leon recalled naming one particular gook Victor Charlie, which stood for V.C., but the dumb son of a bitch was too stupid to get it. They were all dumber than hell, those lousy gooks.

Jonathan stared at him, the kid's eyes not so wide and round as they used to be, but now slanted and squinty and dark. Funny, Leon thought. He had never noticed how Oriental Jonathan looked. The kid might even have Vietnamese blood! Sonofabitch, it had never occurred to him before that Grady might have married one of those filthy Vietnamese women who used to hang around the American soldiers. All he had ever learned was the woman's first name, and it was easy enough to change a name. He had always known Vietnamese women couldn't be trusted. Those lousy bitches were all spies.

Leon quickly shot a glance across the street at Maria. She stood on one foot, using her right toe to scratch the back of her left leg. What was taking so goddamn long? Leon felt the sweat dripping into his eyes. Why was it so hot in the van?

Suddenly Cozelli's door opened a few inches and a little face peeked out. Maria talked and pointed across the street to the van. The door opened wider and a boy about Jonathan's size stepped into the doorway.

"Hot damn," Leon said. "It's the kid. That's better than her having to explain everything to his mother."

Maria kept talking and pointing, but the kid didn't budge an inch. He just stood there looking at Maria and occasionally glancing over at the van. What in hell was Maria saying to him?

The door opened all the way now, and a woman dressed in a white bathrobe yanked the boy away from Maria. She kept her hands on the boy's shoulders, protectivelike, and began talking to Maria.

Maria looked down at the floor of the little front porch and hopped back onto one leg again. She always did that when she was nervous. What was Cozelli's old lady talking about? Leon figured she was asking a lot of nosy questions. The woman pushed the kid around behind her, practically back into the house, but the kid popped into view on her other side. Something was wrong. She wasn't going to let the kid play with Maria.

This was it. He was going to have to take them out from a distance. The woman would slam the door in Maria's face in another second, and this would be his last crack at Cozelli's kid. He raised the rifle to his right shoulder and tried to steady it with his left hand. Suddenly a bolt of pain pierced like a flaming arrow into his wounded shoulder. He steadied the rifle, instead, on top of the sideview mirror and peered through the scope. There they were, almost on top of him. He would have no trouble taking the boy first and then his mother. If Maria tried to get away, he would get her on the run. She would never have time to outdistance the scope.

Somewhere Leon heard a remote whirring sound, like the slapping blades of a Cobra helicopter. It was about time they came to rescue him. He had rotted half his life away in this hellhole. Leon squinted through the scope, aiming for the boy's heart, and slowly squeezed the trigger.

Just as the shot rang out, the rifle popped off the sideview mirror and slammed upward against the top edge of the window opening. What the hell? Then he realized someone had shoved his elbow, hard. Leon looked back at the house in time to see the front door slam. The woman and the boy and Maria were gone.

He was in a landing zone. A jeep, or maybe it was an army tank, was approaching, right across the road. He could hear the choppers getting closer and closer. The noise was driving him crazy. A firefight would follow, and it was up to him to save his own ass. He knew he couldn't count on any of his men. Suddenly he heard a tinny squeak, and he looked to his right. A gook had slipped into the jeep next to him, that's who had bumped his arm, sabotaging his mission. This was soon to be one dead gook.

Leon saw the wiry little figure, they were all so goddamn little, slip off the seat next to him and take off hell-bent down the road. Painfully, Leon slid over to the other window. He rolled down the glass and leaned out far enough to get a sight on the V.C. spy who was dashing away. Dumb son of a bitch didn't know enough to jump into one of their stinking spider holes. He just kept running and hollering.

Pain sliced through his shoulder; his scalp was on fire with a raging headache, but the crosshairs were right on the enemy's head. He wouldn't take any chances. He lowered the rifle slowly until he had the runaway's back clearly centered. There was no one to bump him this time. Leon squeezed the trigger, hearing the sharp crack of gunfire echo through his ears.

Chapter 41

KIRA felt everything was moving much too slowly, like a fog rolling in from the sea. But Wentzel had turned on his siren and the flashing red light in his rear window, and was racing through the morning traffic in the capital city. Now that he was in range of the dispatcher, he barked orders into the car radio between squawks of static. Kira clenched her teeth, hoping they wouldn't be too late.

A mile from their destination, Wentzel cut the lights and the siren, and in a matter of seconds they turned onto Winston Road. He drove slowly now, hugging the right-hand curb.

The street was quiet, almost too quiet. A few cars were parked in the short driveways leading to little boxlike garages, but the first block had none parked in the street. The tranquil neighborhood still had a wintry look about it, in spite of a few scrawny daffodils pushing through the soil in several of the yards. Towering old chestnut trees lined both sides of the street. It looked like a good place to raise kids, safe from the blight and congestion of the city.

"The house is in the next block," Wentzel said. "On our right." He stopped at the first intersection and pointed. "The fifth house, halfway down this block. There's a yellow van parked on the other side of the street." He smiled. "I think we've got him."

"Where in the hell's the stakeout?" Wentzel bellowed into the radio. The dispatcher's voice explained that the car should be there any minute, some kind of mix-up. . . . Kira tuned out the radio; her eyes were on the dilapidated van parked in the block ahead.

"Can you see the license plate?" Kira asked.

Wentzel shook his head. "We don't require them on the front of a vehicle. Mistake, if you ask me. How do you want to handle this?"

She checked Wentzel's rearview mirror, and sure enough a car was crawling into place behind them, still a half block away. Their backup had arrived.

"What do you think, Paul? Approach on foot so he doesn't freak?"

Paul nodded to her and then spoke to Wentzel, "Pull around the corner and get the car out of his sight. Kira and I will do the lover routine and move in a little closer."

"I hope it's not too early in the morning to convince him we're lovers just casually strolling down the street," Kira said.

"Don't worry, it's never too early for romance," Paul answered, and then half to himself, "and never too late either."

Using the radio, Wentzel ordered the backup to stay put while he drove his car around the corner. Kira and Paul got out and walked back to Winston Road, where they could see the van. Paul unbuttoned his jacket and unsnapped the flap on his shoulder holster.

"Are you ready?" he asked.

Kira adjusted her shoulder bag, her right hand inside, clutching her .45. "Yes, let's go."

Paul slipped his arm around her and they saun-
tered down the street, stopping, supposedly to admire a well-kept front lawn two houses away from
Cozelli's. A girl stood at Cozelli's front door talking to
a boy and a woman. Nothing seemed out of place,
yet something about the scene was all wrong. Curi-
ously, Kira had the feeling she was a member of an
audience, watching a play. All the while, she felt the
steady throbbing of her own heart pounding in her
ears.

Kira glanced over at the van, but at this angle the
sun reflecting on the windshield made it impossible
to see inside. She looked again at the people on the
porch. That might be Mrs. Cozelli and her son. She
wanted to warn her, but if Hoffman was in the van,
she didn't want to tip their hand.

Inside her purse she tried to relax her fingers to
get a more comfortable grip on her handgun. "You
want to walk a little closer, so we can get a better
look inside the van?"

Before Paul had a chance to answer, Kira saw the
barrel of a rifle slowly edge through the window of
the van, pointing toward Cozelli's house. Instantly,
the sharp crack of gunfire ruptured the quiet on
Winston Road.

Paul drew his weapon and pulled her toward the
protection of a tree. He crouched and studied the
scene. To Kira the scene was a disjointed film, the
frames frozen one at a time, in rapidfire succession.
Out of the corner of one eye she saw Wentzel creeping through a nearby backyard. The backup car
crossed the intersection and rolled closer. In the
distance she heard the rhythmic slapping of the ro-
tary blades of a helicopter.

Within seconds the rifle jerked back, pulled inside the van and away from the window. Kira

was vaguely aware of the people on the porch to her right scurrying inside the house, but by now she was advancing, too, her .45 extended toward the van.

Chapter 42

Jonathan had watched as Maria crossed the street. He had wanted to yell out, to tell her to run for her life, but the words froze somewhere in his brain. Leon was crazy. Jonathan was sure of it now, and he didn't know how to deal with a crazy man. He watched as the glazed look in Leon's eyes turned from a distant, vacant sort of stare to a piercing glare filled with hatred and anger. Leon had little bubbles of spit drooling from his mouth, making him look fierce and rabid. Perspiration flowed freely down his face and neck; his eyes twitched, blinking strangely. Jonathan was too scared to move.

He was going to die without ever having a chance to see his grandma again, or Ginger. He missed his dog so much, and at that moment he wanted nothing more than a chance to run his fingers through Ginger's soft coat and snuggle next to her on the carpet in front of the fireplace.

Maybe when Leon finally killed him, he would once again be with his parents. Isn't that what was supposed to happen in Heaven? He wasn't sure what Heaven was, or where it was, but it had to be better than being terrorized by a crazy man.

Across the street the boy and his mother were talking to Maria, but they didn't seem too interested in Leon's story about the puppies. That was a stupid story anyway, and it served Leon right. Jonathan hoped Billy had been grounded for getting an F on his report card and wouldn't be allowed out of the house. It was a terrible thing to wish on the kid, but he knew anything was better than the sort of fear Leon could provide.

Then Jonathan saw Leon slide the rifle into position. "No," he cried, but the word was hardly more than a groan caught in his own throat.

Leon steadied the rifle and peered into the scope. He was going to shoot the boy, maybe Maria, too! Jonathan saw Leon's trigger finger tremble slightly, then he began to squeeze.

Jonathan lunged toward Leon, slamming the butt of the rifle down toward the seat. The barrel bounced upward against the top edge of the window.

Jonathan fully expected Leon to reach out and hit him with the butt of the rifle, or at least to belt him in the face with his fist, but Leon just sat there looking dazed and confused. This was his chance to run.

Jonathan pushed open the door of the van and jumped to the ground. There were no sidewalks. The grass came all the way out to the curb. He darted forward, running so fast the heels of his shoes slapped hard against his behind. He drew air into his lungs and screamed, but most of his breath was consumed by the explosions of his rapid gulps for air. He passed two houses, then three, wondering if Leon was chasing after him. He had to get away; he ran faster and faster. Everything on the street was a blur of colors; he wasn't able to think of anything except getting away from Leon. He cried out for help. The words may have been a whisper or a scream or only in his mind; he wasn't sure.

Suddenly his mind cleared for a split second. Run

to a house, he told himself. Get help from one of the houses. There was a driveway a few feet ahead.

He veered, skidding on the slick grass, feeling his balance waver. In the next instant he heard shots ring out, loudly echoing between the little houses up and down the street. Almost as if the world had suddenly shifted into slow motion, his feet slid out from under him and he felt a lightning bolt of pain shoot from his head down his spine.

Chapter 43

K IRA heard Cozelli's front door slam shut. The girl on the porch might have been Maria Mendoza. Had the shot been intended for her? Kira stepped into the street; Paul was to her right, circling away from her. Suddenly the passenger's door on the van opened and a boy jumped out. Oh, dear God, she thought, it's Jonathan.

The boy bolted forward, but Kira focused on the driver, who had just slid to the other side of the front seat. She was no longer protected by the tree, but that was not important. Hoffman—and she was certain it was Hoffman—didn't seem to be taking any notice of her. When she spotted his rifle pointing out the side window at the boy, she carefully aimed her own weapon, praying her trembling hands would not betray her. Shooting through the window, she had no choice but to try to hit him in the head. Clenching her right wrist with her left hand, she held her arms steady. She wished she had a bigger target, but Hoffman's head would have to be big enough. She took a deep breath, checked her aim, and squeezed the trigger. The retort seemed to echo, then she realized Paul had gotten off a shot, too.

Hoffman slumped forward and hit the horn. Terrified faces appeared in the windows across the street, but no one ventured outside. Kira finally remembered to breathe.

Her eyes quickly shifted, searching for the running boy. The boy had to be Jonathan, but where had he gone? She began to walk. Farther down the block she spotted something, a little form lying facedown on the grass.

Chapter 44

"**J**ONATHAN, Jonathan, are you all right?"

Jonathan vaguely heard the words, a soft voice, a woman's voice, but he was first aware of a pair of hands, then two pair of hands, touching him, searching over his body.

"I don't see any blood. I don't think he was hit," a man's voice said.

"Thank God. What about Hoffman?" The woman's voice was louder now. Jonathan opened his eyes.

"The son of a bitch is dead. You were great. You nailed him right through the temple."

Jonathan saw the woman smile. The man lifted him to a sitting position. "I think he just slipped on the wet grass. He was running like a bat out of Hell."

"What happened?" Jonathan asked, finally focusing on their faces. He didn't know who these people were, but they weren't Leon. "Where's Maria?"

"We'll find her. Was she in the van with you?"

Jonathan nodded. "I think she went into Billy's house. I'm not sure."

The man helped Jonathan to his feet and dusted him off. "You got a nasty bump on the forehead, but I think you're going to be just fine," he said.

Jonathan didn't feel fine. He felt dizzy, like he was going to throw up.

"Jonathan," the lady said. "We're from the FBI. I'm Kira and this is Paul."

The dizziness began to wane a little, but Jonathan hesitated. He still felt weak in the knees, the way he always felt after he got off the roller coaster at Six Flags Over Georgia. "Leon killed my parents," he finally blurted out. "I think he killed Maria's, too."

The lady named Kira put her arm around his shoulder. "Leon was a terrible, evil man, but he didn't kill your parents. They're both fine; they're in a motel, not too far from here."

His throat was almost too dry for him to speak. "They're not dead? Leon said there was an accident, a big explosion and a fire, but I thought he killed them."

"Neither one. They're very much alive, waiting to take you home."

This whole nightmare with Leon had all been a lie. Tears began to run down his cheeks but he wasn't even sure why.

"What about Maria's parents? Are they dead?"

"No, they're alive, too." Kira hugged him closer.

Paul said, "Let's take him back to Cozelli's place."

Paul slipped his arm around Kira and squeezed her so hard, Jonathan felt Paul's grip all the way to his own shoulder. With Kira in the middle, they crossed the street. Jonathan liked the way Kira had one arm wrapped around Paul's waist and the other over his own shoulder. It felt right. The way it felt when he walked through the park or along the beach with his mom and dad. It was finally sinking in: his parents were not dead; everything was going to be all right.

A short, fat man yelled something about the Gradys and the telephone from the house next to Billy's. The man was grinning ear to ear.

Just then the door to Billy Cozelli's house opened

and Maria stepped out onto the porch. Billy was right behind her. She squinted into the bright morning sun for a moment and then waved to Jonathan. Jonathan waved back, and Maria dashed toward him.

"Paul, I think we have some good news for the Mendoza family," Kira said, placing her hands on Maria's shoulders.

Finally, Maria was smiling, really smiling. Jonathan looked around. People he had never seen before appeared as if out of nowhere and inched closer to Billy's house. They milled about in the dazzling sunshine, exchanging whispers.

"Jonathan," Kira said. "Mr. Wentzel has your mother on the phone."

Jonathan ran inside the little white house next door to Billy's. The same fat man stood in the living room, his arm extended, holding the telephone receiver out to him.

Was it true? Jonathan could hardly believe it. His parents, alive and well, were waiting to talk to him on the other end of the line.

Jonathan smiled at the man and took the receiver. Tears suddenly filled his eyes even though the smile remained on his lips. He inhaled slowly, taking the air deep into his lungs. He remembered how anxious he had been to tell Brian and his grandmother how he had shot Leon and how he and Maria had run away, but somehow he didn't want to talk about the events of the last two days. At least, not yet.

He took another deep breath before he spoke. "Hello, Mom? It's me, Jonathan."

AN IMPORTANT MESSAGE TO THE READERS OF THIS BOOK

What you have just read is a work of fiction. But the nationwide problem of missing and exploited children is very real—and can be far more complex and insidious than the events in a novel could possibly portray. It is also important to know that there *is* a full range of services available to assist families in the event their child is abducted.

As a society, our efforts to prevent crimes against children have not kept pace with the increasing vulnerability of our young citizens. In May 1990 the U.S. Department of Justice released a study reporting that there were as many as:

- 114,600 attempted abductions of children by nonfamily members
- 4,600 abductions by nonfamily members reported to police
- 300 abductions by nonfamily members where

the children were gone for long periods of time
or were murdered
- 354,000 children abducted by family members
- 450,700 children who ran away
- 127,100 children who were thrown away
- 438,200 children who were lost, injured, or otherwise missing

The National Center for Missing and Exploited Children (NCMEC), established in 1984 as a private, nonprofit organization, serves as a clearinghouse of information on missing and exploited children; provides technical assistance to citizens and law enforcement agencies; offers training programs to law enforcement and social service professionals; distributes photographs and descriptions of missing children nationwide; coordinates child protection efforts with the private sector; networks with nonprofit service providers and state clearinghouses on missing persons; and provides information on effective state legislation to ensure the protection of children per 42 USC 5771 and 42 USC 5780.

A 24-hour, toll-free telephone line is open for those who have information on missing or exploited children: **1-800-THE-LOST** (1-800-843-5678). This number is available throughout the United States, Canada, and Mexico. The TDD line is 1-800-826-7653. The NCMEC business number is (703) 235-3900.

A number of publications addressing various aspects of the missing and exploited child issue are available free of charge in single copies by contacting the National Center for Missing and Exploited Children's Publications Department, 2101 Wilson Boulevard, Suite 550, Arlington, Virginia 22201-3052.

Families need to know that traditional messages

of "Don't take candy from strangers," "Don't be a tattletale," and "Be respectful to adults, they know what they're doing" are incomplete and can lead to the abduction and sexual victimization of children. Children and families do not have to live in fear of these crimes, but they do need to be alert, cautious, and prepared. The key to child safety is communication. A child's best weapon against victimization is his or her ability to think and preparation to respond to potentially dangerous situations. By learning and following the safety tips listed below, children can empower themselves with the skills, knowledge, and abilities to better protect themselves.

BASIC RULES OF SAFETY FOR CHILDREN

As soon as your children can articulate a sentence, they can begin the process of learning how to protect themselves against abduction and exploitation. Children should be taught:

- ▶ If you are in a public place, and you get separated from your parents, don't wander around looking for them. Go to a checkout counter, the security office, or the lost and found and quickly tell the person in charge that you have lost your mom and dad and need help in finding them.
- ▶ You should not get into a car or go anywhere with any person unless your parents have told you that it is okay.
- ▶ If someone follows you on foot or in a car, stay

away from him or her. You don't need to go near the car to talk to the people inside.

▶ Grownups and other older people who need help should not be asking children for help; they should be asking older people.

▶ No one should be asking you for directions or to look for a "lost puppy" or telling you that your mother or father is in trouble and that he will take you to them.

▶ If someone tries to take you somewhere, quickly get away from him (or her) and yell or scream. "This man is trying to take me away" or "This person is not my father (or mother)."

▶ You should try to use the "buddy system" and never go places alone.

▶ Always ask your parents' permission to leave the yard or play area or to go into someone's home.

▶ Never hitchhike or try to get a ride home with anyone unless your parents have told you it is okay to ride with him or her.

▶ No one should ask you to keep a special secret. If he or she does, tell your parents or teacher.

▶ If someone wants to take your picture, tell him or her NO and tell your parents or teacher.

▶ No one should touch you in the parts of the body covered by the bathing suit, nor should you touch anyone else in those areas. Your body is special and private.

▶ You can be assertive, and you have the right to say NO to someone who tries to take you somewhere, touches you, or makes you feel uncomfortable in any way.

WHAT YOU CAN DO TO PREVENT CHILD ABDUCTION AND EXPLOITATION

▶ Know where your children are at all times. Be familiar with their friends and daily activities.

▶ Be sensitive to changes in your children's behavior; they are a signal that you should sit down and talk to your children about what caused the changes.

▶ Be alert to a teenager or adult who is paying an unusual amount of attention to your children or giving them inappropriate or expensive gifts.

▶ Teach your children to trust their own feelings, and assure them that they have the right to say NO to what they sense is wrong.

▶ Listen carefully to your children's fears, and be supportive in all your discussions with them.

▶ Teach your children that no one should approach them or touch them in a way that makes them feel uncomfortable. If someone does, they should tell the parents immediately.

▶ Be careful about babysitters and any other individuals who have custody of your children.

▶ Talk to your child in a calm and reasonable manner, being careful not to discuss the frightening details of what might happen to a child who does not follow the safety guidelines.

▶ Take an active interest in your children, and listen to them. And, most important, make your home a place of trust and support that fulfills your child's needs—so that he or she won't seek love and support from someone else.